Bolan worked his way to a side door, then back to the street

He glanced over his shoulder at the small building. He had accomplished three things this night: he had destroyed a small fortune of powdered death, killed a handful of street thugs and begun his campaign to take terror back home to the Triads.

As he quit the scene, the Executioner realized he had done something else. Knowing the paranoid mentality of the Chinese Mafia, he was certain the Triad leadership would place blame on one of their rivals, or at the doorstep of the young Golden Triangle warlord who was interfering with their heroin distribution rights.

It was time to go fishing, and Mack Bolan knew he had the right bait—death.

DON PENDLETON's
MACK BOLAN®
HELLFIRE STRIKE

A GOLD EAGLE BOOK FROM
WORLDWIDE®

TORONTO • NEW YORK • LONDON
AMSTERDAM • PARIS • SYDNEY • HAMBURG
STOCKHOLM • ATHENS • TOKYO • MILAN
MADRID • WARSAW • BUDAPEST • AUCKLAND

First edition August 1999

ISBN 0-373-61467-5

Special thanks and acknowledgment to
David North for his contribution to this work.

HELLFIRE STRIKE

Men rise from one ambition to another;
first they seek to secure themselves from
attack, and then they attack others.

—Niccolò Machiavelli:
Discorsi, 1531

As the wolves circle one another, nipping at heels,
looking for a weak spot, I'll be mounting my
campaign from the shadows, seeking to bring them
down.

—Mack Bolan

To the ceaseless efforts of the
Drug Enforcement Administration.
God keep.

PROLOGUE

Moscow, Russia

Plainly dressed men and women shivered in the early spring evening as they hovered around the dozens of makeshift stands lining the road that ran alongside Ismailovsky Park. Peddlers sold everything from Polish-made umbrellas to caviar from the Caspian Sea. Copies of American brand-name sneakers from Korea, Spanish imitations of Levi's denim jeans and Western boots from Taiwan were on display.

Less than a dozen miles from central Moscow, the preserve contained more than three thousands acres of grass and a vast ancient forest. The park was a pleasant escape from the harsh reality of the struggle to survive in Moscow.

An unshaven man pushed his way through the nighttime crowds that filled the walkway rimming the park. Ismailovsky Park was a perfect place for him to hide from his father, and anybody else who might be trying to capture him.

Arkady Chernov had been running from imaginary

enemies—and his father—for a long time. Ever since the Afghanistan campaign.

He had met his true love in Kabul many years earlier. He was then a captain in the Spetsnaz, working as an aide to his father. Decorated for bravery and for the number of rebels he had slain, he had also been wounded in action.

It was in the Russian military hospital that he had first encountered the grayish-white powder that was to possess him. It helped him forget the pain of his wounds and his disgust at the hundreds of men, women and children he had helped slaughter.

The native attendant who had offered him the drug called it *fin,* which he later found out was the local nickname for opium. Whatever its name, it did the same to him as it had done to all of his men.

It became his mistress, his love, his slaver.

A PAIR of Moscow militiamen strolled near the entrance to the park. One of them pointed out the young man in tattered clothing, wandering aimlessly nearby. "Look at his face."

The other did, and saw desperation and hopelessness. As the pair watched, the young man approached two Asian men and whispered something. The three vanished into the woods.

"Another drug addict looking for heroin or opium," the first militiaman commented.

"Probably a veteran of the Afghanistan war. Too

many of them discovered the unholy white powder from the Afghans. Should we go after them?''

''That's the job of the narcotics squad. We'll call it in when we get back to the car.''

The second man agreed, then added, ''If that damned radio the government bought from the Hungarians decides to work.''

Turning their backs on the path the young men had taken, the uniformed cops continued their stroll.

NIGHT HAD ENVELOPED the park. One of the Asian youths scanned the area to make sure they were alone. ''You brought the money?''

Arkady Chernov knew the routine. He'd been dealing drugs ever since he returned from duty in Afghanistan.

''Do you have the stuff?''

The smaller man, named Fast Eddie Ma, nodded to his companion. ''Show him.''

The heavyset man who had accompanied Ma reached under his coat and pulled out a thick plastic bag. The pouch was filled with a quarter kilogram of a dirty-white powder.

''Best China White made,'' Ma boasted.

The tired-looking Russian's eyes became hard and glistening. He had to force himself not to show how desperate he was for the heroin.

From his jacket pocket he extracted a large closed knife and opened the blade. Forcing the knife tip into the bag, the Russian extracted some of the powder and inhaled it.

The rush of instant relief flooded his body. Suddenly relaxed, he smiled happily.

"Good quality," he agreed. "My customers will pay well for this."

"The money," Fast Eddie Ma insisted.

Chernov reached into an inside jacket pocket. The money he had stolen from his father's safe was still there—twenty-five thousand dollars, U.S. He handed the bills to the Chinese youth.

Ma carefully counted the bills, then handed them to his companion. "It's all here," he stated.

"The bag, please," Chernov said, holding out his hand.

"Sorry, no bag." The younger man pulled a silenced 5.45 mm PSM pistol from under his jacket and fired two rounds into Chernov's chest.

As blood gushed from the fatal wounds, the Russian managed to gasp a question before he collapsed to the ground.

"Why?"

"We don't trust drug addicts," Ma replied, firing a pair of lead tumblers into the dying man's face.

FORMER GENERAL Mikhail Chernov studied the reports from the republics. The news from his partners was the same—poppy processing was up almost sixty percent. Several hundred tons of raw opium would be sent to refineries for conversion into heroin.

At any other time the news would have been cause for major celebration. The potential of earning more than the equivalent of four billion U.S. dollars, after taking care of corrupt officials, should have made him ecstatic.

The heavyset, bald ex-general had created a network of corrupt officials who saw nothing when his laboratories turned the raw opium into heroin, or when his couriers smuggled the kilo bags of the white powder across the borders in Europe and Africa.

He had begun to establish distribution in the United States, using the gangsters who had emigrated out of Russia. In cities like New York, Chicago and Los Angeles, heroin flowed from the Russian émigré communities into the mainstream of American drug traffic.

The stumbling block had been the Asians.

They had established distribution channels in North America and Europe long before Chernov had created a major illicit drug industry. Using the Chinese triads, the warlords of the Golden Triangle had created a network that defied infiltration by police agents.

The former Russian general could accept that his syndicate had an uphill struggle to compete for distribution with the Asian dealers. His men had been able to make some deals with American Mafia leaders. But Chernov accepted the fact that it would take time to get his heroin network established.

Now, however, the Asians had begun to dare to smuggle their drugs into the one-time Warsaw Pact countries. Members of the Chinese triads had infiltrated Moldavia, Chechnya, the Ukraine, Azerbaijan and Georgia.

They had even been spotted in Russia, disguised as tourists.

Chernov knew better. They hadn't come to Eastern Europe and the former Soviet republics to see the sights. They were there for only one purpose—to set up distribution networks for their opium products.

Until now the Russian mob had been in control of the sale of drugs throughout the old Soviet empire. Chernov's income had risen a thousand times since he'd returned from Afghanistan and retired his post with the military.

It was better to be a very rich private Russian citizen than a decorated but poor Russian general. The special commandos—the Spetsnaz—he had trained for duty in Afghanistan had left the military when he did. Like himself, none of them had a desire to attempt to survive on a government pension.

The Chinese had to be dealt with before they took over any more territory. Already he had paid off the various police groups to maintain surveillance on Chinese visitors to their countries, and to eliminate any they found selling drugs.

The door to his office opened, and Chernov looked up from his chair at the grim-faced man who entered his office.

The drug lord was annoyed at the interruption. "Can't you see I'm busy, Tremenko? What is it?"

Former Captain Oskar Tremenko had been an aide to Chernov for many years. He knew instinctively when to interrupt the general and when it was wiser to leave him alone. It was the wrong time to bother Chernov, but the news he brought had to be shared immediately.

He hesitated, then spoke quietly.

"I'm afraid I have bad news, General. It's about your son."

"What kind of trouble has that junkie gotten into now?"

"The police called." Tremenko looked uncomfortable. "They found him."

"I hope so. I've just gone over the accounts. Arkady has stolen $25,000 from the safe. He'll get a lesson he won't forget when they release him."

"I'm sorry, General. His learning days are over. He is dead."

Chernov looked stunned. "Dead? How?"

"He was shot in Ismailovsky Park. The police caught the men responsible."

"Send some men to deal with the killers' families. It's the least I can do for my son."

"Their families, unfortunately, are in Thailand. The killers were from Asia. Drug dealers, the police claim."

The retired general exploded. "First they try to cut into our territory with their Asian garbage. They underprice us and bribe officials to look the other way when they smuggle their opium into Russia and the neighboring countries. Now they murder my son. This is too much.''

"I'm afraid I have more bad news," Tremenko stated.

"What else can go wrong?"

"Our friend in the Foreign Ministry called. One of his contacts in Washington, D.C., informed him that the Americans are sending a top official to Thailand to meet with the top men in the Golden Triangle."

Chernov was outraged. "Who is this man?"

"A senator named Robert Firestone. He is chairman of the Senate Oversight Subcommittee on Narcotic Traffic."

"It's time we teach the Americans and these Oriental barbarians a lesson," Chernov snapped. "The same kind of lesson we were teaching the savages in Afghanistan until the government became too involved in public opinion."

He twisted and glared at his aide.

"Cancel all vacations for the men. We're leaving on a mission to Southeast Asia."

CHAPTER ONE

Stony Man Farm, Virginia

Thirty-six hours earlier, Mack Bolan had been air-lifted by helicopter to the rural Virginia complex called Stony Man Farm by the few who knew it existed.

Hal Brognola, the Justice Department official who had been given the job of overseeing the Sensitive Operations Group headquarters, had asked Bolan to meet him there to offer his expert advice on a problem the government was facing.

Intimate with the senior Fed's methods, Bolan knew he was about to be asked to undertake a mission. That was all Brognola could do. The Executioner had severed all ties with the federal government so that he could pursue his War Everlasting on his own terms, unhampered by the red tape of government regulations.

Bolan took the initiative. "What's this all about, Hal?"

"The Golden Triangle. Opium production is up.

Almost fifteen hundred tons last year, and most of it destined for the U.S. and Eastern Europe.''

"You mean Poland, Hungary and the other former Soviet bloc countries?"

"Exactly. Freedom from their Communist masters brought their citizens a lot of benefits. But it also made heroin easily available, whereas before, using drugs was punishable by death."

"Is opium still mostly coming out of Yunnan Province in southern China?"

"The climate and conditions are perfect for growing poppies. And the Chinese Mafia in Thailand, Laos and Myanmar are more than willing to help refine it into heroin and smuggle it out of Southeast Asia."

"Opium is China's most profitable export," the big Fed went on, "but there's a new boy running the show. A General Lu Shu-Shui. He was an aide to General Li, who was the head honcho until somebody knocked him off last year."

"One of Beijing's new stars?"

"Not like you think. From what our sources tell us, Lu Shu-Shui isn't even Chinese. He's a product of the hill tribes who live in the Golden Triangle. But he's young and ambitious, and turns over half the profits to his red partners. Which leaves him with hundreds of millions of dollars for himself." The chief Fed looked discouraged. "Lu is only thirty-three years old, according to drug enforcement sources over there, but it only took him ten years to get from lieutenant to personal aide to General Li to getting him knocked off and becoming the head man.''

''How does he get along with the Yi Kwah Tao Triad? I assume they still control the distribution of Southeast Asian opium.''

''Things have changed more than you can imagine, Striker,'' Brognola replied. ''Lu has set things up so that he's got three of the triads distributing his poison. The top three Chinese crime syndicates—the Chui Chao, the 14K and the Yi Kwah Tao, now bid against one another for inventory. And high bidder gets to set the price for all three triads.

Bolan narrowed his gaze. ''It's a long way from the days when the triads were the powers and the growers were just the suppliers.''

''General Lu has convinced them that the other triads are trying to cut them out of the distribution channels.''

''The bosses must like that,'' the soldier commented cynically. ''The Chinese godfathers with their fancy titles must be just waiting for a chance to get to him.''

Bolan referred to the grandiose titles the syndicate heads gave themselves, Elder Brothers, and the names they assigned to their territorial commanders, Incense Masters. Even the heads of their strong-arm squads had elegant-sounding titles—Red Poles.

''The Elder Brothers tried a number of times. They ordered the regional commanders, the Incense Masters of Thailand, Laos and Burma, to send their troops into the Yunnan mountains. Somehow Lu got wind of the conspiracies. None of the triad hit men ever made it back alive. I don't think Lu is a Communist, but the Yunnan governor keeps sending him People's Revolutionary Army troops every time he runs into trouble. Money talks. Even among Marxists.''

"So we need to take out this General Lu, not the triad bosses," Bolan commented.

"Kill him and somebody else will move up the ranks to replace him. The replacement might end up being twice as vicious as Lu. We've got to hit him where it hurts, and maybe he'll listen to reason.''

"You mean in the pocketbook.''

Brognola nodded. "And that means shaking up his triad channels of distribution.''

Bolan knew the history of the Chinese crime syndicates. About the same time the Sicilians organized the Italian Mafia, the Chinese started gathering together in triads. These secret lodges had as many rituals as did the Mafia, all focusing on the total obedience of their members to the whim of the leadership.

The trio of men who ran each lodge were the Elder Brother, the Incense Master and the Red Pole. Despite their names, the Elder Brother was simply the godfather, and the Incense Master his chief capo. The Red Pole was responsible for carrying out sentences imposed by the Elder Brother.

As the triads spread from China to Hong Kong, then to foreign countries, an Incense Master became the representative of the Elder Brother, responsible to him for the success of the organization he oversaw.

The chain of command was inflexible. If the Elder Brother died, a conference of the Incense Masters selected a replacement, often accompanied by brutal battles between foot soldiers of their lodges.

The selection of Incense Master was less bloody. The Elder Brother made the decision and it wasn't disputable. Nor was the selection of a replacement for the strong-arm leader of each triad.

The communications network between the Elder Brother and his various lodges was often complicated by attempts by authorities to find out what the Chinese crime syndicate was planning.

Like the Sicilians, what had been a variety of income sources—prostitution, gambling, blackmail and protection—had evolved into the distribution of heroin, with the other rackets mere sidelines.

The triad leaders were imaginative in the distribution of the narcotic, and they employed a variety of means to get the white powder to those who sold it to drug addicts: "mules," couriers who carried the narcotic on or in their bodies; the cavities of animal and fish carcasses; cases of crates marked as holding a great variety of agricultural and manufactured products; trawlers and oceangoing freighters, even airplanes.

THE STOCKY HEAD of the Stony Man Farm complex had only two arguments with which to persuade Bolan to take on an assignment: their long-term friendship and mutual trust and respect.

Chewing on his ever-present but unlit cigar, Brognola had wasted no time getting to the point.

"The request for your help came right from the top. The Man thinks you can put a dent in the triad distribution network."

"The only way to stop them permanently is to get rid of the demand of the customers who crave the poison."

"Exactly what I told the President last night. But he was so disgusted at the reports that there were more than a million heroin addicts in this country alone, that he's decided to do something about it."

Bolan remembered his own reaction when he had first heard the figure.

"Short of burning up the poppy crops, then powdering the growing fields with long-lasting herbicides, the problem won't go away."

"Maybe not. But he's planning to hand the drug barons an ultimatum."

"And he expects me to deliver the message?"

"No. He's got somebody to do that."

The soldier looked surprised. "Anybody I know?"

"You should. It's Senator Bobby Firestone, chairman of the Oversight Subcommittee On Narcotic Traffic."

Bolan whistled in surprise. "Why did the Man pick someone like him?"

"He didn't. The senator insisted he be the one to personally present the President's offer and demands."

Bolan shook his head. "Do I get to know what the head Man wants the senator to tell them?"

"I think you'd better know. It's pretty straightforward. He's offering to buy all the unprocessed and processed opium in inventory, as well as poppy production at current wholesale market prices."

A look of disbelief washed across Bolan's face.

Brognola held up a hand. "Hold off till you hear the rest. In exchange, he wants all laboratories and refineries destroyed, all distribution channels shut down and all poppy production halted. He's willing to send in agricultural specialists to help the hill tribes switch to more acceptable crops."

"No way are they going to buy that deal," Bolan warned.

"There's a last part to the President's message. If the drug barons reject the offer, we'll send in as much personnel as it takes to destroy the fields, the labs and the drug warehouses, no matter how many lives it costs."

"Any reaction from the warlord?"

"General Lu said he was willing to meet with Senator Firestone and discuss the proposal." He made a face. "He doesn't know the details, but what's he got to lose listening? If nothing else, it'll elevate his prestige in the Southeast Asian drug world to be getting an offer from the President of the United States.''

Bolan got right to the point.

''What's my role in this?''

''The problem we've got is that too many of the East Asian thugs consider us a paper tiger. They think we talk tougher than we're willing to fight.'' He stared directly at the Executioner. ''We have to give them proof that they're wrong.''

''How about the combat forces?''

''That's the final commitment. Something simpler would reinforce the meetings the senator is planning to hold with the drug barons.''

Bolan wanted to make sure he understood the request. ''What did you have in mind?''

Brognola handed Bolan the stack of papers near him.

''It will have to be a big statement this time. A slap on the wrist won't do. When you're through, the drug barons will have to really know you were there.''

''Anything in mind?''

''I'll leave that up to you. Go anyplace you want. Do what you have to do. You always seem to come up with a way of making a lasting impression on the opposition without kicking off a full-fledged war. But I can at least point you in the right direction,'' Brognola added. ''There's a man at the embassy in Bangkok. Joe Collins. He's Drug Enforcement Administration and as tough as they come. And so far as we know, well informed and honest. He can steer you to the warehouses of the different triad syndicates.''

Bolan felt uncomfortable about exposing someone else to the dangers he was willing to face. Even someone accustomed to life-and-death struggles fighting organized drug syndicates.

''Tell me about him,'' he said.

''His brother was Pete Collins, a San Francisco narcotics cop. Ten years ago Collins was in medical school, studying to be the first doctor the Collins family ever had when somebody found Pete, his wife and two young sons under the Golden Gate Bridge. Somebody had carefully sliced their bodies into strips with razor blades—death of a thousand cuts. The medical examiner said they were alive through the torture.''

He shook his head.

''Collins hates the triads. There's an unconfirmed report that he was personally responsible for the deaths of more than a dozen youth gang and Tong members. Before anyone could question him, the DEA signed him up for training and then shipped him off to Bangkok to run their shop there.''

Mack Bolan had met victims of the triads. Most had been dead when he got to them. Those who managed to stay alive carried a deep burning hate inside that the soldier understood. He had felt the same way when the only woman he'd ever loved was brutally slain by American traitors.

"I'll call him if I need information," he promised.

It was Mack Bolan's way of saying he'd accept the mission.

"Call him when you get in," Brognola suggested. "He's put together a list of prime targets in the Bangkok area."

"What about the opium refineries in Burma? The poppy fields in the Golden Triangle?"

"You make the decision about what would tell the other side we mean business. You've got the President's backing on this one."

"Does he mean it about no CIA interference?"

"They've been alerted to confine their activities to keeping the senator alive," Brognola replied.

There were no farewells. The big Fed and Bolan had seen death touch their lives too often to talk about it.

The Stony Man Farm chief pushed back his chair and stood.

"I'm sorry there isn't time to finish dinner."

The soldier stared up at his old friend.

"Finish dinner? We never started."

Ignoring Bolan's pointed observation, Brognola checked his watch. "You've still got to pack, and a helicopter is waiting out at the landing pad to get you to Andrews, where a jet is standing by for you."

Bolan stood and gathered the papers from Brognola. The two men shook hands. As in times past, both knew this might be the last they saw each other alive.

CHAPTER TWO

Bangkok, Thailand

Chen Chi-Li gathered together the troops. As chief enforcer for the Bangkok lodge of the Chui Chao Triad, it was his responsibility to make sure everything was under control while he accompanied the Elder Brother and his right hand, the Incense Master, to the meeting in Chiang Mai.

"Someone will be staying at the American safehouse on Maekon Road. He must not be permitted to leave there alive."

One of the foot soldiers raised his hand. "Any suggestions?"

"If the house were to explode as he entered it, a possible problem would be gone."

The instructions were clear to the six men in the room—booby-trap the American safehouse.

"It will be done," the most senior of the troops promised.

BOLAN HAD CARRIED one small canvas bag when he checked into the run-down Patpong District hotel earlier in the evening. Paying in cash for two nights erased the suspicious stares of the young Chinese desk clerk, and a thick stack of Thai bahts made the hotel employee conveniently forget to ask the big American to deposit his passport.

The Oriental Palace usually catered to prostitutes who rented rooms by the hour. Occasionally, a tourist wandered in by accident to stay the night. To keep peace with the local police, the desk clerk rarely turned away such customers.

Brognola had given Bolan the address of a safehouse on the edge of Bangkok.

"You can rent a car at Don Muang Airport," the big Fed had said. "The phone at the CIA retreat is checked daily for bugs or taps."

There was no house when the warrior drove up to the address, just smoldering rubble and the body of a Thai cleaning woman.

It was obvious that the woman had detonated explosives and leveled the structure. She had no way of knowing the entrances had been booby-trapped.

Bolan mentally reviewed the list of people who knew his travel plans: Brognola, the President and the DEA agent, Collins.

Nobody else.

LOCKING THE DOOR that led to the shabby hotel corridor, Bolan listened to make sure no one was waiting for him to set aside his weapons and take a shower. After a few minutes, he was satisfied that the bored clerk downstairs considered him a nuisance who had picked a hotel in the red-light district by error.

Opening the small bag, the soldier withdrew a black, one-piece form-fitting garment. Made from space-age fabric developed by NASA scientists, the blacksuit kept Bolan cool in humid weather and warm when the temperature started to fall.

The blacksuit served other functions, as well. It helped mask Bolan's movements at night, and to those who saw him in it, the blacksuit inspired fear.

The Executioner checked the stainless-steel watch strapped to his left wrist. It was time to get ready.

Stripping out of his casual clothes, the big dark-haired man stepped into the musty-smelling bathroom and turned on the shower. Without waiting for the water to get warm, he stepped into the rusty tub and let the cold water bite into his body.

Even at night, the humid air from the Gulf of Thailand cast a heavy blanket over the Thai capital. And Bolan suspected he'd be sweating heavily before this night was over.

Still feeling fatigued from the nonstop flight to Bangkok, Bolan dried off, pulled on the one-piece blacksuit, then slipped into a pair of lightweight pants and put his arms through the combat vest that would carry his spare magazines of ammo.

It was time to suit up for that night's mission. The soldier opened the camera case. Inside, wrapped in sheets of foam, were some of the weapons he preferred to carry on missions like this. He slid his arms through the straps of the rigid leather shoulder harness that held the silenced 9 mm Beretta 93-R. The massive .44-caliber Desert Eagle fit easily into the belt holster.

Lifting his left pant leg, he strapped a chamois sheath around his lower leg. The combat knife it held was razor sharp, a silent assassin for occasions when even the slightest sound would reveal his presence.

Bolan put on the light jacket, specially cut loose enough to conceal the shoulder holster, and filled his pockets with full magazines for the two handguns. Then he opened the door of the hotel room and quickly checked the corridor for unexpected visitors. Clear.

He closed the door and hurried to the window. Two husky locals had taken up positions near the hotel entrance, and both wore loose-fitting jackets. To Bolan's trained eyes they hadn't bothered disguising the weapons they were wearing under them.

It wasn't much of a leap to conclude that if two gunners were guarding the front of the building, two more were waiting at the back exit.

The soldier wasn't sure he was the one they were after, but it was smarter to start with that premise.

Back at the door, the hallway was still empty.

He avoided the rickety elevator and slowly worked his way down the stairs until he could see the entrance from the shadowed mezzanine landing. One of the two men on the street strode into the empty lobby, a squat, bulky weapon clenched in one meaty fist.

Bolan recognized it immediately as a 9 mm Ingram MAC-10. Once reserved for use by Secret Service and FBI agents, copies became available to the public when the agents replaced the bulky submachine guns with mini-Uzis.

Grabbing the desk clerk by his shirt collar, he shouted, in Thai, "Are you sure the American is still in his room?"

Shivering from fear, the young hotel employee stuttered, "Yes, he must be up there. The only way out is through the lobby."

The heavyset thug shoved the clerk into the partitioned mail unit hanging on the back wall, then shouted toward the door.

"I'm going up after him. She will be angry that we have not brought him to her by now."

She? Bolan wondered who "she" was.

It was something he could ask about later. Right now he was preoccupied with getting out of there.

Stepping into the shadows, the soldier slipped the Applegate-Fairbairn knife from its sheath and waited until the burly hood passed him. Then he grabbed him around the neck and with a smooth slashing movement cut his neck into a wide, bloody smile.

Bolan held the struggling man for several moments, then released the corpse, easing it silently to the floor.

The SMG fell from the hit man's limp fingers. Bolan picked it up, then searched the dead man's pockets for extra magazines. Finding three, he slipped them into his jacket pockets and dragged the body deeper into the shadows.

Ten minutes passed. Bolan waited, watching the floor below from a corner of the landing.

The dead thug's partner hurried into the lobby, glaring at the Chinese clerk.

"Where is Mong?"

The young man pointed to the stairs. "He went up to the American's room."

In a sudden burst of fury the raging street fighter slashed the edge of his callused right hand across the neck of the young man behind the counter. With only a muffled gasp, the desk clerk slipped to the floor— dead.

Muttering to himself, the hardman turned and headed up the steps. As he reached the mezzanine landing, he saw his partner's body.

Then he turned and looked in horror at the muzzle of the SMG pointed at his head.

"Time to give up," Bolan said quietly in Thai.

The thug stared in silence at the big American, then lowered his chin and bit into a pellet hanging from a chain around his neck—a cyanide suicide capsule.

Bolan tried to force open the hit man's jaws, but seeing the empty grin on the thug's face, he knew it was too late.

As the gunman fell to the carpeted floor, a duplicate of the MAC-10 his dead partner had carried tumbled from his jacket to the ground.

There wasn't time to waste picking it up or to wonder how they found him and what they wanted. He had to assume someone along the way had sold him out. Quickly, he searched the second thug's pockets and found two more full magazines for the SMG.

His first instinct was to contact Brognola and tell him the mission had been compromised. But Bolan was more determined than ever to carry out his part of the assignment. It would take more than a quartet of hit men, and someone one of them referred to as "she," to stop him.

He knew he would have to deal with this unexpected threat, but he had too much to accomplish to give it more than a moment of thought.

He made a quick decision about his next move. There were still two more gunners out back, but Bolan decided he didn't need to get into a lead duel with so many innocent pedestrians on the streets.

Sliding the knife back into its sheath, he slipped the submachine gun under his jacket, pocketed the additional clips and calmly walked out the front door of the hotel.

He had to stop and pick up the bags he had left at the airport bus terminal, then meet the DEA agent at the small bar Collins had selected to obtain the list of heroin warehouses.

The Executioner was in a hurry to get started.

CHAPTER THREE

By nine in the evening, the small factories and ware-houses in the waterfront district of Bangkok had been closed and stood empty.

Except for the one-story corrugated metal building that backed onto the river. Inside lights were slightly visible through the thick, dirt-smeared windows, while a half-dozen armed thugs patrolled the interior.

The faded sign over the main entrance read Thai Agrochemical Products. Inside, neatly stacked cases of pesticides and insecticides lined the aisles of the structure.

Hidden inside the sacks of farming chemicals was the reason for the armed guards—plastic kilogram bags filled with heroin. More than fifty million dollars' worth of pure heroin, nicknamed China White by dealers and addicts, was waiting for a small fleet of trawlers to arrive and transport the narcotic to sea-going freighters waiting at the southern end of the Gulf of Thailand.

Chan Tse-Chao thought he heard a noise outside. Gripping the American-made 9 mm Ingram SMG in his right hand, the scar-faced thug opened the side door of the waterfront warehouse and carefully studied the immediate area. Satisfied, Chan shut and locked the thick metal door.

The other guard stared at him, a cynical expression crossing his face.

"Hearing things again?"

"Just checking," Chan grumbled. "Someone has to make certain no one attempts to steal our precious bags." He was getting tired of Kung Sa making fun of him just because he was being cautious. After all, until Chen Chi-Li returned he was in charge of the guards.

"The warehouse is full of powder," he reminded his comrade. "You can't be too careful. The other triads are jealous of the success of the Chui Chao."

"If you mean the 14K or the Yi Kwah Tao, you know the triads have signed a sacred oath pledging never to steal from the other triads."

The triad soldier had studied the sacred vows that accompanied the elevation of rank in the Chui Chao. Someday, he knew, he would move up in the ranks to Red Pole—perhaps even Incense Master of Bangkok—as he proved his worth. In preparation for those events, he learned all he could about what was expected of him.

Most sacred was the ceremony in which a candidate for one of the higher ranks was asked three hundred questions, covering the lifelong commitment to the Chui Chao. To an outsider, the ceremonies were similar to those held by the Italian Mafia, except that the Asian syndicate didn't exchange kisses on the cheek or the intermingling of drops of blood as evidence of a lifelong bonding.

"Pledges are made to be broken," Chan warned.

Kung decided to change the subject before he said something the other soldier would pass onto the Red Pole.

"Where did Chen Chi-Li go?"

"North with the Incense Master to Chiang Mai for a meeting," Chan replied.

Kung looked skeptical. "What kind of meeting requires Luk Ming Sang to bring the enforcer with him?"

Chan chose not to answer.

"It must be a very important meeting for the Red Pole to leave his post in Bangkok," the thick-necked guard added.

Chan was getting tired of being interrogated by someone he considered beneath his position in the triad.

"Why don't you ask him when he gets back?" he retorted.

The beefy guard knew better. Chen Chi-Li wasn't the kind of man of whom you asked questions. Not if you wished to live.

Kung Sa knew of the Red Pole's rapid rise through the ranks of the Chui Chao. Starting as a foot soldier, he moved up to become the leader of the strong-arm wing of the triad, second in command to Luk Ming

Sang, the head of the triad's branch in Bangkok—its Incense Master.

Someday Kung knew that Chan would move up the ranks to Red Pole, when Chen moved up to Incense Master or died in a battle. But the heavyset thug had his own secret ambitions. He knew things happened that could change careers.

Like Chan's death.

"It is time for you to check to make sure that the others are patrolling the warehouse," the scarfaced guard leader ordered, interrupting Kung Sa's thoughts.

The Red Pole had left seven trained warriors behind to guard the triad's precious inventory of heroin.

Kung's cousin, Chin Ma, who helped keep the financial records for the Incense Master, had told him in confidence that this was the largest shipment of the white powder the triad had ever exported. All was destined for a dozen major cities in the United States, where affiliated Chinese Tongs and youth gangs were anxiously waiting to resell the shipments to local distributors and dealers.

Each of the men had been promised a substantial bonus. Kung planned to use his to fly to Macao, pay off his gambling debts and try his luck again at the casino tables in the Portuguese enclave. This time he was positive he would win a small fortune from the casino owners.

Grumbling, the beefy foot soldier shoved the 7.62

mm carbine under an arm and shuffled his feet down one of the warehouse aisles.

BOLAN HID the confiscated Ingram SMG under his jacket and walked out the front door of the hotel and made his way to the side street where he had parked the rental car. Almost swallowed up by the teeming hordes of tourists and locals, he stared at the spectacle in depravity that surrounded him.

The City of Angels, as Bangkok was nicknamed by those who lived there, hadn't changed since his last visit. Patpong Road was still crowded with hawkers trying to drag passersby into their establishments, promising them everything from a live sex show to a night with a teenaged virgin.

The glare of neon burned in the night. Promises were shouted by pitchmen in a variety of languages—English, French, Japanese, Korean, even Spanish.

The huge metropolis got its nickname because of the great number of Buddhist temples that crowded every street and roadway.

Its other nickname was the Venice of the Orient, because of the great number of canals that connected the different districts. Almost as crowded with traffic as the streets, the *klongs* reeked of rotting garbage.

There was a third nickname for Bangkok, one it richly deserved—Sex Capital of the World.

Sex was an important commodity. More than

500,000 people tried to sell their wares day and night in every dark corner of the city.

But it was opium and its derivative, heroin, that created prosperity. In one way or another, most of the city's inhabitants thrived on the illicit drug trade. Bankers continuously found new ways to launder the illegal income of the drug syndicates. The boom in commercial construction owed its growth to investment funds funneled through intermediaries.

Underpaid policemen supplemented their meager salaries with bribes from distributors. Drug pushers fed the local addicts with the desperately craved white powder.

Even airline crews weren't immune. Thousands of flights left Bangkok for foreign cities every month. On many of them, hidden in the baggage or in the body cavities of passengers and crews or dissolved and hidden in liquor bottles, hundreds of kilos of opium and heroin were smuggled into the United States, Canada and Europe.

The profits from the poppy derivative were enormous. A five-thousand-dollar purchase of raw opium from the hill tribes who grew the colorful poppy plant, became nearly two million dollars after deducting processing and smuggling expenses.

THE SOLDIER HAD MADE his way to the side street where he had parked the small Nissan he had rented at the agency on Wireless Road, checking to make sure no one was tailing him. Satisfied he hadn't been observed, he'd driven through the crowded streets to the airport bus terminal, where he picked up one of the two canvas bags he had stored in separate public lockers.

Now the canvas carryall he had picked up sat in the back on the floor of the car. The one he'd left behind contained money he had confiscated from crime bosses and terrorists to finance his missions. This one contained his traveling arsenal. The appropriated MAC-10 and its clips were safely tucked under the front passenger's seat.

As he stopped for a red light, two ten-year-old Buddhist monks in saffron robes stepped into the street and silently held out collection plates to him.

Dropping a handful of Thai coins in their plates, the Executioner looked around for the small café where Collins had said he'd meet him.

Finally, the light changed and he turned the corner. The shabby-looking bar was at the far end of the street.

Yunnan Province

LU SHU-SHUI WAS annoyed at the interruption. He had been in bed with his favorite concubine, a British woman.

The Chiang Mai meetings wouldn't start until late the following day. His villa outside the northern city in Thailand was being prepared for the men who would be his guests.

Showing his irritation, Lu sat up in the bed and snapped, "What is it, Colonel?"

"The governor of the province has just landed in his helicopter. He needs to talk to you, General."

Lu wondered if the Communist official was going to demand more money for permitting Lu and his forces to use the vast lands of the Golden Triangle to grow their poppy crops. This would be the third time in two months that Governor Zhao Jafar Bun had arrived unexpectedly at the base camp Lu called home with demands for additional contributions to his personal bank account.

Slipping into his uniform, the handsome young hill tribesman checked his appearance and walked out into the morning sun.

Zhao was waiting for him in the mess tent.

Lu shook the gray-haired man's hand and ordered tea for the two of them.

"Is something wrong?"

"Beijing is demanding more contributions to help support their efforts to rebuild the country."

Lu smiled. He could feel the scar that crossed his right eyebrow start to twitch. It always did when he was working on a solution to a problem.

Giving away more of his profits from the opium production would be a problem. He thought of having the Yunnan governor killed. But he knew all that would do was bring in a replacement, and perhaps create unnecessary problems between the Communists and him.

Aside from the monetary donations, all that the Beijing government demanded was that no incidents occur in Yunnan Province. If there were conflicts, it was important that they happen in the bordering countries—Thailand, Laos and Burma.

So far, Lu had been able to resolve disputes by a simple rule—he had both parties in the disagreement killed by one of his personal troops.

"That could be a problem," Lu warned. "Already the triads are demanding we lower our prices on the white powder so they can maintain their profits on distributing the heroin."

"Perhaps it is time you found some other way to distribute the opium," Zhao suggested.

Lu smiled. A man was coming to the Chiang Mai conferences who could do just that. He had waited a long time to meet the man, who was a United States senator. Robert Firestone was a powerful man, who was in charge of investigating narcotics distribution. From what his Intelligence sources had told him, Senator Firestone had the ear of the American President.

In fact, one of his contacts in Washington, D.C., reported there was talk that the senator might run for the presidency when the current officeholder completed his term.

"I am meeting with the triad leaders in Chiang Mai tomorrow. A special representative of the American President has contacted me with a proposal."

"What does he suggest?"

"I don't know. He said he would reveal the offer when the triads and I met with him. It doesn't matter what deal he brings. I think I have the means to convince him it would be to his advantage to help me find a more direct way to distribute the refined opium."

The governor stood.

"I assume you will take some of our People's Revolutionary Army troops with you."

"Only the special ones. It would be foolhardy to go alone."

The general had selected the best hundred soldiers from the force of five hundred men under his command and given them better accommodations, women and additional money to protect him and the poppy plants.

"Beijing expects a reply from you this week. I have done everything I can to stall them. But you know how impatient the central government can get."

"They will get the reply from me before the week is ended. And I think that they—and you—will be pleased with what I can offer."

"I have faith in you," the governor agreed, then added, "I assume you made the usual deposit to my Swiss account."

Lu Shu-Shui smiled. Like all Communist officials, the Yunnan Province official was a practical man.

Bangkok, Thailand

BOLAN WAS STARTING to feel the lack of sleep. The cacophony of car horns and loud music from the rows of bars that lined the red-light district of Bangkok kept him awake.

His rented Nissan was jammed in late-night traffic, and he looked around with interest. At an hour when families should be sitting down to an evening meal, single men and women, as well as large families, walked aimlessly down the street, oblivious to the shouted offers from peddlers and hustlers.

Like the rest of the city, Patpong Road resembled one huge shrine to Buddha. Giant statues of the heavyset, serene-looking founder of Buddhism were located at almost every corner.

The soldier watched as young men raced in and out of traffic on small Japanese motorcycles or mopeds, their hair long and whipped by the wind, each wearing the same uniform of faded jeans and workshirts, deliberately trying to irritate the more traditional, older generation.

Bolan finally reached the corner, which he turned, then found a parking spot. Moments later he slipped into the small bar where he was to meet the DEA contact.

Inside the tiny bar, whose atmosphere was permeated by rock and roll music from a jukebox, he spotted a tall, brawny man with neatly trimmed sandy-blond hair sitting alone. He wore casual slacks and a loose jacket.

"Collins?"

The seated man looked up and studied the tall man who had appeared at his table.

"You must be Belasko," he said icily.

Bolan nodded as he sat. He could tell that Collins was angry, but he had too much to get done to worry about that now.

The agent handed the soldier two sheets of paper, the supposed locations where the triad stored its drugs. There were twenty listed.

When he had finished scanning it, Bolan looked up at Collins.

He had questions to ask. Before he could, however, Joe Collins asked a question of his own.

"Are you CIA, Belasko?"

"No," Bolan replied.

"Then you must just be crazy," Collins decided, still sounding irritated.

"I've been accused of that before," the soldier admitted. "Why?"

"Look, I don't care if the reason you're here is to go out in a blaze of glory. Getting this list cost me a lot of points with contacts I've been building for the past five years. So you better be planning to use it."

"That's why I'm here."

"What do you plan to do—knock on the door and walk inside? It doesn't work that way. The warehouses have squads of top killers guarding them, and the trawlers coming to pick up the heroin will be covered by armed guards, as well. All of them are triad foot soldiers, dedicated to their godfather, to borrow a phrase from the Italians.''

The Executioner didn't reply.

"You don't act like a CIA cowboy or contract hit man, but I keep wondering what you're doing here if you're not," Collins continued.

The soldier couldn't think of an answer to give him, without lying. And Collins didn't look like someone who trusted easily.

"I could ask you the same question," he replied. "From what I've been told, you could have a cushy job back in D.C., instead of working in this back-water country."

"I've got my reasons," he said, sounding evasive.

"Do they have something to do with your brother and his family?"

Collins looked stunned. "That's my business."

"You can't go forward trying to get revenge on the men who killed them," Bolan commented. "You'll waste a lot of your life if you do."

"What do you know about it?" he asked bitterly. "You didn't see their bodies at the morgue, sliced up like slabs of beef. And when the cops caught the killers, they were all under sixteen, part of a China-town youth gang, so they got off with a couple of years in jail."

The soldier knew the drill from personal experi-ence. He had witnessed the murder and degradation of his own family.

The DEA agent flashed an icy smile.

"But they got theirs," he reminisced. "And now the men who sent them are getting payback."

"Let it go," Bolan advised. "There's no lasting satisfaction in revenge."

Collins shook his head. "Strange words coming from a hired gun." Then he studied him.

"Why are you here?"

"To help give a million and a half junkies back in the States a chance to get clean. They'll never make it as long as the triads find ways of smuggling the poison into the United States."

"I thought that was why the President sent Senator Firestone here. To cut a deal with the bigwigs." A look of disgust crossed his face. "It won't work. Whatever they promise, they won't keep their word."

"That's why I'm here. To show them what will happen if they renege."

"One man against a thousand thugs." The skeptical expression returned. "You don't have a snowball's chance in hell of succeeding."

"At least I can try," Bolan said.

Collins suddenly became quiet. Finally he spoke again.

"You're on a suicide mission. The odds are against you. Why don't you pack your bags and go home?"

"Like you said. Not a snowball's chance in hell," the soldier replied bluntly.

The DEA agent kept staring at him, studying his

face, his expression, his eyes. Collins was impressed by the physical appearance of the man who sat across from him. He looked even larger than the six foot three he had been told Belasko was. If he weighed two-hundred pounds it was more in muscle and toughened sinew than in body fat.

The man was larger than life. Collins had met many mercenaries, but none with the self-confident expression, the cold, dead eyes Belasko wore. He looked like someone who had taken care of himself and others for a very long time.

The one thing Collins was certain of—Belasko wasn't someone he wanted to face in battle.

"You really mean it, don't you? About not packing up and going home."

Bolan nodded.

"You are crazy. I hate watching someone commit suicide."

"Nobody invited you to join. I work alone."

"That's a shame. You need somebody who can steer you to the right contacts, get you to the right places." He hesitated, then continued. "For instance, do you know where the senator is right now?"

"No," Bolan admitted.

"He's on a helicopter flying to Chiang Mai to meet with General Lu and his triad partners."

"That's what he came to do."

"Maybe. But I don't think he was expecting to have the enemy show up at his hotel and offer him a helicopter ride there."

"How'd they know where to find him?"

"There's a snitch in the embassy," Collins informed him.

"Do you know who?"

"Positively? No. But my hunch is an old-timer with the CIA trying to put away a private retirement fund. His name's Dave Weyant, if my contacts are telling the truth. But there's no proof. And if you know anything about government, you need proof to take somebody out."

Bolan didn't offer an explanation. But that was exactly why he didn't work for the government.

"Are you saying he was kidnapped?"

"No. I think whoever contacted him promised to get all the drug barons together in Chiang Mai."

"Why there?"

"For one thing, it's close to the Chinese border. Also, General Lu has a private villa just outside town. I don't know what else he said to con the senator to come north, but it had to have been pretty good."

A cynical expression crossed Collins's face as he continued. "Maybe he waved a picture of his mother in front of the senator and promised him a date with her. From what I hear she's a pretty hot-looking lady for someone in her late forties."

"What's she got to do with this?"

"She raised Lu, and from what I hear, used stolen drugs to finance his career. That's hearsay, of course. On the surface she is a very successful exporter of

Thai silk and art. And very rich." He smiled cynically. "A lot richer than any rice or silk merchant you'll ever meet."

"Maybe I ought to meet this lady. What's her name?"

"Mai Ling. Sounds Chinese, but she isn't. Comes from one of the tribes that grows poppies in the hills on the Thai-China border. And she's someone you want to avoid. She's got a personal army of trained thugs who like hurting people, even if they haven't done anything wrong."

"You're making the meeting sound too much fun to miss."

Collins shook his head in exasperation. "I knew it. You are crazy."

Like a fox, Bolan thought.

The key to General Lu was his mother. Know how she thought, and you could predict how her son would react.

He wanted to meet her. But the meeting would have to wait until he had completed his primary mission, which was to wipe out warehouses that belonged to the three prime triads.

And Bolan was pumped to get going.

CHAPTER FOUR

Parking the small car on a side street, Bolan shed his outer clothes. The lack of streetlights would cover his movements, while he reconnoitered the warehouse Collins had claimed was a major heroin distribution center for the Chui Chao Triad.

After circling the one-story building, he paused to evaluate the situation. A loading dock faced the street, and a door on the opposite side of the warehouse led to a parallel street. A smaller platform at the rear of the structure faced the river, making it easy to receive the deadly merchandise from the small pirogues that plied the brackish water, and move the plastic kilo bags filled with the white poison hidden in cases of legitimate merchandise.

The windows of the warehouse were streaked with dust and dirt, making it difficult for the Executioner to peer inside and get an accurate count of the number of triad soldiers guarding the building.

The only thing Bolan was sure of was that he had to be ready for anything that happened.

He pulled a mini-Uzi machine pistol from the car-

ryall. Sliding the sling over his left shoulder, Bolan
decided it was better to be alive and ready than dead
and sorry.

His mission was to destroy the heroin cache inside,
and the plastic explosives in the carryall should accomplish that. A thin nylon rucksack shoved in a
corner of the carryall would make carrying them easier and leave his hands free to use his weapons if he
ran into enemy gunners.

He had a full plate ahead of him. Brognola said
he wanted to make a lasting impression, and the soldier had a simple solution.

Destroy everything he could.

Digging deep into the canvas bag, he took out four
blocks of C-4 plastique, already fitted with detonators
and timers.

Bolan slipped the bag on his back and worked his
way back around the building to the small loading
platform.

He had noticed a glass-paned door to the right of
the dock. Gently, he turned the handle. The door was
locked, as he had expected it would be. However,
the barrier posed no challenge. He had brought a
small glass cutter and a roll of sticky tape. Carefully,
he scored the glass pane nearest the door handle, then
tapped the cut edges and separated the glass from the
frame. He attached several lengths of the sticky tape
to the pane to pull it out.

Reaching through the small opening, the Executioner felt around. There was only a door-handle

lock. Surprised at the lack of security, Bolan wondered if the group wasn't worried because its members were dumb or because the warehouse was full of armed guards. He opted for the latter.

Easing open the door, the soldier slipped inside. He let his eyes get used to the darkness, then went to search for possible live opposition.

FOUR MEN in sweat-stained fatigues sat around a small table in the office. A double deck of cards was in front of one of them, weapons nearby on the floor.

A short, slender man smiled at his companions and started shuffling the cards.

"Another game of blackjack?"

"You've been hypnotized by gambling ever since you got back from Macao, Tsung," a stocky man complained.

"I do not wish to waste time talking. Are we going to play?"

The third, a wide-faced man who was missing his upper front teeth, offered an observation.

"I think you lost your money in Macao and wish to win it back from us."

The small slender man was getting annoyed. "Do you want to play? Yes or no?"

The stocky man sighed. The game had already cost him a thousand bahts, but it was better than sitting around dying of boredom.

"We can start again when Shen and Wong finish checking the warehouse area."

"And find nothing," Tsung stated. "Who would dare invade a warehouse of the Chui Chao Triad?"

He stood and grabbed the AK-47 assault rifle from the back of his chair, where it had been hanging.

"Well, let's give them a hand so we can get back to the game that much quicker."

He turned to the man with the missing upper teeth. "You wait here in case there is a call from the Red Pole."

Tsung and the stocky foot soldier shouldered their weapons.

"If the Incense Master calls, get his number and tell him I'll call him back when I have the time," Tsung called out as he and the other man headed out the door into the warehouse.

The man looked disgusted. "If I tell the Incense Master what you just said, you will not live long enough to call him back."

Tsung didn't hear the remark. He and his partner had already vanished into the warehouse area.

THE SOLDIER MOVED silently through the warehouse. He had planted two of the plastic explosive blocks among the heroin stores, and he had thirty-five minutes to finish and get out.

Moving down a wide aisle between two rows of wooden crates, Bolan heard voices speaking Chinese. He moved quickly to the end of the aisle and pressed himself against a wall, hiding in the shadows of the large wooden boxes.

He eased the Uzi from his shoulder and waited for the gunners to appear.

"Nobody here, Shen," the nearer voice called out.

"Good. We'll just swing past the crates of rice and then see if we can win some of our money back from Tsung," the second voice replied.

Bolan lowered the weapon and gripped it tightly. The Uzi had a habit of pulling up as it was fired, unless it was kept under control.

He heard the footsteps come closer, then stop.

"Hey, you been walking around here, Shen?"

"Not for a couple of hours. Why?"

"Looks like somebody stirred up the dust."

"Maybe one of the other men did when they made the rounds," Shen replied.

"Maybe."

Bolan readied himself as vague shadows appeared on the floor in front of him.

The first shadow became a tall, thickset man built like a wrestler who held a Chinese-made AK-47.

Bolan pushed the Uzi at him.

"Who are—" The man froze.

The second voice called out. "What's wrong, Shen?"

Bolan stepped out in front of both men.

"I'm what's wrong," he said calmly.

The second man bared his toothless gums in a snarl and hastily brought his Russian-made AKS-74 U shorty assault rifle into target acquisition. Anticipating the move, Bolan spun out of the path of the clattering slugs. The shooter tried to follow his adversary's movement, but he was having trouble keeping the submachine gun from shooting its rounds into the ceiling.

Bolan drilled three rounds at the gunman. The first punctured his sternum and shoved the man into a stack of wooden crates. The second and third slugs punched holes in his stomach.

Stunned at the swiftness with which death came, the shooter dropped his weapon and crumpled to the ground.

The second guard took advantage of the distraction and fired at Bolan. Like his dead comrade, he was having trouble controlling the rounds fired at the target.

By the time he could pull down the gun barrel, Bolan was no longer in front of him. The Executioner didn't waste time aiming carefully. Instead, he let the Uzi's tendency to ride up create a vertical pattern of holes from the guard's stomach to his face.

Momentarily unaware he was dying, the guard tried desperately to return fire. His trigger finger wouldn't respond to his brain's command. He started to say something to Bolan, but his words were cut off when death claimed him.

As the soldier turned to retrieve his rucksack, he felt a blow across his shoulders. Staggering from the unexpected attack, Bolan lost his balance and fell against the wooden shelving. The Uzi fell from his hands.

A second blow followed the first.

Still stunned, Bolan turned and saw a slender man slashing down at him with the metal stock of an AK-47. He rolled away just in time to avoid a third blow.

The angry-faced man hovering over him quickly reversed the weapon in his hand and rammed his finger in front of the trigger.

The soldier kicked upward, between the attacker's legs, and smashed his booted toe into the man's genitals. Grunting with pain, the guard staggered backward, but managed to hold on to his weapon.

Bolan knew there was no time to retrieve the Uzi. He released the Applegate-Fairbairn blade from its sheath as he rolled sideways again.

The furious guard, still grimacing from the blow to his groin, pulled back on the trigger. The muzzle of his rifle jerked toward the ceiling as a continuous stream of lead tore from the barrel. The slender shooter was shoved backward from the recoil.

Bolan took advantage of the momentary confusion and wrapped his hands around a wooden upright, feeling the pain of the bruised shoulder as he pulled himself to his feet.

Jumping at the man, the Executioner wrapped an arm around his neck and pulled the razor-sharp combat knife across his adversary's carotid artery.

Fresh red blood spurted like a fountain from the severed vessel, soaking the man's shirt and spattering blood on Bolan's hand. Releasing the man from his iron grip, the soldier watched him sag into a nearby stack of wooden boxes, then slide along them to the ground.

As Bolan wiped his bloodied hand with a rag he found nearby, a question popped into his head. How many more he would have to face before he could get on with the business of eliminating the heroin cache?

He picked up the fallen Uzi and checked his watch.

Getting rid of the three men had taken fifteen minutes. Only twenty minutes left before the timers set off the planted plastic explosive charges.

He moved back to where he had set down the rucksack.

As he kneeled, a too-familiar sound alerted the soldier and he spun. A large man with an expanded stomach that reflected years of overeating started firing the 9 mm Skorpion machine pistol in his massive hands.

Only Bolan's quick reaction saved him from being stitched by projectiles from the Czech-made weapon. Dropping the Uzi, he threw himself toward the shooter as soon as he heard the metallic click of a trigger moving. The concrete floor behind him kicked up a pattern of dust as the rounds chopped into it.

There was no time to compare the relative merits of the various arms he was carrying.

Without worrying if it was the right choice, Bolan

yanked the .44 Magnum Desert Eagle from its rigid side holster, flicked off the safety and fired twice.

Both rounds ripped into the stocky man's right side and made him stumble. Bellowing in rage, the shooter unlimbered an assault rifle and started to aim it at Bolan's head. Before he could pull back on the heavy trigger, the soldier quickly corrected his aim and unleashed a trio of slugs into the enraged man's chest.

Bits of shattered breastbone and tissue flew from the newly opened crater in the guard's chest. Thick red fluid flowed from the gaping wound.

The Executioner retrieved the Uzi and slung it over a shoulder, then expelled the clip on the Desert Eagle. Snapping in a fresh clip, he pulled himself to his feet.

Ignoring the pain in his shoulder from where the guard had rifle-butted him, he picked up his rucksack, then moved quietly down the wide aisle, stepping over the bodies and making his way to the small door ahead.

Gun ready, he braced himself and kicked open the door. With his .44 Magnum pistol held in front of him, he made a quick survey of the area.

The room was empty. Only a double deck of cards and an ashtray filled with cigarette butts sitting on a small wooden table indicated that anybody had ever been in there.

The former occupants were dead. All of them, he hoped.

A second door led from the room. Carefully, Bolan opened it and listened. Nothing.

He had a simple rule. Check first. Die later. It had kept him alive all these years. He followed it now.

Working his way around the door and along the adjacent wall, he steadied his weapon, ready to take on anyone who might be there.

Stacked to the ceiling all around him were crates, mostly sealed. The markings on the sides indicated they had originated in Thailand and were filled with rice. But all of them were filled with death in the form of heroin.

Quickly, he moved up and down the aisles, alert for hidden attackers. Finally satisfied he was alone, the soldier started to plant the rest of his explosive charges and to set their timers.

An aisle filled with crates clearly marked as weapons and ammunition from the United States, People's Republic of China and Russia was a bonus discovery. After checking the labels, Bolan forced the lids from two of them.

Inside were layers of RPG-22 light antitank missile launchers and 73 mm HEAT rockets.

The soldier slung a pair of the launchers and put several rockets into his rucksack. Then he pressed the final block of C-4 against the bottom of one of the stacks of crates.

Finally done, he checked his watch—less than ten minutes remained.

Feeling the bone-deep pain in his shoulder, he

thought of leaving without forcing his injured shoulder to support the weight of additional supplies. Another dozen fragmentation grenades might come in handy, he decided, as he changed his mind and packed them in the remaining space in the rucksack.

Several cases of high-powered 9 mm ammunition caught his attention. He grabbed a couple of boxes from an opened crate and packed them beside the grenades, then worked his way back through the side door to the street.

Bolan reached the car, got in and dropped the shoulder bag next to the canvas carryall on the floor.

He started the engine, then looked back at the small building. He had accomplished three things this night: he had destroyed a small fortune of white-powdered death, killed a handful of street thugs and begun his campaign to bring terror back home to the triads.

As he drove away, he remembered something else he had accomplished. He had planted seeds of suspicion about who was responsible for the soon-to-be demolished warehouse. Knowing the paranoid mentality of the Chinese Mafia, he was certain the triad leadership would place blame on one of their rivals, or at the doorstep of the Golden Triangle warlord.

Loud thunder roared through the air as the plastic explosives released their destructive energy. Through his rearview mirror, he could see flames shooting into the sky. The fire rapidly consumed the large storage facility, saturating the air with the strong aroma of burning heroin.

Several minutes later as he quit the area, fire trucks rushed past him, heading for the holocaust. He slowed to let them pass, then accelerated again.

It was time to go fishing, and the Executioner knew he had the right bait.

Death.

CHAPTER FIVE

Rangoon, Myanmar

Former general Mikhail Chernov knew more about what was now called Myanmar than he let on to his contact at the Russian embassy.

In his business, one had to know who the competition was and where to find it.

In Myanmar the competition was the peasants under the control of the Shan army.

The Shan States formed the border between Myanmar, China and Thailand. All the opium processed in Myanmar was shipped for export through Thailand to avoid confrontation with the puritan government authorities.

The Shans were Myanmar's largest minority group. Denied independence when the country rid itself of the British, the Shan people had formed their own government. Although not officially recognized by the authorities in Rangoon, direct conflicts were scrupulously avoided.

The sale of opium financed the Shans' continued

struggle for independence from the government in Rangoon.

The Shan United Army, one of the two major military forces on the border with China and Thailand, was led by one of the minor warlords named General Tuan Weh. Tuan controlled a number of the major opium refineries in the region. But because he was isolated from drug distribution networks, the Shan general was satisfied to be a junior partner of the supreme warlord in the Golden Triangle, General Lu Shu-Shui.

Tuan's refineries had been described to Chernov by agents who had visited them with the excuse of being potential buyers. They were relatively primitive laboratories, filled with a minimum of apparatus and a great number of underpaid workers from the hill tribes.

Only the chief chemist had the experience and expertise to reduce bulky raw opium into the two types of heroin most popular among addicts—Opium No. 3, used by those who preferred inhaling the snowlike chemical, and Opium No. 4, the choice of those who injected the drug directly into their veins.

The process reduced the bulk by ninety percent, making the smuggling of the opium concentrate a less complicated task.

Trucks transported the drug through the mountains and into Thailand to where the kilo-sized bags were smuggled by air or boat into foreign countries as far away as Russia.

Chernov's review of what he knew about the opium trade in Myanmar was interrupted by the former KGB officer.

"I heard about your son," Yuri Maleshnikoff said.

"When one loses a child, the world weeps," Chernov said quietly. Then he added, "But when one loses a son, the future of his family cries bitter tears."

The two men hugged, a Russian tradition that was supposed to prove their closeness. Usually, however, it became an expected formality, as it was this time.

"Do they know who killed him?"

"Two drug dealers from here," Chernov lied. "Unclean hoodlums."

Maleshnikoff smiled. As a member of a faction of the reorganized KGB, he was very much aware of the retired general's new business venture.

"And you are here to avenge his death."

"Would you do less?"

"No, of course not," the Russian cultural attaché said quickly. "How can I help you?"

"The murderers came from the north. My men and I need a way to get there, and the proper equipment for when we do."

Maleshnikoff held up his hands in protest. "The government frowns on killings, no matter how just the reason."

Chernov reached inside his jacket and took out a thick wad of bills.

"Swiss francs. There should be enough here to

buy us transportation and anything else we might need.''

Quickly, the embassy official thumbed through the money. ''More than enough, old friend.''

''What is left please keep as a token of my affection.''

''I will remember you after I retire as a dear friend and former comrade in arms,'' Maleshnikoff promised.

The two men had served together in the early years of the Afghanistan campaign. Chernov as head of a Spetsnaz battalion, Maleshnikoff as a deputy director of Russian Intelligence.

''But gather what we need quickly.'' He handed the government representative a list.

Maleshnikoff ran a finger down the page. ''Everything you request is available, except Hind Mi-24 helicopters. The only Hinds in this country are the ones our government donated as a token of our affection.''

''We can accept a reasonable substitute that will carry my friends and me.'' Then he paused before adding, ''And Yuri, I presume that being the military Intelligence resident here is not the profitable position it once was.''

Maleshnikoff was surprised by the blunt comment.

''No. Everything has changed since the Soviet Union ceased to exist.'' Then he added, ''It will take me twenty-four hours. I've rented you a large house in the best part of Rangoon. Enjoy the sights while I get busy.''

As he turned to rush away, Chernov stopped him. ''While you are taking care of our needs, could you arrange for us to meet a representative of the Karin United Revolutionary Army?''

The embassy officer looked puzzled. ''Why a Karin, specifically?''

''I am told they hate those who deal in opium.''

Like their Shan neighbors, the Karins were at constant war with the Myanmar government. The Karin army was predominantly Christian. Because they refused to grow or trade in opium, they financed their activities with a five percent border tax.

''They do. But none of them are in Rangoon. I can have someone set up a meeting for you in some village north of Mandalay.''

''Good. Do it.''

Chernov reflected on the events that led him into this new and profitable career.

The Azerbaijanis had tried to dominate the drug traffic. But Chechens like Chernov, who flocked to Moscow from northern Caucasus, had driven them from competition, killing those who refused to get out of their way.

To anyone who would listen, Chernov claimed that he and his men were only trying to help veterans of the unfortunate war to save Afghanistan from American-backed rebels. Thanks to their government, the soldiers had acquired a drug habit, as

American soldiers had acquired during the Vietnam War.

The Soviet government had refused to help the addicted veterans after the conflict had stopped. They even refused to acknowledge that these heroes were drug addicts.

The Afghans were more than willing to supply the Russian soldiers with as much opium as the veterans could afford to buy. That much was true.

Former general Chernov had actually seen the rapid growth in drug addiction firsthand, when he commanded the Third Spetsnaz Battalion stationed just outside the Afghanistan capital of Kabul. His own son, Arkady—a first-rate lieutenant—had become addicted to opium.

His personal solution to the problem was simple— execute all of those caught using heroin.

When the Third Battalion was returned to the Soviet Union and disbanded, Chernov saw how many veterans had come back to Russia and the other former Soviet republics with a serious drug habit.

Searching for a way to supplement the meager pensions he and his men were offered by the government, he saw an easy opportunity to create a major new industry—the growing, refining and sale of opium.

His answer to the Golden Triangle was the Golden Crescent. Luxuriant poppy fields sprouted across the former Soviet republics of Kazahkstan, Uzbekistan, Turkmenistan and Tajikistan. Thousands of square kilometers were filled with the deceptively beautiful blossoms, blessed by a climate that permitted two crops to be grown each year.

More than a million and a half addicts consumed much of the refined opium, but still there was more than enough of the poison left to export. In deals with the American and Sicilian Mafia, Chernov and his associates were able to move the rest of the processed drug at a profit of more than five hundred million dollars.

And ran into the tough competition created by Chinese triads.

Chernov had sent skilled ex-soldiers to eliminate competition in Europe and the United States. But that only resulted in the loss of lives on both sides.

When the triads began to infiltrate territories that had been the exclusive province of the Russian mob, the former Soviet general had stepped up his war with the Chinese drug distributors.

The news that the American government was sending a senior official to negotiate a deal with the warlord and the triads handling distribution made his next decision obvious—wipe out the triads, the refineries and the poppy fields that supplied them.

This was one cold war that was going to get hot quickly.

He had decided to personally lead a well-trained force of former Soviet commandos to where the Asians grew and refined their poppies and destroy everyone and everything involved.

The solution was simple when examined with a military strategist's mind. The twenty Spetsnaz commandos he had smuggled into Myanmar were the elite of the old Soviet warriors. Well-trained, emotionless, resourceful, they had proved themselves in Angola and Afghanistan. Now they would prove themselves again in Southeast Asia.

The first task was to eliminate the refineries that converted the opium into the more-easily-shipped heroin. The small primitive factories would consume several hours of his men's time at most. Then it was across the border to the southern sectors of the Yunnan Province of China.

There, in the mountainous region, were the poppy fields of the Golden Triangle. The poorly defined national boundaries made it impossible to determine which land belonged to Thailand, Laos, Myanmar or China.

To Chernov it didn't matter. If poppies grew on the land, herbicides were to be sprayed to destroy them. The chemicals Chernov had brought had been banned by the United Nations for destroying people as well as agricultural pests. But the bleeding hearts of that international body couldn't distinguish between peasants and human beings.

Which was all the hill tribes of the Golden Triangle were—peasants.

The death of his son, Arkady, provided him with the perfect excuse for traveling to Southeast Asia. He was a grieving parent seeking revenge.

At least the Russian embassy resident in Myanmar, Yuri Maleshnikoff, seemed to buy it. Chernov hoped others would, too.

If they didn't, too bad. They would have to join the Azerbaijanis, who complained when he took control of the heroin trade.

In hell.

Before leaving to negotiate for the supplies on the list, the cultural attaché led Chernov and his men on a stroll through Rangoon.

To the Russian, Rangoon was a pleasant but boring experience. Wandering along the broad boulevards of the capital was duller than strolling through the area surrounding the Kremlin in Moscow. It was like walking through a time in history when the British ruled the country, much like when the Russians ruled the other Soviet republics.

Surrounded on three sides by the Rangoon River, a tributary of the Irrawaddy River, the city had a gentle climate, kept pleasantly cool by breezes from the Bay of Bengal, twenty miles away.

Laid out like a grid, finding addresses in the capital was a simple exercise. Unlike those in other major Southeast Asian cities, Rangoon streets and roads were clearly marked. No traffic jams interfered with the movement of vehicles. And after midnight, the city virtually came to a stop.

Factories and warehouses were mostly located in the Okkalapa section of the city, on side streets near the Pazundaung Creek.

The only legal way to enter or leave Myanmar by commercial flight was via Rangoon's Mingladon Airport. Airflot's Moscow-Tashkent-Vientiane-Rangoon flight operated once weekly.

As he led the sightseeing tour, the ex-KGB official made a comment.

"It is too bad you cannot stay for the Water Festival. A most charming and childlike occasion."

Chernov had heard about the Burmese holiday. Celebrating the arrival of some mythical god wasn't of primary importance to him. The only god he worshiped was the one who provided him with the money and power to live better than he had ever lived.

Yuri Maleshnikoff, the former general decided, had grown soft. There was a time when the spy in charge of a station spent his time killing enemies of the Soviet Union, as well as dissidents and traitors. Now Maleshnikoff seemed to fill his time mooning over some local festival.

"But now it is time to eat, before you leave for Mandalay and the Myanmar border," the ex-KGB officer suggested.

IT WAS OBVIOUS that the people of Myanmar took their food seriously. The meal consisted of a bowl of steaming fish soup and rice noodles, seasoned with lemon grass, banana stem, fried garlic, chili powder and a squeeze of fresh lime juice. Fruits and salad were served as side dishes. And large cups of tea helped wash away the searing sensations of the overpowering spices.

"When and where do we pick up the helicopters?"

"I've arranged to rent a pair of Mi-24s from the local civil air authorities. There is a small military airfield just outside the city. They and their crews will be waiting there for you."

Chernov was surprised. "How could you rent Hinds from the government?"

"We have no friends in the government, but we do have a lot of high-level mouths we feed regularly."

Now Chernov understood. Useless gunships made excellent gifts for future favors.

"And everything we requested will be aboard?"

"Without any inspection from the government representatives. They have been properly rewarded for their lack of diligence. As have the crews."

Chernov smiled. Maleshnikoff hadn't forgotten everything he had learned in the KGB's training program.

Standing, the ex-general stretched and commented, "Then it is time I retrieved my men and got on my way. We have a lot of work to complete in very little time."

Maleshnikoff moved to his side.

"And when I officially retire, I can presume you will have some position available in your organization for someone with my skills?"

"For you there will always a significant job with me," Chernov lied, making a note to eliminate the man when he and his men were leaving the country.

CHAPTER SIX

Whatever else the DEA man might turn out to be, Collins's information was accurate, Bolan decided, watching from the dark doorway as crews loaded large wooden crates into the rows of trawlers bobbing in the water.

The trawlers were operated by Thai captains, but the stocky men loading the boxes on them were Chinese, all foot soldiers for the Chui Chao Triad.

They were pure syndicate. Each man carried a side arm, while several wore carbines slung across their chests in leather slings.

The crates were marked with a variety of content labels, ranging from rice to silk, but their contents were all the same. Intermingled with the indicated products were thick plastic bags of refined heroin, with a street value of several hundred million dollars.

Bolan knew what the crates contained. He had checked several before positioning himself in the nearby doorway.

The dark-haired American, dressed in a blacksuit, his face masked with combat cosmetics, knew the value of the shipments. He had seen similar shipments in prior visits to Southeast Asia.

He studied a dozen men, dressed in the military fatigues of members of the People's Revolutionary Army, who kept themselves separate from the others and watched stone-faced as the crates disappeared into the large holds of the trawlers. They were speaking to one another in a Chinese dialect that Bolan had never heard before.

They acted like their brethren the world over—suspicious, humorless, hands constantly hovering near their side arms.

It took somebody with power and connections to keep inquisitive local police from accidentally coming upon the busy transfer of drugs. Bolan wondered who held that position now.

At one time it was the head of the Thai military police, who was finally exposed as a partner of the Golden Triangle warlords in the distribution of opium products.

The soldier turned and checked the armament he had brought with him: the Beretta 93-R was snug in its shoulder holster, while the huge Israeli-made .44 Magnum Desert Eagle was safely ensconced at his hip.

He had replaced the Uzi with an M-16 A-2. He needed a weapon that would be effective at a long distance. The rucksack on his other shoulder held one of the RPG launchers he had confiscated, and three 73 mm HEAT rockets.

A half-dozen fragmentation grenades and C-4 plastic explosive, along with small timers and detonators, completed his arsenal.

He mentally reviewed his options.

To attack the ships with missiles would sink them in port and destroy their illegal cargo. But he would probably die in the effort, leaving the triad and Golden Triangle warlords free to replace the cargo, and continue without interference the business of ruining lives around the world.

He could attempt to eliminate the triad and PRA guards, then notify the authorities about the cargo.

He dismissed the thought. They were trained killers and wouldn't stand still while he picked them off. And he was certain the police—at least some of them—were in business with the smugglers.

Workers swarmed all over the deck, securing covers and storing equipment. Bolan saw the captains, hard-faced Thais who seemed indifferent to the deadly cargos they would be carrying through the Bay of Thailand to a point in the ocean where the heroin crates would be transferred to awaiting ocean-going freighters.

As a group, eight of the trawler captains walked down the gangplanks and headed for the triad troops.

To get their payoff, Bolan suspected.

The Executioner had worked out a battle strategy. First he'd mine the trawlers with C-4 and set the timers. The next move was to eliminate the captains and the guards.

The sound of gunfire would terrify the dock workers. After they scattered, he could come down from the roof and launch the HEAT rockets at the opened door of the dockside warehouse.

The final step was to escape, leaving any survivors to explain their armed presence to the police when they arrived.

After locking a rocket into position, he made his way to the exit. Cautiously, he worked his way down to the side entrance.

Walking between high stacks of cargo, he worked his way to the heroin-laden trawlers.

Working quickly under the cover of darkness, he sliced a wedge of the plastic explosive and pressed it to the undercarriage of the first vessel. Inserting the miniaturized detonator and timer, he gave himself a half hour to complete his mission.

Because they were interfering with his ability to work quickly, the soldier hid the rocket launcher and the M-16 behind a stack of crates, then rose to his feet and moved back onto the dock.

The stench of fish and diesel oil filled his nostrils as he worked his way toward where the ten thugs were gathered with the captains.

As he approached the dockside meeting place, he heard a noise behind him. Whipping out his silenced Beretta as he whirled, Bolan spotted a triad hunter behind him.

"I found the intruder we were warned about," the hardman shouted as he unleathered his side arm.

Bolan fired first, three quick shots that tore through the gunner's breastbone and shattered his heart muscle. Without a sound, the dead man slid to the wooden planks.

A voice called out in the Fukien dialect. Although he couldn't translate the words, Bolan could hear the mocking tone. The soldier stood still.

"Hey Chu," the voice called out, this time in Thai, "did you get him? The man on the phone asked us to call and let him know."

Bolan could translate most of the question.

Man? Nobody knew his destination.

Except for Joe Collins.

Collins was DEA, not Triad. Had he been bought?

This wasn't time to ponder the identity of the informer.

The Executioner pulled the body behind some crates, then moved closer to where the others stood.

The voice called out again. "Stop hunting for the American. We need to finish loading and get out of here."

Bolan could see the dock workers scurrying on the deck and the sound of the guardsmen moving toward him.

He moved away from them, toward the trawlers.

A man in work clothes shouted. He had found the body.

Bolan saw the frightened Thai captains run for their trawlers. It was time to turn the captains' terror into a rout.

He retrieved his M-16 and rocket launcher from their hiding place, then lowered his eye to the carefully calibrated sight on the combat carbine.

One of the triad soldiers had run after the nearest trawler captain and was trying to reason with him. The Executioner guessed at the distance and swept the gangway with a brief burst of 5.56 mm fire. The triad gunner turned his head to talk to the other guards, then, looking surprised, fell from the gangway into the filthy dockside water, his lifeless corpse punctured by lead-created cavities.

Shouting erupted from the other trawlers, the terrified Thai sailors yelling in fear to one another.

A triad gunman tried to shut up the loudest sailor with a burst from the 9 mm MAT 49 submachine gun in his hands. The Executioner took careful aim and fired. He could hear the Chinese guard cry out in pain as he slid out of sight.

Someone had started the engines of the trawlers. Bolan knew that the drug-smuggling captains had decided to flee the field of battle. Only the triad guards would be left.

And him.

He heard sounds coming closer. Bolan grabbed his gear and moved deeper into the shadows. One of the People's Revolutionary Army soldiers strode into view, and the Executioner tore him in two with a burst from his weapon.

The big American reached for a new clip when he sensed someone behind him. As he turned, his assailant jerked the trigger of his weapon and fired at him, scorching the arm of the blacksuit. Bolan felt the burning sensation and, knowing the M-16 was empty, threw himself to the ground. He rolled behind the stack of crates, while the angry Chinese hit man fired repeatedly at his disappearing form.

Bolan tugged at his combat vest and freed a grenade, quickly yanking the pin. He stood and tossed the bomb over the crates, then fell to the ground and hugged a huge wooden box.

Bits of human flesh and bone rained on him moments after the grenade exploded.

He heard a sound coming toward him and knew it was the leader of the triad guards. The movement stopped. Bolan yanked out the Desert Eagle and held the heavy handgun with both hands, waiting patiently.

The sound started again, slowly, carefully. Bolan turned his head toward it, then lifted the handgun and squeezed the trigger.

The bulky man who hovered over him, holding a .45 ACP Colt Government Model pistol, looked shocked as the bullets tore into him. He stared at Bolan with hate in his dying eyes, then fell facedown into a pool of his own blood.

Pulling himself to his feet, Bolan gathered his equipment and moved quickly to the dockside.

The trawlers that were still able to were pulling away from the docks. The soldier could see the panic in the faces of the Thai crews.

To lighten the weight of the trawlers and make their escape swifter, the captains had pitched everything movable overboard, including the bags of heroin.

Satisfied, Bolan went about setting the blocks of plastic explosive around the rear perimeter of the Chui Chao building.

He glanced at his watch. Only five minutes remained to finish the job and get away before the waterfront vanished under the impact of the explosions.

The soldier moved around a low stack of crates and saw one of the triad guards, little more than a teenager. His face was filled with fear.

Bolan saw the teenaged boy cock his head at the sound of distant police sirens.

The young man held a 9 mm Heckler & Koch pistol. Bolan knew how deadly it could be used by an expert. He looked at the terrified youngster and realized he was no expert. He was a little boy playing a grown-up game. The Executioner's huge pistol seemed to mesmerize the Chinese youth.

One of them would have to make a move soon. Bolan didn't want the police to find him there, and from the expression on the boy's face, neither did he.

"Throw the gun away and give yourself up. I won't hurt you," the soldier shouted.

Bolan could see the decision process working as he watched the young man's facial muscles twitch. The face became hard. He'd made a decision.

The youngster quickly raised his gun. Bolan set his body to withstand the recoil of his huge weapon and started to squeeze the trigger. He stopped. The teenager had rammed the H & K against the side of his head and fired.

Glancing at his watch again, Bolan realized only two minutes remained before hell unleashed its fury here.

No time to mourn the wasted life on the ground in front of him.

He had one final gift to give the triad. Lowering the RPG to his shoulder, he took careful aim and unleashed the HEAT missile into the warehouse.

The entire building vibrated as the rocket released its awesome power on whoever and whatever was inside it.

Bolan raced for the rented Nissan, jumped behind the wheel and floored the gas pedal. The small car shuddered at the sudden rush of fuel and tore across the dock and onto the road in seconds.

As he raced toward downtown Bangkok, the soldier felt the earth shake, then heard the gargantuan explosions pummel the air with their violent anger. The sky was lit up with flares and rockets crossing one another, while exploding ammo created a cacophony of rage on the collapsing wooden dock.

Bolan didn't con himself into believing he had won a major victory in the continuing war. It was only a temporary setback for the enemy, though a very expensive one.

Many more battles would have to be won to even make a dent in the operations of the powerful drug barons who were the opposition.

But the triads now knew that the Executioner had spoken again. In a loud, explosive voice.

And this wouldn't be the last time this night that they would hear the thunder of his fury.

CHAPTER SEVEN

Bolan dialed the unlisted number Joe Collins had given him. Good battle tactics required that he have the latest intel.

The DEA man answered the phone.

"Belasko," Bolan said softly.

"The local radio is full of your adventures, Belasko. For a mercenary, you're a pretty gutsy guy. What do you need?"

"It's going to take more time than I anticipated. Can you find me a hotel room. Nothing conspicuous."

"You can bunk on my couch."

"I'm dangerous to your health," the soldier warned. "I think I'd prefer the hotel room."

"Your choice. Call me in a half hour. What's new on your end?"

"The best is yet to come. My next target is going to be special. The syndicate won't forget me for a long time." He paused. "I'd better get going. I'm twenty minutes away from becoming the greatest nuisance the triads have ever had to face."

There was admiration in the DEA man's voice as he commented, "You've already forced the Chui Chao to rush a replacement supply of heroin to one of their Bangkok warehouses. And I'm pretty sure the other triads will be searching for more product before morning."

"There are only two places to hit these guys. Their wallets and their lives." Then Bolan added, "Any intel on where and when the new inventory arrives?"

The DEA staffer gave him the details he had received from one of his snitches.

"Any other storage places I should know about?"

Collins ran down a list of possibilities from memory.

Bolan's next question took Collins by surprise.

"Any recommendation for a good local doctor?"

"Yes. Me. Why?"

"Sorry. I forgot you dropped a medical career when your brother and his family were killed. I caught some metal slivers in my shoulder when a car exploded, and I have a slight bullet wound."

"Get here as soon as you can. You probably need a tetanus shot as well as some antibiotics."

"Not right now. I'll see you when I see you," Bolan replied, and hung up.

Collins placed a call. The American Embassy did a lot of business with the Narai Hotel, on Silon. A room for Michael Belasko would be held in his name.

Collins's phone rang again. The caller was Scarface Tommy, one of his best snitches.

The nickname came from the scars that covered the young Thai's face and body, inflicted by drug dealers who suspected, but couldn't prove he had sold them out to the Americans.

Collins forced himself to sound casual. "Twice in one night. You must be running hot. What's new?"

"The 14K is planning a big surprise for some American agent they expect to raid them tonight."

"Really? I hadn't heard. What kind of surprise?"

"Worth lots of money, yes?"

"I've always treated you fairly, Tommy."

"This time double fairly. Dangerous information. Tommy may have to leave Bangkok fast."

Collins gave in. "Double fairly, Tommy. Now what's up?"

"Somebody tipped off the 14K that some American mercenary is coming to destroy one of their drug warehouses tonight. So they got fifteen—maybe twenty—men hiding inside to catch him and kiss him with their knives."

Collins shuddered. The knife kiss was a particularly vicious revenge ritual. The triad foot soldiers took turns easing the skin of the victim from his or her flesh, while the captive was kept alive. Eventually, the victim died of shock, but not before he or she begged the torturers to kill them and stop the agony.

For Collins the ritual had a personal meaning. His

brother, sister-in-law and nephews had been forced to suffer a variation of the ritual. The reawakened memory made the DEA agent jump out of bed and scramble into his clothing as soon as he finished talking to his source.

Grabbing a 9 mm Glock 17 and a handful of magazines, Collins shoved them into his jacket pockets and hurried to the front door of his apartment. Then he stopped and picked up a small bag from the coat closet that contained medical supplies.

Perhaps he could get there in time to stop Belasko. Or if not, to kill him before triad torture destroyed his mind and whatever mission he was really on in Bangkok. To do that he'd need more stopping powers. He decided to make a stop at the embassy.

SUN SURVEYED the triad hardforce he had assembled for the ambush. The Red Pole of the Bangkok lodge of the 14K had called him from Chiang Mai and ordered him to get the men ready for an attempted attack on their warehouse.

"We saw nobody lurking about when we checked the outside," one of the men reported. "Where did the Red Pole get such information?"

Knowing how the chief enforcer operated, Sun shrugged. "Probably from the Incense Master. He would never give such orders without the permission of Luk Ming Sang."

The temporary battle chief knew more than he admitted. From what he'd been told, the Incense Master had contacts even in the American government. Supposedly, a CIA agent was on the 14K payroll to provide just such information.

"Get the men ready," Sun ordered. "When the American mercenary is inside the building, we will capture him and learn everything he knows."

"The usual way?"

Sun smiled with anticipation. "Yes."

The other man, a new member of the triad, shuddered. He had only seen one inquisition, but the screams of pain from the victim still rang in his memory.

Hastily, he grabbed his carbine. "I will go and check on the others."

The temporary leader grinned. The best way to stop members from betraying the 14K was to have them witness what happened to those who did. This would be a good lesson.

DAVE WEYANT HAD SPENT the past ten years as an Intelligence officer in Bangkok. Like his CIA predecessor, the prune-faced agent supplemented his government income with gifts from a variety of groups. Of all of them, the 14K Triad paid the best.

There was never an argument when he named a price.

Unlike Madame Mai.

She had given him half of what he had asked for for the information on Senator Firestone and the American mercenary.

But, Weyant rationalized, every little bit of money deposited to his secret account would make his soon-to-come retirement more pleasant.

Working late, he decided to see if the DEA staffer Collins had come up with any more information worth peddling. Based on information the DEA had gathered from his sources, Weyant had already earned ten thousand dollars from the triads.

Checking to make sure that no one was on the second floor, Weyant used a duplicate key and opened the DEA agent's door.

Collins, the CIA agent knew from past incursions, kept his confidential information in a small safe built into one of his desk drawers.

Fortunately, Collins's predecessor had left the combination on the desk one night after a drinking bout with some secretaries at the embassy.

Weyant eased the safe drawer open and spun the combination lock. At the very top of a pile of papers was a copy of a confidential memo regarding triad drug warehouses. Two of the locations had been checked.

The CIA man wondered if that meant they'd already been hit. The third one was the main drug storage facility for the 14K.

The information could be worth a lot of money. He studied the list. There were other unchecked locations, operated by the other triads.

It wasn't as if he were selling out fellow Americans. This had to do with Chinese and Thai gangsters. Then, remembering that Belasko was probably an American, he rationalized that selling out American gangsters didn't count as breaking the oath he had taken when he'd joined the Central Intelligence Agency.

The CIA fielder lifted the phone on the desk. The information he had should easily be worth another ten thousand dollars to the triad leaders.

COLLINS SAW THE DOOR to his office open. The cleaning staff was his first thought, but he knew that they weren't allowed to enter the room without his presence.

Easing the Glock from his waistband holster, he pulled back the slide and jacked a round into the chamber.

The man's back was to him, leaning into the telephone clasped to his ear.

"This is Weyant. Is the Incense Master there?"

Collins raised the pistol.

"Put the phone down, Dave."

"Collins," the CIA agent said, without turning. "I was walking by and saw your door open. I was just calling security."

The brawny DEA man wasn't buying the explanation.

"The phone. Put it down, Dave."

Weyant lowered the receiver onto the cradle.

Collins saw the man's shoulder move slightly, then

watched as Weyant spun in the chair, a 9 mm Smith & Wesson Model 459 in his hand.

The DEA agent didn't hesitate. Pumping two rounds at Weyant's face, he watched as the CIA staffer's features shattered into a mass of bloody tissue and fractured bone.

He knew the sounds of gunfire would bring security, but he didn't have time to answer questions. They would have to wait until he got back to the embassy. The gun in the rogue agent's hand, the opened security vault, should provide whoever found the body with clues about what had happened, and why.

He got a MAC-10 and a handful of loaded magazines from his arms locker, then switched handguns, replacing the Glock with a .45 ACP Colt Government Model pistol. Collins grabbed four clips for the gun and raced out of his office.

Right now he had a life to save. If Belasko wasn't already dead.

MACK BOLAN SCOUTED the streets around the large metal warehouse. A great number of Japanese and American vehicles were parked nearby, all of them the latest models.

Something was wrong. Bolan could sense an ambush waiting to happen. He knew too much about how the triads tortured their victims to allow himself to fall into their hands.

Reaching into his canvas carryall, he grabbed a

block of C-4 plastique and carefully cut it into small rectangles. He fitted each with a detonator and miniaturized timer.

Setting the timers for fifteen minutes, he moved quickly from the rented Nissan to the warehouse. Squatting, he worked his way around the building, affixing blocks at the various door and window openings. Then he pasted one where two of the outer walls met.

Moving quickly back to his car, he got behind the wheel and shut the driver's door. He had plenty of time to drive away, and a great need to do so. When the C-4 detonated, the building would blow up with a gigantic clap of thunder and would spew debris in all directions.

Shoving the ignition key into the lock, he started to turn it, then felt the blow of something hard against the side of his head.

And felt nothing after that.

CHERNOV CLIMBED aboard the nearer of the two combat helicopters with the embassy staffer.

"Everything you requested is here," Maleshnikoff said, pointing to the cases of weapons and chemicals. "Some of it, I might add, was very difficult to obtain without a clever excuse." He paused, then added, "The pilots are being well-paid, and both are members of the Myanmar Communist Party."

"Yes, yes," the general said impatiently. "I'm

sure you did an excellent job. But it is time for us to go.''

The station chief started to climb down from the helicopter, then remembered something.

''There were stories from Bangkok about the bombing of triad warehouses that supposedly stored heroin.'' He smiled cynically. ''This wouldn't be the work of some of your men?''

''No, but that is good news.''

Perhaps a war had broken out between the leading triads. Chernov rejected the notion. He was impatient to get going. What was keeping the representative of the Karin army?

A Land Rover, painted olive drab, drove up to where the Russian warbirds were parked. A wide, mustached man got out and ambled toward Maleshnikoff and Chernov with the confidence of a senior military officer,

''I am Colonel Ne Win, of the Karin United Revolutionary Army,'' he said. ''I decided to come to Rangoon to meet you.''

The Russian knew how to handle this barbarian.

''I am General Mikhail Chernov, head of the Third Spetsnaz Battalion.''

Both men studied each other with suspicion. Then suddenly, the Asian man held out a hand and smiled.

''Your local Russian Intelligence official,'' he added, ''tells me we have a common cause.''

Warily, the Russian asked, ''And what is that?''

''The elimination of heroin from Burma.''

"Absolutely true. That is why we are here."

Ne Win looked pleased.

"This country has close to one hundred thousand heroin addicts. It doesn't need more drugs or more addicts."

Chernov nodded, then turned to Oskar Tremenko. "Captain, have the men check the supplies. Make sure there are enough weapons and ammunition. But more important, that there is enough herbicide to complete our mission."

The pilot turned his head and grinned at the Russian general, his mouth filled with gold crowns.

"Ready to fly, Comrade?"

"In a moment..." He hesitated, then added, "Comrade."

The head of the drug syndicate watched as the Spetsnaz took inventory of their supplies. Dressed in the dark jumpsuits and thigh-high boots that were part of their combat uniforms, the muscular ex-commandos moved about the rear of the modified Russian gunship with confidence.

Colonel Ne Win smiled as the man who led the field forces shouted his report.

"We've got enough supplies to burn down central Moscow and wipe out all the plant life for twenty miles around it."

The general considered the image and smiled for a moment, then wiped the warm expression from his face.

"Then it is time to leave."

He clapped a hand on the pilot's shoulder.

"We go. Now."

COLLINS COULD FEEL the ground shudder as a great eruption resounded from the waterfront area. He knew what had happened. Somehow Belasko had managed to set off explosives before the 14K Triad thugs got him.

Forcing his car around stalled traffic, the DEA agent worked his way to where a large warehouse had once stood. Uniformed Thai police had blocked off the area.

Abandoning his vehicle, Collins slipped past the police cordon and moved closer to the shredded sheets of corrugated metal and wood that had once hidden bags of heroin.

Bits of body parts were strewed everywhere. Paramedics forced themselves to load the pieces of human remains onto stretchers and carry them to vans. As he studied the wreckage, Collins saw no one he recognized. Certainly not the American mercenary.

Someone in Washington, D.C., had to be notified, but he didn't know whom.

Sadly, he turned and walked away.

Something caught his eye—a body wedged in the narrow space between two factory buildings. It was too small to be Belasko.

He moved closer to study it. It was a small person and the head was missing—severed from the body. Collins had seen similar victims before, men and women condemned by the triads for violation of some minor regulation.

Reaching into a pocket, the DEA agent found the small flashlight he had brought with him and shone it into the space.

The head was there, bloody gore dripping from severed vessels. The expression on the face was one of horror and terror.

Collins recognized Scarface Tommy.

Forcing back the vomit that had pushed its way from his stomach into his throat, Collins turned and walked back to his car.

Starting the embassy-issued vehicle, the DEA agent drove slowly toward his office and to the hours of answering questions about Dave Weyant.

CHAPTER EIGHT

A thousand demons kept pounding sledgehammers
against the interior wall of Bolan's head. He could
smell dried blood, then tried to reach up and touch
the wound.

He couldn't. His hands were tied behind his back.

Slowly, the soldier opened his eyes, lowering his
lids to protect them from the bright bare ceiling bulb
that burned high above his head.

He was in a small, empty room. A basement room,
judging from how high in the wall the small, barred
windows were set.

A tall woman entered. Wearing a heavy silk jacket
and pants, she fingered the large gold-and-silver
necklace around her neck.

At first Bolan mistook her for Chinese. But she
was too tall. His second guess was Mongolian, but
her legs and arms weren't thick enough.

Finally it dawned on him that the woman was from
the hill tribes. Judging from her features, he spotted
her as a member of the Hmong tribe. Their women

were beautiful, even on the verge of being breathtaking, and tall.

This one, who Bolan guessed to be in her late forties, hadn't lost her beauty. Only her youth.

Still, something was wrong. He studied her face, then realized it was her eyes. They were cold and emotionless, the eyes of a reptile ready to strike.

"Now we can talk, American," the woman said coldly.

"About what?"

"About why you are here. About why you have destroyed the inventory of our customers. About who sent you."

"I'm only a guy on vacation," Bolan replied. "I don't know about destroying things."

The woman smiled icily. "I won't insult your intelligence by pretending to believe you. You came here to destroy the heroin we sell to distributors. Bags intended for the United States and Canada. That makes you, or the men who employed you, our competitors. Am I not right?"

Bolan said nothing.

"You look somewhat Italian, but I will assume you were hired to do this job." She paused, then admitted, "You are good at what you do. Too bad you already work for the American Mafia. I could have offered you a much more profitable position. And your life."

"I wasn't hired to give lectures," Bolan stated,

deciding to go along with her assumptions until he could figure how to escape.

The woman stifled a yawn. "I am growing bored at our little game. And I have a long trip ahead of me."

She turned and pressed a button mounted in the wall. A man responded, almost as tall as her and costumed in the garb of the Lahu, a sister tribe to the Hmong.

"Gather two men and take this man to the farm, then return and watch the villa. I will be back in three days."

She turned and left the basement room.

AT THE TOP OF THE STAIRS, the woman stopped and studied her image in the long mirror mounted on the brocaded wall.

She liked the idea of being tall. Only Chinese women were tiny and weak, unlike Mai Ling. Her name was Chinese, but she wasn't. The slender beauty had descended from the hill tribes who lived in the Golden Triangle.

Despite her real age of fifty, Mai Ling knew she still looked like she was in her midthirties. So many men—and lovers—had told her so.

Her long glistening black hair was meticulously styled by the visiting Parisian hairdresser who maintained a small salon at the Shangri-La, on New Phetchabui Road. The clothes she wore were made of handwoven Thai silk, styled in the fashion of the Hmong.

Her villa, once the pride of a French diplomat, was built of lacquered teak and set in a wooded area just off Mittaphap Road, the superhighway that led north from the capital. A wall of two-inch steel, covered with a layer of stucco, surrounded the compound.

She felt perfectly safe when she was in residence here.

Armed guards maintained a twenty-four-hour watch on the property, carefully examining all visitors, including those making deliveries.

Inside the compound, an armored 1989 Mercedes-Benz sedan sat in the driveway, facing the front doors of the villa.

The handsome mistress of the property stepped out on the patio and lit a cigarette. Pacing along the covered patio that circled the building, she smoked one cigarette after another.

Mai Ling was nervous, perhaps for the first time in her life. Certainly since she had moved to Bangkok.

She didn't know why. Nothing had made her nervous for many years. Not since she had moved here from the Thai-Chinese border.

Perhaps the American barbarian was responsible. He hadn't treated her with either respect or fear, the two emotions she cherished most.

The only person from whom she could accept any other emotion was her son, the wildly successful warlord of the Golden Triangle, General Lu Shu-Shui.

From him she expected love and affection, as well as respect and fear. After all, she had created him. His career, his successes, had really been her successes. But in a society where men were so dominant, Mai Ling was satisfied to let her son receive the credit, while she shared in the power and the financial rewards.

As she headed for her suite to pack, she remembered clearly the life she had led before. She had been the daughter of a peasant farmer, and her family had grown the opium poppy for as long as she could remember.

Opium wasn't some dreaded poison, but a way to survive in a harsh world where death came too quickly to many.

If outsiders used the poppy sap to destroy their minds and bodies, that wasn't the concern of the hill tribes. It was their own doing.

Few outsiders came for any other reason than to steal or buy the opium. The only one Mai Ling could remember as being different was a wounded American cargo pilot who worked for a CIA cover called Air America. He had landed in a small field during the bloody conflict taking place east of them.

While his wounds healed, the American had helped the others in the tribe raise their crops and hunt for food. And after he had recovered and flown away, he had returned occasionally to bring them food and other essential supplies.

And to visit a beautiful teenaged girl named Mai Ling.

Then during one visit, he gave Mai Ling a small satchel filled with money and flew away for good.

After he had left, she discovered she was pregnant. Although she wasn't positive, she decided that he would be the father of blame. Filled with shame, her family used some of the money the American had given her to buy a husband.

Despite their humiliation, Mai Ling personally felt no shame at being pregnant and unwed. Somehow she knew that the child she was carrying would be an important person. He or she would be worthy of a better life than the one the child would live in her tiny, isolated village.

Packing several woven sacks of unrefined opium, she had bought a mule and moved to Bangkok to seek a new life for her newborn son and herself. That was thirty-three years ago.

Soon she would meet that pilot again—the man who she believed was the father of the powerful warlord to whom she'd given birth.

Robert Firestone.

The pilot had become an important man, just like the son he had never met.

A United States Senator.

Better still was his unique position in the American government—chairman of the Senate Oversight

Subcommittee on Narcotic Traffic. And he was a personal friend of the United States's President.

Now he was back in Thailand, about to negotiate with their son. Over the years she had sent the man brief notes about Lu, so the senator knew he had a son. From time to time he sent money, but it was a pittance compared to the millions they earned from the drug trade.

The CIA agent in Bangkok had passed on information from his contacts in the American capital.

"The senator is coming here as a representative of the President. He's going to demand that General Lu shut down the heroin distribution channels and destroy the poppy fields," Weyant had reported.

"And if my son doesn't?"

"They'll send planes and troops to back up the President's demands."

Mai Ling smiled. Her son wouldn't mind getting rid of the Chinese triads who took such a large share of his profits for moving the drugs through their connections in the United States. As far as destroying the growing fields went, the woman was sure her son could convince his father that was impractical.

He would easily agree to cutting out the triad gangsters if his father would find an appropriate substitute.

If not, Mai Ling was certain her son would be willing to expose the connection between him and his still-respected father to get what he wanted.

She had taught him well.

Something else the American CIA man had said concerned her.

"There's a rumor that another American will be arriving at about the same time. No one knows who sent him. It could have been the President or the American Mafia, but someone wants to destroy the network of distributors operating in Thailand."

"The name of this so-called miracle worker?"

"I'm told he calls himself Mike Belasko. But who knows what his real name is? All I know is that he is supposed to be a one-man army, and has come to Bangkok to prove it."

The woman had been considering the information all evening. The senator was about to meet with her—his—son in Chiang Mai. The only stumbling block could be this American mercenary.

This Mike Belasko, or whatever his name really was, had to be stopped before he could ruin her plans.

She had summoned the leader of her personal guards and outlined the problem.

"Find this Mike Belasko," she had ordered. "He is somewhere in Bangkok."

All the husky Mongolian ex-wrestler had asked was, "And kill him?"

"First we'll find out what he has planned. Then," she had promised, "you can kill him. But first Phrom shall have his turn."

And Khan had done what she had demanded.

Now it was time for this Belasko to die. Even if he wouldn't talk.

CHAPTER NINE

Chiang Mai, Thailand

Four hundred miles north of Bangkok was the city of Chiang Mai. Nicknamed "the city that opium built," Chiang Mai was also famed for having more than three hundred Buddhist temples in a town with only 1,565,000 residents.

Unlike its big sister Bangkok, prostitution and pornographic spectacles were relatively nonexistent in Chiang Mai. Its biggest attraction was its proximity to the Golden Triangle and the hill tribes who tended the poppy fields.

From the air, Senator Firestone could see the secluded estate where he would be holding the meeting. Large sugar palm logs covered the top of the huge villa set in a rain forest just fifteen kilometers east of the city. In the moonlight, the varnished roof glistened like a mirrored lake.

Once owned by the French provincial governor of the northernmost region of Thailand, the now well-maintained estate had changed hands many times

since the Thais declared their independence and
drove their French rulers out of their Southeast Asian
country.

More than thirty years had passed since he'd last
been in Thailand. Everything seemed different—quieter, for one thing, without the distant sounds of explosions and gunfire.

To get his mind off his mission, Firestone reflected
on the past. In 1960 he had been Lieutenant Bobby
Firestone, a combat pilot with more than forty attack
missions to his credit.

As deliberate as he had been in his search-and-destroy missions against the North Vietnamese army
and its guerilla teammates, the Vietcong, he had been
just as compassionate toward the innocent victims of
the war—the women and infants whose bodies he
could spot strewed across paddies every time he flew
at low altitude.

Weekends had been spent flying a borrowed cargo
plane and airlifting as many mothers and babies as
he could to safe havens away from the killing zones.

Several of the Southeast Asian governments had
embarrassed the lieutenant by presenting him with
humanitarian medals.

He remembered the prime minister of Thailand
calling him "the finest example of a human being."

What the government official handing him the
medal couldn't have known was that Bobby Firestone was really a coward. At least when it came to
his personal life.

SEATED IN THE LIVING ROOM of his hotel suite in Chiang Mai, Tan Suan Chi stared at the Bangkok Incense Master with a look of disapproval. The Elder Brother of the Yi Kwah Tao had listened as Lao Su told him about the call he had just received.

"Do we know who destroyed our warehouse?"

"One of the soldiers who survived the explosion claims he saw a large American near the building."

"A large American? There are more than ten thousand American tourists in Bangkok. What made the fool decide this one was dangerous?"

"He looked dangerous, Master."

"Foolish evidence," Tan commented. "But find this American and question him."

"In the usual way?"

Tan lost his patience.

"Of course in the usual way. What other way is more effective?"

The Yi Kwah Tao's inquisition torture techniques always got information from those who were forced to submit to them.

The head of the triad looked at the clock on the mantel of the fireplace in his hotel suite. "Meantime, I have a meeting I have agreed to attend."

"It could be a trap, Master."

"Naturally." The man with the wispy gray beard smiled. "Which is why I had you surround the warlord's villa with our men. Now it is time for me to be driven to this meeting with the senator from

America. He is supposed to land near the villa any moment.''

SUN JEE HAD FLOWN IN from his Hong Kong headquarters to meet with the American senator. As his Incense Master, Luk Sang rode with him in the new Mercedes, the head of the Chui Chao Triad heard the news about the destruction of their opium inventory.

"This is, indeed, bad news. We have customers waiting for the shipments. Why did you not stop him, Luk?''

"We tried, but the information about him arrived too late, according to the men who survived the attack.''

"Our predecessors had difficulties with an American mercenary a number of years ago,'' Sun Jee remembered. "Could it be the same man?''

"Didn't we kill him?''

"No. The ones who died were the Elder Brother and your predecessor, the Incense Master.''

"The issue, Master, is who hired him?''

"Excellent point, Luk. It could be one of a number of organizations. The Italians who run the syndicates in the United States could be behind the attack.''

"Why would they do such a thing? We are a valuable source of the white powder.''

"True,'' the Elder Brother agreed. "Perhaps one of the other triads is behind the destruction. We know that both the Yi Kwah Tao and the 14K have been trying to gain exclusive distribution rights from General Lu.''

Luk Sang looked as if a bolt of lightning had suddenly struck him.

"It must be the general. He is trying to destroy whatever power we have and take over the distribution himself.''

The gray-haired Elder Brother nodded.

"Then we must find and kill this American before he can do more harm.''

The Incense Master bowed his head.

"It will be done, Sun Jee. That is a sworn promise.''

The gray-haired man had lived to reach seventy by being cautious. The godfather of the Chui Chao Triad had avoided making rapid decisions about anything.

As Luk Sang kept proposing possible responses to the destruction of their heroin depot, Sun listened in stony silence. Weighing the suggestions, he finally made his decision.

"I do not think the general is behind these attacks. We are a valuable source of income for him. It is obvious that the other triads are trying to wreck our distribution channel.''

"What about the Russians, Master? They are increasing their activity in the opium trade.''

"Since their defeat in Afghanistan, the Russians have maintained a low profile in this part of the world. Besides, they have their own growing fields in their former Asian republics.''

The Elder Brother paused.

"Let me make another—" Luk Sang began.

"Stop!" the Elder Brother snapped. "You give me a headache with all of your possibilities." He glared at the Incense Master. "*I* will tell you what we are going to do. Nothing!"

The Incense Master looked stunned.

"Nothing. We will go to the meeting with the American and hear what he has to say, then sit in council and make a decision."

Luk Sang looked worried.

"Doing nothing is not the same as not being prepared to do something. I assume you have our men stationed about General Lu's villa."

"Just as you ordered, Master," Luk replied in a humbled tone.

THE AMERICAN in room 207 of the Dusit Inn paced the floor restlessly. The tall distinguished-looking man wondered if he had been smart to come here. Since his arrival in Bangkok, he had been haunted by the feeling that eyes were watching him.

Senator Robert Firestone wasn't prone to paranoia, so he was certain he was right. And he thought he knew who it was.

A knock at his hotel door interrupted his thoughts.

"Time to get going, Senator," a voice called through the door. "The meeting is scheduled to start in twenty minutes."

"Be with you in five minutes," he replied loudly, then slid a tie around his neck and began to tie it.

He had come to deliver a verbal offer from the President of the United States to the warlord who controlled the growth of opium from that mountainous corner of Southeast Asia that encompassed the northern parts of Laos, Thailand and Myanmar, and the leaders of the triads that distributed the drug.

As he stood before a mirror and knotted his tie, he was surprised to see that his hands shook.

It wasn't as if someone had forced him to come. This was a mission for which he had volunteered. When the man in the White House gathered a group of his closest advisers to discuss possible ways of keeping opium, and its heroin derivative, from leaving Asia, Firestone suggested that he was the logical bearer of the offer.

The man in the Oval Office had looked surprised. "Why you, Bobby?"

"For one thing a lot of people in that part of the world remember me for my rescue missions during Vietnam."

The handful of top government officials had nodded their agreement.

"Even more important, I have a personal connection with General Lu, who controls the drug trade."

One of the group, Hal Brognola, asked, "How would you know someone like Lu?"

"Since I head up the Senate Oversight Subcommittee on Narcotic Traffic, I have come across his name many times. After all, there aren't many men who grow over seventy percent of all the opium in the world. And we have other connections.''

Brognola had known from the expression on the senator's face that was all the man would say.

"It's a tough message, Bobby," the President had warned.

"The tougher the better. What do you want me to tell him?"

"If he destroys the poppy fields, we can offer his people financial aid to find new crops with which to support themselves."

"If he refuses?"

"Then legal or not, we'll send our best-trained men to wipe out him and his army."

The others in the room turned their heads and stared at the senator, who ignored them.

"Sounds like a fair offer to me," he commented quietly.

"And you're sure you can find him to deliver the message?" The President paused. "I can get the CIA over there to locate him for you."

"You won't have to bother," Firestone replied. "He'll come looking for me."

Brognola had jumped in with a question. "What makes you so sure?"

"I have something he wants."

The President had looked surprised.

"Which is?"

Firestone couldn't bring himself to tell the absolute truth. Not yet.

"A direct link with you, Mr. President," he lied.

And, he had added silently, a chance to meet his biological father.

CHAPTER TEN

General Lu Shu-Shui was running late. General Tuan Weh, who controlled the jungle laboratories in northern Myanmar, had, at the last moment, insisted on meeting with him. There was some problem with a group that was trying to destroy his refineries.

As Lu reminded Tuan, somebody was always destroying opium refineries. If it wasn't Myanmar government troops, then it was soldiers from the Karin United Revolutionary Army. In his paranoia, Tuan claimed the attackers spoke Russian to one another.

There were always problems. It came with the responsibility of controlling almost 150 thousand square miles of poppy fields and forest.

But for now Lu had left those problems back at the base camp on the Chinese side of the Thailand-China border.

He leaned back in his seat and let his pilot ease the Russian-built Mi-28 combat helicopter to the makeshift landing pad near the northern villa. Already he missed the concubines he had living with him across the Thai border.

The handsome young warlord turned to his aide, Colonel Kwong Lee.

"Your men are driving down from the border?"

"Yes, General. They arrived this morning and moved into the dormitory quarters. They should be on duty by now."

"They are properly equipped?"

"Full combat gear."

"How many?"

"A dozen. I would have had more come but, as you know, this is the time for picking the poppies. I was certain you didn't want any of the hill tribes to give less than their fullest effort."

A vague smile crossed the young general's face. Despite his relative youth—thirty-three—Lu didn't like anybody, especially those who served him, being able to predict his actions. The colonel was a special case. The People's Revolutionary Army had sent him to be its representative in the general's organization.

The thin, long scar that crossed his right eyebrow began to twitch. It always did when he had a difficult decision to make.

It was time to change aides. This one had started to believe he was destined to take over from the young general. Lu had discussed the problem with the Yunnan governor. He had agreed with Lu's solution.

Easing a silenced 9 mm Calico M-950 pistol from his waistband, the general raised it to line up with Kwong Lee's left ear and pulled the trigger twice.

There was an expression of disbelief on the dead man's face, as if he were asking, "Why?"

"Ambition is not always a good thing," General Lu told the corpse. "You can discuss it with the man I replaced when you get to hell."

LU HAD WAITED for this moment for more than thirty years. The years between had been filled with death and suffering. Joining the staff of his predecessor, General Li, he cheated and lied his way up through the ranks until he became a personal aide to the elderly general.

He waited for the right moment, then switched loyalties to the People's Revolutionary Army.

It made him the perfect candidate to take control of the military forces when the obese old man died in bed with one of his concubines.

Ruling eight hundred soldiers and the hill tribes took all the conniving and salesmanship he could muster, plus some help from the squads of interrogators he had recruited to keep his people in-line.

As he stepped down from the helicopter, Lu knew that the foreign bank accounts containing vast fortunes still didn't satisfy him. There was one last thing he had to do. And this night he could finally close the book on his past.

As he let his pilot lead the way to the huge villa, the general could hear the sounds of helicopters approaching the landing pad.

WHILE THE HIND WARBIRDS hovered over the make-shift structure practically hidden by the jungle foliage, the Karin Army representative, Colonel Ne Win, pointed to it.

"There is a typical jungle opium laboratory," the slight man with long black-gray hair said.

Chernov clapped his hand on the pilot's shoulder.

"Find someplace to land."

The pilot turned his head and stared at Ne Win.

"There is a small open field about two hundred yards west of the building. You can land there."

After the helicopters landed, two dozen Spetsnaz commandos in full battle dress, each armed with an AKS-74 U assault rifle, jumped from the copters and gathered in a circle. The former general shouldered his AKS-74 U and gave them orders.

"Consider this an assault on the enemy. Search and destroy everyone and everything you find in the area."

Ne Win looked concerned.

"Except for a handful of chemists and technicians, those who work in the refinery are merely peasants, struggling to make enough money to feed their families."

"They should have chosen a different occupation," Chernov snapped, and signaled his men to follow him.

A PAIR OF MEN, struggling to carry heavy canvas sacks into the structure, saw the uniformed men rushing at them. In panic they dropped the bags and began to run.

A young commando washed the air in front of him with lead, tearing both peasants into bloody carcasses.

Men and women poured out of the roofless building in terror.

Aiming carefully, Chernov's troops picked off the luckless workers as they scurried for cover.

Like straw dummies, the once-living fell to the ground, soaking the soil with their life fluids.

Ne Win led the way into the jungle laboratories. Fifty-five-gallon black metal drums lined the wooden walls.

"They contained the chemicals used in processing opium," the guide explained, seeing Chernov's stare.

The laboratory was a makeshift one-story structure, without a roof, which permitted the noxious fumes to escape in the jungle air. It was filled with a collection of tubes, flasks and measuring devices. To Chernov it looked more like a rural school lab in one of the remote former Soviet republics than a refinery where the dried poppy sap was converted into heroin.

As Ne Win explained, without such crude refineries built near the growing fields, the raw opium would have to be shipped in bulk to Hong Kong or some other refining center. It was an unnecessary expense in a region where life was cheap.

When the process was complete, the final products

were a tenth the size and weight of the raw opium that had been delivered.

Chernov stared in disgust at the filth and contamination.

"How much heroin can a place like this produce?"

"At least two hundred kilos of heroin a day. That is more than two tons of processed opium daily."

"How many factories like this are in Myanmar?"

"No one really knows. At least three more. As you see," Ne Win replied, pointing to the contents of the large room, "it doesn't take much equipment to start a laboratory."

"Then we should push on," Chernov commented, signaling his men to get back on the helicopters.

He still had herbicide to spread over the growing fields, and a host of competitors to eliminate.

MAI LING'S HARDMEN had tied Bolan's hands behind his back with thick rope. Until the door opened, he didn't know why they had left his feet unbound.

A short wiry Thai entered the room, grinning at the trussed Executioner. Despite his relatively slender build, Bolan recognized him for what he was.

A kickboxer.

The hardened sinews in his arms and legs from countless hours of practice gave the man away.

Bolan was no expert in the cruel sport, although he could hold his own in a fair competition. Often the fight wasn't fair, and the high incidence of death and severe injuries had led authorities to prohibit the sport until new restrictive rules could be imposed.

Kickboxing wasn't a complicated sport. All parts of the opponent's body were considered fair game. But unlike American-style boxing, punching was considered the weakest attack of all in competition.

Telling blows included high kicks to the neck, elbow thrusts to the face and head, knee hooks to ribs and low crescent kicks to the opponent's calves.

Fighters were permitted to grasp the other fighter's head and pull it down to meet an upward knee thrust. Kicking was merely a way of softening an opponent for the decisive blows—knee and elbow strikes.

Bolan studied the small man. He was wearing loose white clothing, the traditional exhibition costume of a kickboxer. Then he looked down at his feet. Instead of soft leather shoes, the new arrival was wearing steel-capped boots.

Now, the Executioner understood. A kickboxing exhibition was about to begin.

And Bolan was the main attraction.

The small Thai bowed stiffly.

"I am Phrom," he said formally, then waited for the soldier to reply.

Finally, he spoke again.

"You should introduce yourself," he continued, "so that I know who it is I have killed."

"Just get on with it," Bolan said, while his mind and eyes searched for a solution. With his hands bound behind his back, no answer came quickly.

"This is not like your American boxing. We are not animals like your fighters," Phrom snarled, standing directly over the warrior.

The Executioner kicked upward, between his attacker's legs, and smashed his booted toe into the man's genitals. Grunting with pain, the slender man staggered backward.

Still grimacing from the pain of the Executioner's kick, Phrom tugged a 5.45 mm PSM police pistol from a pocket and started to squeeze the trigger.

Bolan lurched to the left, and the bullet drilled into the teak-inlaid floor. He felt the agony of the bruised shoulder as he pulled himself to his feet and threw a hard kick to the side of his adversary's head.

Phrom staggered backward, dropping the pistol to the floor. Bolan used a knee hook to floor the slender Thai, then took advantage of the moment, knocking over a precious porcelain vase.

Turning his back on the fractured art treasure, he grabbed one of the fragments and sawed against the cords.

Strand by strand, the heavy rope released its grip on his hands as the Thai kickboxer forced himself to his feet.

Before the soldier could plan a defense, the Thai threw his right foot at Bolan's head. Only a last-minute twist of his neck saved the Executioner from a concussion. Even so, he was stunned at the swiftness and power of the blow.

The Thai kickboxer pushed his opponent away and snarled, "Now you die, American."

With a sudden kick to Bolan's shinbone, the Thai knocked the Executioner to the floor, then threw a powerful kick at Bolan's rib cage.

Prepared, the soldier grabbed the other man by the ankle and twisted the leg until his opponent screamed in pain.

The tables had turned. Bolan threw the kickboxer to the wooden floor, then, as the fighter started to get to his feet, slammed his combat-booted foot at the other man's ear.

In a screech of anger and agony, Phrom jumped up and threw himself at his adversary.

It was time to end the charade, Bolan decided.

Wrapping an arm around the neck of his assailant, he began to squeeze.

"That is enough," a woman's voice called out. "Let him go."

The Executioner could see the guns the tall, silk-clad woman and the two huge Thai thugs at her side were pointing at him.

There was no alternative. Bolan released the semiconscious kickboxer.

The woman turned to a Mongolian-featured man.

"This one is yours," she said coldly. "I would come along for the sport, but I have to leave for Chiang Mai."

She turned to the kickboxer. "I want all of his weapons dropped in the crocodile pond."

Phrom started to argue with her, but saw the expression of anger on Mai Ling and nodded.

"If the Thai police decide to search this house, I don't want them finding anything that would connect the American with us."

She walked through the open doorway and vanished down a corridor.

The soldier turned to the two armed men.

"What's next?"

Phrom had recovered his pistol. Without a word he rapped the weapon against the back of Bolan's head.

BOLAN DIDN'T NEED his eyes to tell him where he was. He could smell the rank odor of reptiles in front of him. From the soft, splashing noise he knew exactly what kind they were.

Crocodiles.

Mai Ling's henchmen had driven him to a crocodile farm, on the outskirts of Bangkok, locked in the trunk of an ancient Silver Wraith Rolls-Royce. He had been there before. As an observer, not as a meal for the loathsome creatures.

The next step would be to throw him into the huge pond. He moved his hands and legs. No ropes.

Bolan wondered if the thug Phrom called Khan decided he didn't need them, or had left in too much of a hurry to bother tying his hands and ankles.

It didn't matter. What lay ahead for the Executioner was a slow, painful death in the jaws of the huge reptiles.

A crocodile didn't usually kill its victim. It grabbed its prey in its huge jaws and dragged it under, rolling it over and over until it drowned. Then the crocodile shoved the body under a convenient stump or rock to let the water rot the flesh until it was soft enough to satisfy the crocodile's appetite.

Bolan knew he couldn't outswim the crocodiles. As slow as they seemed on land, in water the leathery creatures could move astonishingly fast. And did.

If it was only one or two crocodiles, perhaps there was a chance to survive. But Bolan remembered the guide explaining that almost thirty thousand of the creatures lived in the huge man-made lake.

Bolan heard noises from outside. Somebody was opening the trunk. He decided to pretend to be unconscious until he could find a way to escape.

The Mongolian bodyguard glanced at the still form in the trunk. Furious, Khan decided that the Thai had to have hit the man too hard.

Bolan could sense that a second figure had joined the one who had opened the trunk.

Phrom noticed Khan staring at the American's body.

The Mongolian glared at the Thai kickboxer. "You hit him too hard with your gun. You were told not to kill him. That was to be my job."

Nervously, Phrom checked Bolan's neck for a pulse.

"He's not dead," he replied, relieved. "Just unconscious."

"Good. And throw away the American's handguns. If Mai Ling sees them on you, the next person to go swimming will be you."

The Thai didn't like being here. The thought of being near the reptiles reminded him of his childhood on the river, watching friends being dragged underwater by the monsters.

"What did Mai Ling mean earlier when she said the American politician would have to cooperate with General Lu or be destroyed?"

"I'm not sure," Khan replied. "There is some connection between the two of them that could destroy his career if it got out."

"I wonder what it is?"

"Don't wonder. It's safer that way."

Phrom decided to change the subject. "Let's get the guard to open the gates."

"You're right. My friends have waited long enough for an American meal."

He started to laugh at his attempt at humor, then saw the disapproving expression on the Thai's face.

"All right," Khan growled. "I'll be right back."

BOLAN TRIED to figure out the connection between Firestone and the tall Asian woman. But it wasn't something he had to worry about now. Getting air into the trunk was a greater priority.

The soldier was having difficulty breathing in the

close environment of the Rolls-Royce's trunk. He needed something to force open the trunk lid.

Feeling around in the dark, his hand felt a round metal bar. A tire iron.

Twisting his body, he forced the cold steel tool into the slight space between the lid and frame of the luxury vehicle. Gently, he began to work the tire iron back and forth, hoping to force the lock.

From the conversations he had overheard, Bolan knew that there was at least one Thai thug guarding the vehicle.

Slowly, he kept pulling and pushing with the metal tool. Sweat began to pour down his face. Breathing became increasingly difficult. Still he kept working at the trunk door.

Finally, he heard the soft snap of the lock breaking.

Who else had heard it?

Resting for a moment, he waited to hear the footsteps of one or more guards on the gravel driveway.

Nothing.

He eased the trunk lid open and climbed out.

A man stood in front of the vehicle, cradling Bolan's silenced 9 mm Beretta 93-R.

He recognized him—the Thai kickboxer.

Wiping the sweat from his face, Bolan moved quietly until he was behind the man, then grabbed him by the throat.

There wasn't time for niceties. He wrapped an arm around Phrom's neck, then, with his other hand, forced the man's head in the opposite direction with a slightly audible crack. Bolan slowly lowered the corpse to the ground.

He retrieved the Beretta, and the .44-caliber Desert Eagle, which the kickboxer had tucked into the back of his waistband.

Searching the man's pockets, he found four full magazines of ammo, two each for the handguns.

The soldier pulled the body behind the limousine, then shoved it into the trunk.

Metal clattered on the floor of the storage area as the body rolled over. Bolan looked into the trunk.

The Applegate-Fairbairn combat knife had to have been hidden on some part of Phrom's body. Bolan was pleased to have it back.

The Executioner wasn't sure how many of Mai Ling's hoods had brought him there, but he moved into the shadows and waited for the others to return.

CHAPTER ELEVEN

Bolan readied himself as vague shadows came out of the wooded area in front of him.

The first shadow became a tall, beefy man built like a wrestler. In his hands he held a 9 mm MAC-10 submachine gun. Bolan brought the retrieved Beretta 93-R into target acquisition.

The man froze.

The second voice called out. "What's wrong?"

Bolan stepped out in front of both men.

"I'm what's wrong," he said calmly.

The first man bared a mouth full of large teeth as he snarled, and tore at the trigger of his Ingram. Anticipating the move, Bolan spun out of the path of the chattering slugs. The shooter tried to follow the soldier's movement, but was having trouble keeping the MAC-10 from shooting its rounds into the air.

Bolan fired a triburst at the man. The first round punctured his sternum and shoved him back into a tree. The second and third punched holes in his stomach.

Stunned at the swiftness with which death came,

the shooter dropped his weapon and crumpled to the ground.

The second man raised his hands.

"I only work here," he pleaded.

Bolan motioned for the man to place his hands against the side of the Rolls-Royce.

The crocodile farm guard took advantage of the distraction, snatching a 9 mm Type 59 pistol from his waistband and firing at Bolan.

The soldier had sensed the guard's sudden movement and jumped out of the path of the lead death dealers. Bolan didn't bother wasting time aiming the 9 mm pistol. Locking his finger on the trigger, he released a hail of lead that stitched a vertical pattern of holes from the farm guard's stomach to his face.

The guard tried desperately to fire back, but his trigger finger wouldn't respond to his brain's command. He started to say something to Bolan, but his words trailed away when death claimed him.

MARCEL MARACEL WAS a freelance intel op. Everyone from the local CIA station chief to the Russian "attachés" in Thailand, Cambodia, Laos and Myanmar bought information from him, as did the heads of the local chapters of the various triads and the young warlord of the Golden Triangle.

The short, hairy man made it his business to know who was doing what—and to whom. His network of informants throughout Southeast Asia was larger than the intelligence services of any of the countries in which he operated.

Maracel's past was a mystery. He worked for any side that would pay him—the CIA, the Khmer Rouge, the Pathet Lao. Supposedly he had been a member of an Algerian resistance force dedicated to eliminating French control of their African satellite.

Operating out of a small office in the Patpong District, Maracel contacted the Russian operative in the Rangoon embassy.

"There is a man named Michael Belasko. An American. Probably a mercenary. Word out is that he has been behind the destruction of a number of triad warehouses, but no one knows who sent him."

"Interesting but not very useful."

"Perhaps it will be more interesting to your friend, General Chernov."

"You can talk to him if he comes through Rangoon again," Maleshnikoff replied.

"Too bad. I had some information about the drug triads and the warlord of the Golden Triangle that I know he would have wanted to purchase."

"Tell me. Perhaps I will be interested."

Maracel smiled to himself. Maleshnikoff had taken the bait.

"I happen to have the exact location of where the visiting American senator is meeting with the drug barons. But it will cost you ten thousand U.S. dollars, deposited to my Hong Kong account."

The Russian weighed the offer. The sum wasn't

outrageous. He would charge the general twenty thousand dollars when he contacted him on the helicopter's shortwave radio.

"I will make sure the proper people receive your information. And your bank account will be replenished. It would be valuable to know who sent this man Belasko. And why."

"I'll keep digging," Maracel promised.

Then he gave him the location of General Lu's villa in Chiang Mai.

"It would be worth a little extra if I knew exactly who is there."

Maracel checked the page in his hand.

"The Elder Brothers of the Yi Kwah Tao, the Chui Chao and the 14K Triads. Their Thai Incense Masters and Red Poles. And a half-dozen foot soldiers each.

"Of course, General Lu will be there, with a dozen of his best soldiers guarding the grounds. The American senator will naturally be there, guarded by a handful of local CIA agents.

"And a surprise guest. Or maybe not such a surprise."

Maleshnikoff was growing impatient. "There will be a five hundred dollar bonus in your account if you don't drag this out much longer."

"The general's mother has decided to participate in the discussions. She is flying there right now."

"Good information, Maracel. I'll arrange to transfer funds to your account in the morning."

The freelance intel op smiled after he replaced the receiver in its cradle. He was living the best of all lives. Much better than his life had been before he defected from the Soviets while on a KGB mission to Cambodia and the Khmer Rouge.

Yuri Borodin ceased to exist when Marcel Maracel was created.

THE HEAVY DRAPERIES in the living room of the villa were drawn shut so that outsiders would be unaware of the meeting.

Watching as the American senator entered the room, the drug barons and their right-hand men wondered what the man could have to say that was important enough for General Lu to insist they meet with him in the warlord's Chiang Mai villa.

The senator stood and got right to the point of the meeting. "My name is Bobby Firestone. And if you don't know what I do for a living, I'm your enemy. I am chairman of the United States Senate Oversight Subcommittee on Narcotic Traffic."

The blunt introduction brought expressions of surprise to the faces of the men in the room, including the CIA agents lined along the back wall of the large room.

"The President of the United States has instructed me to make you an offer. An offer, in the language of our American Mafia leaders, that you can't refuse."

The reference to the organized gang leaders caused several of the CIA agents to smile.

"It's simply this. The United States government will purchase your current poppy crops plus your unprocessed and processed inventory at a fair price. Not the price you expect to get from selling it to distributors, but a most generous sum."

Eyes narrowed. What did the American government want in return was the question written across the faces of the Asian drug lords.

"In exchange for which, we expect you to destroy all of your processing plants and every last corner of your poppy fields."

The 14K chief jumped to his feet. Shedding the tranquil expression he usually wore, the thin, bearded old man shouted, "What kind of insanity is this?"

Sun Jee of the Chui Chao dropped his mask of composure and joined in the shouting.

"What makes you think you can stop us from moving the white powder into your country?"

The Elder Brother of the Yi Kwah Tao, Tan Suan Chi agreed with his two rivals.

"We are too powerful for even your government, and we have invested millions in our distribution network."

Firestone stared back at the triad godfather.

"You've invested less than a half-million dollars for your current inventory. And every last penny was blood money taken from dying drug addicts."

General Lu listened carefully to the arguments,

then pushed his way past the seated attendees to stand facing the American politician.

"You are a paper tiger, growling without teeth," he said softly.

His comments brought skeptical glances from the triad leaders.

Sun Jee looked surprised.

"Then you haven't heard that someone—we suspect a mercenary hired by the American government—has destroyed some of our larger Bangkok warehouses?"

The others nodded in agreement.

"You claimed to be coming here with an offer. Now it appears you are only a decoy," Lu snapped.

"I know nothing about these bombings. Perhaps one of you three are responsible," Firestone snapped back.

General Lu was certain the American senator didn't. He had copies of grainy pictures his mother had taken of the captured mercenary. He had shown them to his contacts in Bangkok. Several had identified the man as someone who had come to Thailand before to wage a personal vendetta on the triads.

The warlord turned to the Elder Brothers.

"Destroyed inventory can be replaced. I have enough stored to supply you with twice what you lost." Then he added, "At a price, naturally."

The smile on Lu Shu-Shui's face seemed to reflect his reaction to the destruction of the triad warehouses.

It was good for business. At least, his business.

Firestone turned to the Elder Brothers. ''I suggest you reserve your decision until you hear the entire proposal.''

Lu asked the question. ''What else is your President offering?''

''If you refuse this offer,'' Firestone replied grimly, ''an army of specially trained commandos will drop from the sky with enough weapons and equipment to destroy anyone or anything who tries to stop them.''

CHAPTER TWELVE

Bolan had a message he wanted those involved in the opium trade to get—the Executioner was among them and prepared to destroy anyone who was still involved in exporting the white-powdered poison.

Confiscating the seventy-year-old Silver Wraith, he tried to decide how he could reinforce the messages he'd already left behind in the destroyed warehouses.

The soldier had an immediate destination in mind—where he had parked his rental car, and he hoped no one had stolen it. First, though, he had to make a phone call.

Pulling up in front of the Oriental Hotel, Bolan got out of the vehicle and slipped the doorman some bills to watch the limousine, then walked inside the lobby to find a pay phone.

"Collins."

"We need to talk. Now," Bolan stated.

The DEA field officer was stunned. The man was supposed to be dead. Some of those who had witnessed the gigantic explosion swore they saw a Westerner rush into the warehouse just before the building blew apart.

"How did you escape?"

"Later," the soldier replied, as he checked the magazines in his guns. He named the street where he'd parked the rental car.

"Give me ten minutes," Collins said.

SITTING AT THE large desk in his room, General Lu told his new aide, Major Sung, "This American who is destroying the warehouses could be a problem. Eliminate him."

Sung looked puzzled. "Any suggestions, General?"

Lu stared coldly at the young officer. "If you want to make the rank of colonel, you will not need suggestions. But here is one. Take some of our troops and fly into Bangkok. We have equipment and arms stored in our own depots down there. Then find this man and kill him before he threatens our personal authority."

"What about the Thai military police? We are not supposed to be in their country."

"The deputy commander is an old friend. I will call him. You will find him cooperative. Especially when it means that his personal Hong Kong bank account will be enriched by looking in the other direction."

COLLINS PULLED UP in his embassy-owned vehicle and signaled Bolan, who stood beside a Rolls-Royce.

The soldier checked inside the limousine, then locked the vehicle and got into the DEA agent's car.

Bolan could sense Collins was full of questions.

"Whatever happened at the 14K warehouse?"

"It went to hell, just like the other two."

"You were supposed to go with it," Collins commented.

"What's that supposed to mean?"

"You were set up, Belasko. You were supposed to walk inside that warehouse where two dozen guns were supposed to wash your body with lead soap," Collins growled.

"How do you know?"

"One of my informants," Collins answered. "He called from a pay phone some time ago to pass along the tip." He paused, then added, "You owe me six hundred bahts. That's twelve bucks."

Collins held out his hand. Bolan stared at it in disbelief, then reached into a pocket and found a twenty. "Keep the change in case you get another tip about me," he said wryly.

"I won't. Not from this informant. I found his body and his head, separated from each other."

Bolan turned away to check his weapons. The American DEA agent stared at him.

"Don't you want to know what he told me?"

"Whatever it is won't stop me from going through with the mission."

"The triad godfathers want you dead," Collins

stated, "but it's worse than that. The Dragon Lady wants you dead, too."

It was the first time he had heard the slang name since he'd arrived in Thailand.

"Who's the Dragon Lady?"

"Her name is Mai Ling, which would make her Chinese. But from what I hear she's originally Hmong, from the hill tribes up north. The ones who grow poppy plants."

"I met her. But I couldn't figure out why she was so interested in me."

"You're a threat to her sonny boy and his career."

"Which of the drug lords is her son?"

"General Lu Shu-Shui, the majordomo of the heroin trade. She still treats him like he was a kid in short pants. And my sources say that when he's around her he acts that way."

"So she's in bed with the triad bosses," Bolan commented.

"That's what's so strange. For years she's been trying to get General Sonny Boy to cut out the Chinese syndicates and deal directly with the United States and Europe."

Brognola's comments about the identity of the President's emissary came to mind. He wondered how Senator Firestone was tied into this scenario.

He turned and faced Collins. "What do you know about a Senator Bobby Firestone?"

"Outside the fact that he's my kind of man when

it comes to taking on the drug barons and their lobbyists, and has the clout to do it, nothing."

He paused, then added, "Except that nobody has seen him since he arrived in Bangkok." Hastily he added, "It could mean nothing."

Leaving the bag on the front passenger's seat, Bolan picked up a block of C-4 and a pair of timers and detonators.

"I'll be back in a minute."

"Where are you going?"

Bolan pointed to a small, one-story building. "Isn't that a weapons depot for the Chui Chao?"

Collins stared at the structure. "Yes. Why?"

Without answering him, the soldier got out of the car and walked to the building. He peered through the dust-covered window and saw a tall stack of crates. The markings on them indicated they contained ammo.

Pressing half the block of plastique against the outer wall, then inserting and setting the timer and detonator, Bolan worked the second timer and detonator into the remainder of the rectangle of grayish explosive. Setting the timer for seven minutes, he shattered one of the glass panes, then tossed the C-4 through the opening. He watched it roll until it landed near the ammo crates. Then he trotted back to Collins's car, reached in and grabbed his carryall.

"Let's get out of this neighborhood and have a drink. You know the town. So you lead."

Collins jumped into his sedan and started driving

slowly down the street, away from the warehouse. In his rearview mirror he could see Bolan following.

Suddenly, he pulled up beside Collins.

"I suggest we move a lot faster," he called, and took off.

The DEA agent pressed on the accelerator and turned the corner, only inches behind him.

From behind him he could hear the massive thunder as the warehouse was destroyed by explosives. He pulled alongside the Executioner.

"Follow me," he shouted.

CHAPTER THIRTEEN

Chernov watched as his men showered the small village with a massive barrage of ammo. Villagers fell like trees, and no one was exempt. Women and children died, shattered by high-powered lead.

Within an hour, the small Myanmar village looked like a relic of the days when the Cambodian Khmer Rouge slaughtered everyone in sight.

This was the fourth village to die at the hands of the Russian drug baron and his men.

"The laboratory," the ex-general told his aide, Oskar Tremenko. "Let's burn it down. We can spray the area with herbicide after we take off."

Ne Win, the Karin army colonel, waved to Chernov from the lead helicopter.

"A radio message for you," he shouted.

Chernov wondered what Maleshnikoff wanted. He was the only person in Southeast Asia who knew how to reach him.

Sprinting to the plane, Chernov scrambled into the Hind and spoke into the handheld microphone.

"What is so important that you had to radio me?"

Maleshnikoff told him about the information he had acquired about a meeting in northern Thailand that was supposed to start that evening.

And that someone named Belasko was believed to be responsible for the explosions in Bangkok.

"Is he CIA?"

"My contact in the Intelligence Agency denies any knowledge of the man. He claimed the man must be a freelancer."

"Then why would he risk death by destroying the heroin warehouses?"

"Perhaps a rival syndicate, like the Italians or the Turks, hired him."

"Ask your contact if he can arrange for me to meet with this Belasko. It seems we both have the same goal. And I would feel more comfortable if he was on my payroll."

"It cost a lot to get this information," Maleshnikoff said.

"There will be an additional deposit to your bank account when I return home," Chernov promised. "I can meet with him in the morning. Get me hotel rooms. I prefer the Oriental, which I understand is a very nice place. You can leave me a message about the meeting there."

He handed the microphone to the pilot.

Climbing down, he waved to Tremenko.

When his aide reached him, Chernov told him, "Finish up quickly. We have two more stops to make before we can go home."

"May I ask where, General?"

"Only when we get there."

He smiled. The United States government would lay the blame for the death of the senator at the feet of the Chinese triads.

For him, Chernov decided, it was a win-win situation. Exactly the kind of situation he preferred.

"I'M TIRED OF BEING out of the loop," Collins complained, as he sipped his drink.

"At least you're still alive," Bolan reminded him.

The DEA agent shook his head and smiled sadly.

"It's ironic. I joined the Drug Enforcement Administration to get revenge for the brutal deaths of my brother and his family. And all I've been allowed to do since I came here is gather information."

Bolan only half heard him. Fatigue was starting to set in as the adrenaline in his system slackened.

"You look beat," Collins commented.

The DEA operative stood and dropped some bills on the table.

"Meet me at the embassy. I've got an extra set of keys to my apartment in my office. Just in case you change your mind."

"It might be a little while before I get there. I've got something to take care of first," he said, selecting his next target in his head.

Collins remembered the rogue agent he had shot and the follow-up interview that had been scheduled.

"I'll probably be there half the night, finishing up paperwork."

MAI LING RECEIVED NEWS of the death of her two closest aides by telephone. Livid, she told the caller to check the security cameras. She was certain there were pictures of the American mercenary on the tapes.

"Have copies made and distribute them throughout Bangkok. Offer a reward of—" she paused while determining the right amount "—make it fifty thousand bahts."

For that kind of money, Mai knew that most of the street thugs in the capital city would kill their own mothers.

As she hung up the phone, she knew that it was time to join the meeting. From the arguments she had overheard, now was when she should step in and offer a possible solution.

BOLAN SAW THEM when he walked up the street from the American Embassy. The two young Thais dressed in jeans and thin leather jackets loitered near the entrance to the ultramodern structure.

Ignoring them, Bolan got into the rental car. The two stared at a photograph, then glanced up at him. Quickly they mounted a parked Honda Elite moped and pulled away from the curb.

Starting the engine, Bolan released the brake and turned the wheel hard and clutched into second. The

Nissan squealed a complaint as he raced it down the street past them, then he clutched into third gear and accelerated.

If the pair was following him, Bolan decided he'd lead them on a chase they wouldn't forget.

Threading his way through the heavy traffic in central Bangkok, the soldier narrowly missed a truck as he whipped into the traffic circle at Klang Road. He ignored shaken fists and shouted curses from tourists and locals as he kept his eyes peeled for openings in the endless melange of pedicabs and taxicabs racing around the circle.

In his rearview mirror, he could see the scooter's driver pumping fuel in an effort to keep up with him. Seated behind him, the other youth had his arms wrapped around the front man's waist to keep from falling.

The narrow scooter could have inched through openings in the traffic, but the driver seemed to be satisfied staying behind Bolan's car.

The soldier knew that a few blocks ahead was a series of waterfront dead ends, a good place to take a stand without involving innocent pedestrians. He plowed ahead, aiming his car in the direction of the side streets that ran up to the river.

With his hand pressed hard against the horn, he maneuvered around trucks and passenger cars that threatened to crash into him. Pedestrians, used to the suicidal driving of local cabbies, stepped back on the sidewalks as he crossed Bamrung Muay, then Chakra Bongse Road.

A rush of traffic racing across his path forced Bolan to slam on the brakes. While he waited, he opened the glove compartment, grabbed the Beretta and laid it on the seat next to him.

He could see the passenger on the moped talking into the driver's ear. Suddenly, the driver sped up and tried to close the gap between the rental car and himself. A group of schoolchildren crossing the street scattered as the Japanese-made two-wheeler plowed toward them in its relentless pursuit of Bolan's car.

The soldier jumped the curb and moved around a small crowd, which scrambled out of the way.

The moped raced onto the sidewalk behind him. An elderly woman was knocked to the ground as she tried to hurry out of the path of the scooter. Several people ran to help her to her feet.

Bolan had to accept that the battle was going to take place before he could reach the waterfront.

Looking around, he couldn't see any place to stop that would protect pedestrians from the deadly gunfire that was sure to erupt. All he could hope was that the battle would be brief.

Glancing over his shoulder, he saw the passenger release his grip on the driver's waist and aim a weapon.

Bolan recognized the piece as an MM-1 Multiple Projectile Launcher. He grabbed the Beretta and turned briefly to fire, but too many civilians crowded the area for him to risk a shot.

The Nissan scraped its left fender along the wall, creating a trail of sparks. Bolan steered the vehicle around a small cluster of cowering pedestrians and back onto the roadway. The driver of the moped followed close behind, oblivious to the panic he was creating.

Temporarily stymied, the moped passenger lowered his weapon and wrapped an arm around the driver's waist. Twenty yards later traffic closed in and forced both Bolan and the moped driver to use their brakes.

Bolan looked back and saw the rider pointing the MM-1 again. As the young thug pulled on the trigger, the Executioner dived out of the car. Two grenades narrowly missed contact with the Nissan. Hitting a wall, the bombs chewed open a section of bricks and sent a shower of clay and metal fragments onto fleeing pedestrians.

Ignoring the panic the explosions had created, the Executioner snapped off a pair of shots back at the moped. One missed and tore into the asphalt roadway. The other ripped a bloody path into the intestines of the driver.

The soldier rolled to the ground and whipped three more rounds at the Japanese scooter. Behind him, the Nissan coasted into a brick wall and came to a stop.

One of Bolan's rounds scarred the face of the young shooter. Another slammed into the wounded driver, knocking him off the moped. The final slug punctured the fragile gas tank, sending fuel spewing over the roadway and onto the sidewalk pavement.

People screamed and tried to run from the bloody chaos, but the streets were too crowded for anyone to put distance between themselves and the geyser of gasoline.

"Get out of here," the Executioner yelled in Thai, as sparks ignited the fuel.

The flames inched their way back to the scooter tank. The gunner tried to scramble off the overturned moped, but was too tangled in the wreckage to move.

Bolan charged toward him hoping to pull him away, but had to stop when the flames reached the ruptured gas tank.

The tank blew with a muffled roar, and the moped and its two passengers disappeared behind a huge fireball. Black smoke swirled upward from the wreckage.

Flames covered both young men. The shooter rolled on the ground, screaming in pain as he tried to extinguish the fire covering his body.

Several men ignored the danger to themselves and tried to smother the flames with their jackets. Chunks of superheated metal flew from the minibike, forcing the would-be rescuers back. Several drilled through Bolan's shirt and into his shoulder, slashing the skin where he'd already been injured. He succeeded in yanking out several of the larger pieces. The others were too deeply imbedded to remove without tweezers.

The soldier looked at where the moped had been and saw only twisted pieces of blackened metal. What had once been two young men was now charred human flesh.

A young American, still in shock, approached him.

"They tried to kill you," he said as if he thought Bolan didn't know. Then he asked, "Are you all right?"

Standing slowly, then heading back to where the dented rental car had stopped, he nodded.

The man continued his questioning. "Why were they trying to kill you?"

The Executioner didn't answer. The only thing he was sure about was that the two attackers were dead, and he was still alive.

"One of them was holding this piece of paper," the tourist said. "The man in the picture looks like you."

Bolan took the printed sheet and studied it. It was him, shot from a strange, overhead angle.

He read the reward offer. At least whoever was after him thought he was worth a fair amount of money.

There was a phone number, and Bolan suspected it belonged to an answering service.

Thousands of the reward offers had to be circulating throughout the city, Bolan decided. Somebody wanted him dead, and he wanted to know who that somebody was.

"Perhaps I should call for an ambulance," the tourist suggested, looking at the bleeding cuts that covered Bolan's face. "You look injured."

In the distance Bolan could hear the warbling of police sirens. There was no reason for him to wait for the Thai police.

The young American turned back and looked at what was left of the two. Then, realizing that he was smelling death, leaned against the wall and vomited.

Bolan climbed into the Nissan and backed it away from the wall that had stopped it.

The bits of metal digging into his back felt like shrapnel. He had no time to seek medical attention.

Right now he had a war to continue fighting. All he knew was that the action had been accelerated, and he was the target.

CHAPTER FOURTEEN

Bolan was on a roll. His next target was a one-story sandstone structure located on the edge of Chinatown. He pulled his car to the curb and parked.

Checking his handguns and Uzi, he replaced the magazines with full clips, then set the Uzi submachine gun on selective fire and shouldered it.

The Israeli-made weapon was an ugly but reliable tool. Weighing less than seven and a half pounds, the powerful submachine gun was only seventeen inches long from the tip of its stubby barrel to the end of its folded metal stock. Each magazine clipped into its grip held twenty-five rounds of high-velocity ammo. The little subgun could be fired from a one-hand hold when necessary.

Nine millimeter Parabellum rounds hurtled out of the barrel at the rate of 600 rounds per minute, with a velocity of 1,250 feet per second. Changing magazines took less than a second. Bolan was glad he held one of the subguns now. It was one of the few weapons he trusted in combat.

The building was dark. Bolan tried to peer through

the dirt-streaked windows, but the light inside was too dim to see anything clearly.

The soldier decided to try another tactic. He banged on the door with the butt of his Uzi, then stepped to one side and waited.

The door opened and three Asians in fatigues looked outside. In a Cantonese dialect, they shouted out a question.

"Who is it that knocks?"

Bolan kept silent.

Two of the guards came out of the warehouse and looked around.

"Perhaps it was only a drunk looking for a free drink," one of them told the other.

Bolan stepped out of the darkness, the silenced Uzi grasped in his right hand. Unleashing a torrent of death from the Israeli subgun, he saw the first guard stare at him in shock for a moment, then crumple in a heap on the ground as life pumped out of both arteries onto his fatigues.

The second hood swung his AK-47 at Bolan and shoved a finger in front of the trigger.

"You're it," Bolan said quietly as he quickly moved at the man and chopped at his throat with the karate-hardened edge of his palm.

He could hear the small bones in the neck breaking as his palm pushed past them and ruptured the vital carotid artery. The guard crashed back against the outside wall, then slid to the ground.

The third guard stared at the bodies of his two

fallen comrades, then moved into the street to destroy the man who had committed this unthinkable act.

He had hesitated too long. A burst from the Uzi tore into his face before he could lift his AK-47, and his lower jaw dissolved as the slugs exploded into fragments inside his mouth. He fell forward and collapsed at Bolan's feet.

The Executioner stopped and listened for any sounds that might indicate that more gunmen waited inside the building to ambush him.

There was none. Instead the area was filled with an eerie silence. Cautiously, he began to enter the warehouse.

Four fatigue-clad men had been waiting, and all four charged him. Twenty-five rounds of 9 mm lead drilled into the ambushers, who fell to the warehouse floor in a twitching mass.

Not quite four, yet, Bolan decided as he heard moaning from one of them. He leaned over the blood-covered dying man and asked him a question in Cantonese.

"Where is the American meeting with your Elder Brother?"

In response, the dying man moved his hand to the autopistol in his waistband. Bolan ended the gunner's suffering and desperate attempt to continue the battle with a pair of slugs that tore through the man's heart muscle.

One more thing remained to do. Digging into his

vest, Bolan found slices of C-4 plastic explosives, along with detonators and timers.

Setting the timers for five minutes, he plastered cases of ammo and rockets around the large warehouse, then raced out of the building and jumped into his waiting vehicle.

As he sped around the corner and down another street, he could hear the first of the explosions shatter windows in the area. Pausing momentarily, he looked back.

The sky was filled with flames and bits of wood, sandstone and metal speeding through the air. The impressive display brightened the neighborhood momentarily. Then a cloud of dust began to settle on the streets as the last explosion consumed what was left of the warehouse, and the bodies in it.

BOLAN PULLED THE CAR to the curb and took out Collins's list. There was at least one more place he wanted to hit this night—an automotive warehouse owned by a front company for the Yi Kwah Tao Triad.

According to Collins's notes, the warehouse stored drugs and weapons, as well as auto parts.

The one-story structure was located on Maekon Road on the edge of Chinatown. The soldier checked the Bangkok map for the quickest way to get there. The road wasn't noted. He decided to call Collins from a pay phone.

As he pulled from the curb, he didn't notice the

two men seated in a Mazda, who were studying a sheet of paper. The passenger signaled for the other to follow the soldier's car.

Bolan found a dimly lit restaurant that had a pay phone mounted on a wall. He would call Collins from there.

A slender Thai was using the phone, and he looked strangely familiar to Bolan.

The man turned his head and glanced at the Executioner, then turned his back on him and continued his conversation.

Bolan had ordered a cup of coffee and was sitting at a table waiting for the phone. Finally he stood and grabbed the check. There were other food shops, other telephones, he reminded himself as he walked to where the young female cashier was glancing at a fashion magazine.

A burst of gunfire shattered the large glass window where he had been sitting. The waitress began to scream hysterically but seemed frozen in her high stool behind the counter.

Bolan's .44 Desert Eagle cleared his waistband as he dropped to the floor. Rolling at an angle from the shattered window, he saw two forms spraying steady bursts of lead from the AK-47s they brandished as they charged toward the small restaurant.

The Executioner lined up a shot and took out the lead gunner. The round slammed into the man's face, shoving him backward. A second slug ruined his chest.

Swinging his gun at the surviving thug, Bolan pulled the trigger twice. The guy spun before he could fire the AK-47 he held.

A sudden sense of danger from behind saved Bolan's life. He threw himself into a shoulder roll and turned just as the man who had been on the phone pumped searing rounds of lead from the 9 mm Makarov pistol in his hand.

Bolan aimed the Desert Eagle at the new assailant and fired toward his chin. The gunner's chest exploded in a shower of bloody tissue.

The expression in the would-be killer's face didn't change as the hollowpoint rounds tore through his breastbone and exploded inside into dozens of searing fragments. Even as his lifeblood gushed from the huge cavity created by the Magnum rounds, the hit man tried to fire back.

Throwing himself at the gunner, the Executioner fired again, this time at the would-be killer's stomach. The impact of the two rounds pushed the man backward even while he was squeezing the trigger of his pistol. A series of scorched holes appeared in the ceiling tiles as the man fell back onto a table, then slid to the ground and became still.

Bolan struggled to his feet and looked around the demolished room.

The three attackers had one thing in common— copies of the reward offer with his picture. Whoever wanted him dead was attracting a lot of takers.

Dead takers, Bolan reminded himself, and wondered if the reward money was worth their lives.

His musings were interrupted by the wail of police cars. He didn't have the time for interrogation. He had to leave.

CHAPTER FIFTEEN

The pain in his shoulder was beginning to throb. Every movement of his upper arm created more agony for Bolan.

Trying to ignore the throbbing agony in his shoulder, Bolan followed the highway out of Bangkok, heading for the secluded villa the Dragon Lady called home.

He'd finally called Collins, and according to the DEA agent, Mai Ling was out of the city on business.

Bolan checked the windows. There were only eight Thai guards covering the villa. All were armed.

Professionals, he decided.

He saw the Chinese copies of the 7.62 mm AK-47 carbines each was carrying. Even the imitations of the Russian-made Kalashnikovs were excellent weapons. Fitted with 30-round magazines, the compact carbines could unleash 800 rounds a minute.

One Uzi was no match for the awesome firepower of a half-dozen or more AK-47 carbines. At least face-to-face.

A surprise attack was the only solution.

Bolan stared through the windows at the interior and quickly improvised a plan of action. Digging into the canvas carryall on the floor of the rental car, he took out a small brick of C-4 plastique and carefully cut the rectangle into three roughly equal blocks. Then he fitted them with detonators and miniaturized timers.

Surprisingly, the front door wasn't locked. Obviously Mai Ling had confidence in her guards' ability to keep her villa secure.

Moving carefully through the living room, Bolan walked through an open doorway and stopped. Kneeling, he pressed the first brick against the central power control panel, then set the timer for six minutes.

In a corridor closet, he found a small cache of rifles and ammo. The small pile of ammo boxes was the next receptacle for the C-4. Setting the timer for five minutes, Bolan searched for a final location.

Through one of the windows, he saw a dilapidated truck parked alongside the high wall that surrounded the large residence, and a quartet of men pacing along the patio. Setting the timer for four minutes, Bolan slipped out a back door, worked his way to the ancient vehicle and pressed the final block against the fuel tank.

The Executioner heard the soft scuffle of rubber-soled shoes behind him. Pivoting, he unleathered the Beretta 93-R and stroked the trigger twice. Both rounds tore into the throat of the thick-necked sentry behind him.

As the thug fell to the ground, Bolan heard the sound of leather soles slapping concrete. Turning in the direction of the noise, he switched the selector switch to 3-round-burst mode, then waited for a guard to appear. The soldier who showed up was wearing the uniform of the People's Revolutionary Army. The AK-47 in his hands flew into the air as the impact of three Parabellum rounds ripped through his breastbone and carved paths to his heart muscle.

Suddenly the villa was silent as the remaining guards regrouped.

Crawling fifteen yards, Bolan fired a burst at a shadowy figure near the villa. The sentry dropped his AK-47 with a grunt of pain, then collapsed in a heap.

A barrage of fire washed the darkness as PRA soldiers fouled the night air with the stench of cordite.

Bolan unslung the Uzi and returned the fire from his new location, spraying the space in front of him from left to right with life-stealing lead.

One of the attackers screamed in pain as hot metal tore his chest to shreds and shoved him back against the wall. A second gunner dropped his assault rifle and clutched his midsection, trying to close the newly created cavity.

A third hardman rushed at the Executioner, crazed by the burning lead that had shattered his right shoulder. A quick burst ended his glory run.

The attacker had been carrying a mini-Uzi. Bolan

leaned down and relieved the corpse of the pair of 30-round clips taped together on a canvas belt. The Dragon Lady's bodyguard would have no further need of weapons or ammunition.

It was time to retreat.

Bolan moved swiftly through the side door and headed for the parked Nissan.

A surly faced soldier spotted him and raced to a nearby parked car, a bright red Datsun, to give chase. A second armed soldier jumped into the passenger seat of the vehicle as it began to accelerate.

As he spun around a corner, Bolan wondered how Mai Ling had gotten hold of his picture. Then he remembered the small security camera mounted near the ceiling of the basement room.

Bolan checked his rearview mirror and saw a burly gunner in the passenger seat poke an AK-47 assault rifle out of his opened window. A short burst of hardball NATO rounds tore chunks of metal out of the trunk.

The Executioner began an evasive pattern, swinging his car from left to right, then back again. Hoping to put distance between himself and the chase car, Bolan approached an oncoming corner at racing speed. He twisted the wheel hard toward the inside of the curve and tapped the brakes just enough to push the vehicle into a slide.

The rear end swung to the outside. As he executed a four-wheel drift, he shoved the gearshift to low, stomped on the accelerator and shot out of the curve.

He could hear the tires of the Datsun squeal as the driver skidded and spun out, trying to maneuver through the same turn at high speed.

Bolan maintained the pattern of erratic short turns in the narrow road until he saw a small café a hundred yards ahead. Metal tables and chairs were stacked against the corrugated metal wall. He decided to make his stand there, and spun the Nissan onto the sidewalk.

As the car crashed through the furniture, Bolan grabbed the mini-Uzi and spare clips, and opened the car door. Just before the vehicle came to a complete stop against a wall, the Executioner jumped from the rental car.

The driver of the chase car hadn't expected the sudden stop and jammed his brakes. The Datsun skidded, smashed into Bolan's rented car and flipped on its side.

The big American took refuge behind the hood of the battle-wounded rental, then watched the surly faced passenger force his way out of the Datsun. Nervously, the hardman sprayed a continuous torrent of 7.62 mm rounds at Bolan's car to cover his exit, then dived behind the door of his car.

The Kalashnikov's hammer hit metal, and Bolan could hear the shooter desperately trying to ram another magazine into the assault rifle.

The driver had remained still during the brief attack. Bolan suspected he was either unconscious or dead. Either way, he wasn't a threat. Yet.

Bolan wanted to end the battle peacefully, if possible. The pair of soldiers, if both were still alive, could be a valuable source of information.

"Drop the gun," he shouted.

"Drop dead, American," the burly soldier holding the assault rifle shouted back.

Time for conversation was over. Bolan waited for the AK-47 shooter to raise his head again. When he did, the Executioner unleashed a short burst of 9 mm death from the Uzi. He could hear the soft thud of a body banging into metal behind the passenger door.

Without warning, the burly rifleman stood, his face twisted by anger, and poured lead rounds in the Executioner's direction. Blood pouring from a shattered shoulder, the crazed street fighter started walking toward Bolan.

Surprised at the wounded man's show of courage, the Executioner waited until he got closer, then loosed a trio of 9 mm slugs.

The lead zingers tore into the rifleman's chest and neck. As if he were impervious to bullets, the burly man kept moving forward.

Bolan knew the man was fatally wounded, but he didn't believe in taking unnecessary risks. He fired another two rounds. The impact spun the shooter and slammed him back into the door of his car. He dropped his AK-47 and slid to the ground.

Bolan cautiously made his way toward the other vehicle to check to make sure the two gunners were dead. He felt the pulse on each, and he knew they were.

The Executioner quit the area, deciding he needed to talk to Hal Brognola for an update on how the triads were viewing his hits.

CHAPTER SIXTEEN

Bolan returned to his hotel and made a call to Hal Brognola from a telephone in the lobby. After dialing a series of cutout numbers, he was finally connected to the big Fed.

"You outdid yourself this time," Brognola said. "A lot of stuff went up in smoke over the past sixteen hours."

Because it was a nonsecure line, Bolan coached his conversation carefully. "How's the salesman doing?"

"He called Big Daddy. His first meeting with the boys got the anticipated reaction. He's due for a second session with them tonight. So anything you can do to empty their pocketbooks would be greatly appreciated by the Man."

"I've still got some more tricks up my sleeve," the soldier promised. "Meantime I need a favor."

"Name it."

"Got a call through a mutual friend that a former Russian general named Chernov, I repeat—Mikhail Chernov—wants to have me join his team and help clean out the local dealers. Do you know anything about the man?''

''Negative. But I'll put the hound dogs on it right away. Where do I find you?''

Bolan told him the name of his new hotel.

''Leave me a message to call you back. Or contact Joe Collins and tell him whatever you learn. I'll be at the meet.''

THE MAN WAITING for Bolan at the restaurant displayed his years of military leadership in his ramrod-stiff posture.

Mikhail Chernov used his two decades of experience as a Soviet officer in running his heroin crime syndicate in Eastern Europe. As the godfather of the Chechen Mafia, he ruled his drug empire with an iron hand.

This was why he wanted to meet the man called Michael Belasko. The American was doing exactly what Chernov wanted his men to do, but this Belasko wasn't operating under his control.

The only logical solution was to hire the mercenary to continue his one-man campaign against the Southeast Asian drug cartel.

Sitting at the window table, the ex-general could see his Spetsnaz commandos waiting for his signal. If Belasko rejected his offer, the two on foot would attempt to kill him. And if that failed, the team in the car would chase him down.

Lost in his review of the plan, Chernov was startled to hear his name called.

"Chernov?"

The Russian looked up and saw the big American standing at the edge of the table. He forced a smile.

"You must be Belasko." He pointed to one of the empty seats. "Please sit. We have much to talk about."

"What exactly do you have in mind?"

Chernov smiled. "You Americans. Always getting to the point. We Russians like to take our time before we say what's on our mind."

"I haven't got the time to waste."

The Russian sighed. "Okay. To begin, who are you working for?"

"That's my business."

"I assume you are being paid well. I can double your salary and let you continue doing what you've been doing."

"A waste of good money. But thanks for the offer."

As Bolan started to stand, Chernov spoke quickly.

"The whole story. Okay?"

The Executioner sat.

"My son was a fine young man," Chernov explained, "until Afghanistan. There he started using heroin. Two days ago, some drug dealers murdered him during a drug buy."

"Southeast Asia isn't the only source of heroin.

Turkey, Iran, Afghanistan, northern Pakistan all grow poppies."

"The two who killed him were Chinese from Thailand."

"So you've come over to get even."

"It's the least I could do for my son." He weighed how much more he would have to tell Belasko. "In our limited way, his former military comrades and I have made a dent in the drug traffic here. Mostly in Burma."

"I heard about it," Bolan commented coldly.

"If we could find the various heads of the crime syndicates that grow and distribute heroin in one location, we could get rid of them once and for all time."

The words sounded right, but there was something that bothered Bolan. A smugness? The pat emotional reasons for waging a war against the triads? Something was wrong.

Bolan stood.

"Let me think about it. Where can I reach you?"

Chernov pulled out a travel brochure from his jacket pocket. It was a promotion folder from one of the more popular local hotels.

"We are staying here today. But tomorrow..." He shrugged. "Who knows where we will be?"

The soldier nodded and walked out of the restaurant.

Chernov watched him depart and instinctively knew the American had turned down his offer.

There was only one thing left to do. He gave the signal.

The Russian lifted the left corner of the sheer curtain that covered the restaurant window, then turned and gestured for the waiter to bring a menu.

BOLAN WASN'T SURE who had sent the two men who followed him down the street. They looked European or American.

The one thing he knew for sure was that the bulges in the jackets of the two men were made by weapons. Probably Uzi or Skorpion submachine guns, from their shape and length.

He saw another possible problem making a turn into the side street. A Mercedes-Benz 500. It was too newly purchased to have permanent license plates.

The surge of traffic had forced the German-built car to slow enough that he could look inside. He could see three men, all in their early twenties. All had the icy expressions of Russian professionals, and they stared in his direction.

There were too many innocents on the street to start a battle here, even if he had weapons. He had to draw the foot soldiers and those in the German car away from the center of the city.

The embassy car he had borrowed from Joe Collins was parked at the curb, ten yards away. All of his battle gear was locked in the trunk.

Thinking fast, he formulated a plan. If it worked,

he'll have destroyed some of the enemy. If it didn't, he wouldn't have to worry why it hadn't.

He'd be dead.

Turning from the shop window, he started to walk slowly at an angle toward the borrowed vehicle. The two men followed closely behind. Suddenly, he spun and wrapped a muscular forearm around the neck of the nearer one.

The sudden action had stunned both men. Bolan wasn't sure what reaction his movement had gotten from the occupants of the Mercedes-Benz, but he'd worry about them later. If he survived.

The collared thug's companion whipped a Skorpion SMG from under his jacket and raised it to fire. Yanking open the jacket of the man he held in a throat lock, Bolan brought the slung subgun into target acquisition. There was no time to wonder whether the safety was on. He was certain the weapon had been pointed to be fired when the right opportunity arrived.

He cut loose, the quick burst of rounds drilling into the chest and stomach of his adversary.

Then, letting go of the submachine gun, he twisted the neck of the man he held with a sudden jerk. The neck snapped, and the corpse slumped forward.

Bolan removed the 9 mm subgun from the body. There was no time to search for additional clips. He would have to make do with what he had.

Ignoring the horrified expressions on the faces of passersby, he shoved the key into the Honda's lock, twisted it and jerked open the door. Jumping in, he shoved the key into the ignition, turned it hard, then floored the gas pedal, tearing out of the parking space like a racehorse out of the starting gate at the Kentucky Derby.

In the rearview mirror, he could see the gray Mercedes trying to get around the vehicles that had come between it and Bolan's car. It was only a matter of time before the men in the chase car would get tired of playing games and start shooting at him.

He was certain they had no qualms about killing innocent people, as long as they killed him as well. What he wasn't certain about was why they wanted him dead.

Was it revenge for the dead triad soldiers? He didn't think so. None of the men in the Mercedes was Asian. Nor was the pair who had tailed him.

The one thing he knew was that this wasn't the time to think about it. He had enough on his mind trying to escape.

The first break came when he raced through an intersection before a large truck. He could hear the sounds of gunfire behind him. Checking in the rearview mirror, he saw one of the Mercedes's occupants jump out and, pointing a gun at the truck driver, force him to back up.

The Executioner made a series of tire-squealing turns in and out of the narrow streets of central Bangkok until he finally reached a broad boulevard and turned into it.

He knew he wasn't home free yet. Only when he eliminated the hit men chasing him would he be able to breathe easy. At least for a little while.

He checked the mirror. The German-made luxury car was charging down the broad boulevard in hot pursuit. The eight cylinders under the hood of the Mercedes-Benz gave it the push it needed to catch up with Bolan.

Pedestrians jumped back on the curb as the Honda raced along the roadway, then they waited for the pursuing Mercedes to pass before they ventured into the street again.

The soldier looked around for a battle site.

Picking up the confiscated Skorpion from the seat next to him, he leaned it out the open window and fired back at the larger car. As he expected, the driver ignored Bolan's rounds and increased the speed to try to overtake him.

The tires on the pursuing vehicle were made of thick rubber, but the Executioner knew that no tire was totally bulletproof. Locking a hand on the rim of the steering wheel, he took a calculated risk and poked his head out of the driver's window.

Guns spit lead at him. He returned fire in a constant stream, each round directed at the front tires, until the clip was empty.

Suddenly the Mercedes's right front tire exploded. The vehicle swerved wildly to the right and, before the driver could bring the car under his control, ran into a parked truck at high speed.

The German car spun from the impact, then went airborne before falling back to the road upside down. From inside, Bolan could hear the moans of the injured.

Stopping the car, Bolan walked back to the crash site. Inside he could see the men who had intended to kill him. All but one appeared to be dead.

The still-living assailant tried to poke his gun—a 9 mm Makarov—out a shattered window. Bolan stopped his movement forever with a simple twist of the hit man's neck.

As the would-be killer slumped on the rear seat, dead, Bolan reminded himself that these were killers. The Executioner had no pity for any of them.

Bolan sniffed the air—gasoline fumes.

He looked at the rear of the German car. A rapid stream of gasoline gushed into the street from a ruptured tank.

There was one last thing he had to do.

Standing back from the wreck, he fired several rounds at the stream of fuel, then, when it began to burn, ran for the borrowed sedan.

As he turned the steering wheel to drive the Honda down a side street, Bolan looked in the rearview mirror at the wrecked vehicle. A police car had stopped and its occupants, uniformed officers, were ordering the curious to move back.

The relative quiet of the broad boulevard was suddenly shattered with the violent sound of the exploding gas tank. Bits of torn metal flew in every direction, breaking windows and imbedding themselves into the bodywork of parked cars and into the brick walls of apartment buildings.

The ricochet of fragments traveled like billiard balls from object to object. A large fragment sheared through the front of the Honda, drilling into the radiator.

Flames shot from the demolished vehicle, consuming car and occupants in their fiery embrace.

He left the embassy-owned vehicle where it was, then walked down a side road and signaled a passing taxicab. His destination was the American Embassy. He needed to talk to Joe Collins about getting a replacement car.

He had a meeting later in the evening with a warehouse full of triad killers.

Only the men he'd be meeting didn't know the Executioner was joining the party.

CHAPTER SEVENTEEN

The phone rang at police headquarters. The duty sergeant put down his magazine and answered it.

"Sergeant Siri."

"About that reward poster for the American that I dropped off this morning," the voice said.

Siri recognized the caller. It was one of the street toughs, a character named Sakreepirom.

The poster was still on his desk. He glanced at it.

"What about it?"

"I just saw him on Bangrum Muang Road, near the circle."

"Thanks for the tip."

"He's driving an American Jeep. You'll share the reward with me, won't you?"

"Sure, sure," the police sergeant promised, then hung up the phone and turned to look at the official vehicle location map.

There was a squad car on Bangrum Muang Road, and an armored personnel carrier sitting in the small park off the boulevard, several miles away. It couldn't hurt to see if they were able to stop the wanted man.

He scribbled a message and handed it to the wireless operator.

AS HE DROVE the vintage Jeep, borrowed from the American Embassy motor pool, toward the district where Collins lived, the Executioner was having difficulty focusing. The throbbing pain in his right shoulder kept interfering with his ability to concentrate on the road.

Bolan glanced in the rearview mirror and saw a Bangkok police car moving toward him at high speed. Someone in the vehicle suddenly turned on the rotating roof light.

He would be wanted by the Thai military police for questioning on the deaths of a dozen citizens, despite the fact that they were Chinese drug dealers.

That fact wouldn't make a bit of difference in their relentless search for Mike Belasko. It made sense when Bolan remembered that almost half the population of Bangkok was of Chinese descent. And that the Chinese controlled much of the business in Thailand.

Bolan leaned forward and rammed the gas pedal to the floor. The Jeep responded immediately and picked up speed.

He glanced up at the rearview mirror. The police car had to have been modified too, he decided. It was still gaining on him.

A series of shots exploded from a weapon poked out of the passenger's window of the pursuing police car. Three bullets crashed into the back end of the car.

Bolan scanned the area. Nobody was walking along the boulevard. Those who had the money to party were doing so. The rest of the inhabitants of Bangkok were at home.

The whining ricochet startled him. Through the rearview mirror he could see a uniformed cop leaning out the car, holding a late model 5.45 mm AK-74 assault rifle against his cheekbone. The swerving of the cars caused the continuous spray of lead sizzlers from the Kalashnikov's 30-round magazine to travel wildly.

But Bolan knew that there was always the chance of a lucky shot. The Executioner decided to try to widen the odds without returning fire.

Twisting the steering wheel to the right, he almost ran the small car onto the sidewalk, then wrenched the wheel in the opposite direction.

As he had suspected, the driver of the police car was trying to imitate his actions. Both cars weaved across the wide road at high speed. Suddenly, Bolan spun the wheel and drove the Jeep onto the walkway.

He glanced at the rearview mirror.

As he had suspected it would, the police vehicle followed him onto the sidewalk. Easing the gas pedal, he let the Jeep slow. The cop car kept charging at top speed.

Just as the official car was about to hit him, Bolan slammed on the brakes.

The souped-up Jeep made a hundred-and-eighty-degree turn. Bolan lifted his foot off the brake and pressed the gas pedal to the floor again.

Behind him, the police driver had lost control. Despite his efforts to turn the official car, it stopped hard against the trunk of a wide tree. Steam poured from the ruptured radiator.

The uniformed lieutenant grabbed the AK-74 carbine from the wrecked car and started firing again.

Screaming lead kept tearing into the rear of the surplus military transport. Sooner or later one of them was going to find their target.

Him.

Bolan stopped the car. Shoving open the door, he rolled out of the vehicle and onto the grass and made a quick decision. They weren't interested in arresting him. They wanted him dead.

He set aside all the reservations he had about shooting at policemen. Survival came first. If he could, he'd shoot to wound.

He would have to fight back if he wanted to stay alive.

The two uniformed men charged at him firing the AK-74s from their hips like six-shooters. The soldier hugged the ground, making himself as small a target as he could.

Waiting for them to come closer, he gripped the

Beretta 93-R with both hands and aimed at the nearer man, who wore a lieutenant's uniform.

Several rounds shattered the rear window of the car. Others chewed the boulevard asphalt. Finally, the Executioner decided he could wait no longer.

Switching to autofire, he unleashed a short burst of lead that tore into the officer's legs. Blood streamed wildly from the wounds as the lawman fell to the ground, clutching at his knees and screaming in agony.

The other uniformed man kept charging at Bolan, emptying the 30-round clip. The soldier had changed position before resuming the battle. Now hidden behind the Jeep, he fired another trio of rounds that stabbed into his attacker's shoulder, punching him backward and to the ground. A piece of paper fluttered to the earth.

One glance and Bolan knew what was behind the chase. The reward for him. A lot of people wanted a piece of the action. Even the local police. Somebody wanted him out of the way badly.

The wailing of sirens became louder. Someone had to have called the local cops. There was nothing left to do but get out of there.

Bolan grabbed his canvas carryall and, using the darkened sidewalk for cover, darted between a pair of decrepit apartment buildings and down an alley.

There was a connecting alley at the rear. Running along the side of the buildings, he masked his movements in the shadows of the structures. He moved quickly to where the alley emptied into a side street. Cautiously, he looked around the corner and examined the immediate area. He needed transportation.

Salvation came in the form of a cabby.

The badly scarred ancient Toyota pulled up beside him.

"Taxi, mister?"

"Yeah."

CHAPTER EIGHTEEN

At the rate Bolan was going through them, the American Embassy would soon run out of vehicles. Nonetheless, Joe Collins had come through once again. The Executioner had wheels.

A tip from Collins had brought the Executioner to this place. One of Collins's best sources had passed along the information that the Chui Chao was hiding a large cache of heroin until the attacks on the warehouses owned by the various triads had ended.

The Executioner drove to an apartment building that had been converted to a warehouse after it had been condemned for human occupancy by the Bangkok authorities.

While Collins faced an internal hearing from a representative of the inspector general on the death of David Weyant, Bolan decided to check out the lead.

The soldier sensed that the supposedly deserted building was a setup. He aimed for a remote section of the high wall that encircled the warehouse and parked against it, then rechecked the magazines of the two pistols he was wearing, as well as that of the silenced 9mm Uzi he had slung over a shoulder.

Around his waist he wore a canvas belt. Hanging from it were a trio of M-67 delay fragmentation grenades. The razor-sharp Applegate-Fairbairn combat knife rode in a thin sheath strapped to his right leg.

He eased his way to a small door on the side of the building, using the shadows to mask his presence, then stopped and listened. There was no sound from inside the house. Only the whistling of an evening breeze in the trees disturbed the silence outside.

Still, the soldier wondered how many hardmen were hiding on the other side of the wall. This time they weren't expecting him. He hadn't told anyone that he was going there, not even Hal Brognola.

There was a leak in the support system. He wasn't sure who was passing on information about his movements to the opposition, but somebody had to have told the hit men where he was.

The first name that had to come to mind was Joe Collins, but, as before, he dismissed the notion that the DEA agent was a turncoat. Brognola had deemed the guy clean, and that was enough for him.

Still, he knew he couldn't be too careful. He wasn't taking any more chances. The life he led was enough of a gamble without having to provide the enemy with marked cards.

Bolan had a lot of questions that hadn't been answered. One important one was, how did the triads know about his movements so quickly? There was a possibility that someone had ransacked Collins's private files.

The problem with that answer was that David Weyant, the rogue CIA operative, was dead. And still the opposition could track him.

His reflections faded quickly as he saw the night shadows on the wall begin to move. Bolan stepped away from the barrier and held his 9 mm Beretta in a two-handed grip.

One of the four gunners who sensed the Executioner's presence turned. Then the other three followed his lead. One of them, a man with European features, raised an assault rifle. But before he could release its death dealers, three Parabellum rounds punched into his mouth and out the back of his neck.

Bolan spun to his left and out of the direct path of the carbines aimed at where he had been standing. Muzzle-flashes spit from the assault rifles' bores as all three gunners fired.

The Executioner returned fire from his new location, washing the space in front of him from left to right with a carefully placed volley of piercing lead from the Uzi.

One of the attackers screamed in pain as hot metal tore his throat into shreds and shoved him back against the wall. A second man dropped his AK-74 and clutched his midsection, trying to hold in his intestines. The third gunner didn't have a chance. He took several hits to the chest and quietly sank to the ground.

After checking that the four were really dead, Bolan quickly scanned the area for additional men. Either there were no others in the compound or they were waiting in ambush.

Moving among the shadows, the soldier worked his way around to the front door.

Pushing a hand against the barrier, Bolan watched the wooden door move inward.

He eased his way inside the building, then waited and listened carefully. The silence was almost overwhelming. He decided to move to the rear of the building and check out the rooms on the main floor.

Using the darkness for cover, the soldier worked his way cautiously along the downstairs corridor. At the point where the corridor took a right turn, he exposed his head briefly to check for waiting assassins.

No one.

He cat-footed into the large, open storage area on the ground floor.

Empty.

Streaks of oil were evidence that vehicles had once been parked in here. Shuffled dust remained where once stacks of boxes had to have stood. Only a piece of bailing wire and slivers of wood remained. It was as if the entire gang had suddenly decided to remove what they had stored here and abandon the warehouse.

Something was wrong. Nobody in Bangkok, no matter how rich, just abandoned a building. Families lived in the same apartments, companies occupied the same factory buildings, for as long as they could. Even the wealthy had difficulty finding decent housing in the overpopulated capital.

But the Chui Chao Triad had just walked away and left the building open to plunderers who would steal anything that was removable.

As he continued his careful journey to the rear door, Bolan tried to make sense out of the situation.

He substituted the Beretta for his Uzi. Slinging the Israeli-made subgun over his left shoulder, he wrapped his large hand around the 93-R and tried the door handle. It turned easily and the door swung open.

Empty.

Holding the 93-R in front of him, the soldier opened a smaller door and found the answer to the riddle.

The door led to a small room. Inside he discovered four dead Asian men, each riddled with bullets, in a neat row on the floor.

Bolan moved from the office through a rear door into another hallway and found five more triad gunners, their faces and chests shredded by slugs fired at close range, sprawled on the floor. The walls and ceilings were stained with their blood and body tissues.

Moving cautiously down the passageway, he found himself in front of an ancient elevator. Moving up the stairs that paralleled the lift, Bolan knew he would find additional corpses.

He wasn't disappointed. One thick-necked Chinese hardman, his eyes staring permanently at the ceiling, was sprawled at the top of the first landing.

Searching the immediate area, the soldier found two more bodies.

He was puzzled. These weren't amateurs. It would have taken a troop of trained gunmen to kill the nearly dozen dead.

Bolan checked the next landing for additional bodies and found four more. The warehouse was a cemetery, he decided. Some force large enough to slaughter more than twelve trained hardmen had invaded the building.

Returning to the main floor, Bolan searched carefully for any clues. A possible answer to the riddle was printed in Russian on a sheet of paper he found next to one of the bodies.

Bolan couldn't read Russian as well as he could speak it. He shoved the paper into a pocket to get one of Joe Collins's contacts to translate it later. Then he searched the rest of the room for other clues.

Several small plastic bags had fallen behind a stack of crates. He slit one open with his Applegate-Fairbairn blade and tasted a few specks.

Heroin.

He recognized the packaging. The drug had come from one of the jungle laboratories in Myanmar.

Suddenly he thought about Chernov. Brognola's

message had said he was a major player in the opium trade, and Bolan knew from other sources that Russia was the second largest source of heroin.

He heard a noise from the other room and spun. Through the open doorway, he could see one of the supposedly dead triad members groaning and trying to sit up.

Bolan hurried to the dying triad gunner and knelt beside him.

"Who did this? One of the other triads?"

All the short, stocky man could do was groan.

"Don't let them get away with destroying the Chui Chao," Bolan added, hoping to stimulate a response.

The mortally wounded soldier shook his head. Bolan leaned his ear against the man's lips.

"Tell me," he urged in a soft voice.

"Not triad."

"Police?"

The man shook his head slightly.

"Who?"

The words came out of his mouth in gasps.

"Look like you. Spoke other tongue…"

The triad gunner died before he could finish.

Chernov, and the men he had brought with him from Russia.

The former Russian general was determined to make a name for himself in the international drug trade.

Unless the Executioner stopped him first.

Bolan didn't know where Chernov and his killers had gone.

There were other tasks to which he had to attend—another warehouse, another cache of narcotics. He didn't have time to think about the Russians right now.

But sooner or later, he knew he would have to confront them.

CHAPTER NINETEEN

Chan Se Tsung was nervous. He kept running his fingers over his nearly naked scalp. This was the first time the Red Pole had trusted him to undertake such an important operation.

A pair of helicopters would be arriving from the north, loaded with the largest cache of heroin the 14K had received—replacements for the supplies that were destroyed in the explosion earlier in the evening.

He had been assigned the responsibility of unloading the flying birds, loading the plastic bags of white powder into the trucks and moving them to another warehouse they owned just off Ban Mo Road.

Chan knew that if he did well tonight, he would be in line for a promotion. Not bad for someone so young. He was twenty-five and had already killed a dozen people for the triad.

He had been promised that the helicopters would arrive before midnight, filled with the valuable cargo. But it was already one, and the only sounds he heard were the loud chirping of birds.

Not far from where he was pacing, Chan heard the angry grunting sounds of nocturnal animals searching for food. Six of his men were posted along the perimeter of the camp. They were there to protect the three dozen triad workers from intruders, human or animal. Any Thai soldier who entered the compound would be greeted by a hail of bullets.

Chan was too tense to sit by the large common fire with his men. He stood and brushed the dirt and twigs from his combat pants. It was time to check to make sure the guards were in place. They had been ordered to take care of their toilet needs before they took on guard duty.

He began to move along the outer rim of the temporary tent community.

A teenager, dressed in jeans and denim work shirt, snapped the 7.62 mm AK-47 assault rifle he was carrying into an awkward salute when he saw Chan approach.

Despite his sense of danger, the temporary Red Pole smiled.

"This is your first mission?"

"Yes, Chan." The slim youth was anxious to impress his chief. "But I've been firing my gun at targets every day for more than a month."

"I'm sure you've become an expert."

The boy beamed and tightened his grip on the weapon in his hands.

Chan started to move to the next guard when he

heard the sound of engines in the sky. As they rapidly grew louder, he yelled to the teenager.

"Pass the word to be alert until we get the helicopters unloaded and the heroin into the trucks."

The teenager yelled Chan's instructions to the guard fifty yards from him.

The sentry acknowledged the orders and continued to yell the instructions to the next man protecting the campsite.

Inside the guarded perimeter, men suddenly became busy. Weapons they had laid down were returned to their holsters or slung over a shoulder.

"Have the men dismantle the tents," Chan told one of the men, "so we can concentrate on the contents of the helicopters when they land. We've got a long drive ahead of us. I want to be ready to move as soon as the trucks are loaded."

Within minutes, men started taking down the canvas shelters and carrying them to the trucks.

Without waiting for orders, the men in the campsite area moved to the edge of the clearing where the helicopters were expected to land.

Chan pushed through the waiting troops.

"Get the landing lights on," he shouted.

Suddenly, rows of lights framed both sides of the landing strip.

From the sky, the sound of engines forcing the blades of two helicopters to spin rapidly became deafening. Some of the uniformed men on the ground put their hands over their ears to muffle the noise.

The pair of Boeing Vertol CH-47C Chinook helicopters hovered over the makeshift field. Their sixty-foot rotors churned the powder-dry dirt on the ground into a minidust storm. The two Lycoming T55-L-11A turboshafts that powered the choppers had been eased off their cruising speeds of 142 miles per hour.

As gently as feathers, each of the choppers settled on the ground. The pilots lowered their turbos to idling, then slid back the doors and jumped out.

The temporary Red Pole rushed onto the strip to greet them.

He had to yell to make himself heard over the engine noises. "What kept you?"

"Some engine trouble," the sour-faced man in civilian clothes explained.

"Have the men put out the fires," he ordered one of the guards, "then bring the trucks to the helicopters. I want to be on the road in twenty-five minutes."

The pilot interrupted. "The fuel we ordered. It is here?"

Chan nodded and expanded his instructions. "And have one of the men drive the fuel tanker over here."

BLENDING IN WITH the shadows, Mack Bolan moved swiftly to where the trucks were parked. His face, smeared with combat cosmetics, was expressionless.

Slung across a shoulder was his silenced 9 mm Uzi. Securely seated in the extra shoulder rig he'd carried was the 9 mm Beretta 93-R, fitted with its customized sound suppressor. The .44 Magnum Desert Eagle sat in a spare waistband holster. His combat knife was secured in a sheath on his left forearm. Its blade had been darkened by combat cosmetics to prevent a stray light from exposing its presence.

Four fragmentation grenades and extra clips for the three weapons were hooked to the webbed combat belt around his waist.

The two helicopters carrying the drug shipment had arrived at the small field just as Collins had said they would.

Bolan began his campaign in complete silence. Easily avoiding the handful of guards posted around the now-dismantled compound, he had hidden and let a tall, uniformed figure pass. Intent on dumping the quickly folded tent he carried into one of the trucks, the triad gunner didn't sense the presence of the armed intruder.

Sliding the razor-sharp blade from its sheath, Bolan slipped behind the man, spun him, clamped a hand over his mouth and rammed the blade under his ribs. Shoving it in until he felt resistance from the man's heart muscle, he twisted the knife, then pulled the blade out and let the lifeless form sink to the ground.

Quickly, the Executioner pulled the tent and the body behind some bushes, then, looking around to make sure that no one had seen him, propelled himself under the nearest truck—a fuel tanker.

Digging into his combat vest, he took out a rectangle of plastic explosive and attached it to the metal plate under the engine block. Checking the already attached timer, he set it for twenty-five minutes.

That should give him enough time to complete the plan.

Four trucks stood in the parking area, and a pair of Japanese-built luxury cars.

Each of the trucks got the same treatment as the tanker.

Four rectangles of explosives remained in his vest pockets, and the Executioner had a destination in mind for all of them.

Men were starting to run toward the trucks.

Quickly, Bolan crawled around a truck and moved to the pair of luxury sedans. The explosives and timers were attached just under the gas tanks and set to detonate. He paused to determine the safest route to where the helicopters were parked.

Because so many men were moving back and forth to transfer the cargo to trucks, he decided to circle the compound and reach the cargo choppers from the other side of the landing strip.

He set off between the trees, pausing and pressing his body into the shadows when the enemy came dangerously close. He didn't want to start a shooting war if it wasn't necessary.

The landing lights exposed his presence, but there was nothing he could do about them. To cut the power wires would alert the compound that an intruder was present.

He sprinted past the lighted beacons and hid behind the second helicopter. The perfect place to plant the explosive was next to the fuel tanks. The problem was that too many men were swarming around both helicopters. And he was running out of time.

Moving to the side of the chopper that faced away from the trucks, Bolan saw the copilot, a swarthy Arab, sneaking a smoke.

There was only one way to get to the cockpit.

The soldier eased the combat knife into his hand and moved silently to the copilot's back.

Some sense of danger alerted the smoker. He stared into the dark jungle, then began to turn.

Bolan wrapped a hand around the man's head and quickly pulled the razor-sharp blade across his throat. Keeping his hand clamped over the dying flyer's mouth to prevent a final outcry, the Executioner lowered the body to the ground, then dragged it under the helicopter. He resheathed his knife.

Men were climbing in and out of the cargo area in the rear. Bolan slid on his belly under the copter and plastered the explosive against the fuel tank wall, set the timer, then slid out from under the aircraft and repeated the procedure on the next one.

Bolan rolled out from under the second chopper, then started across the field toward his own vehicle, parked several hundred yards away from the compound.

"Hey, you!" a voice shouted. "What you doing there?"

The Executioner turned his head. The man who shouted held a 9 mm TEC-9 in his hands. The soldier hesitated, then started to pull the trigger.

Bolan zigzagged into a broken-field run, shifting the Uzi from his shoulder to his hands as he ran.

His weapon was set on continuous fire. The Executioner turned as he tightened his finger on the trigger and stitched the shouting man with 9 mm Parabellum rounds before his adversary could unleash the deadly power of his street weapon.

Even with the suppressor, Bolan was sure the sound of the rounds had been heard.

The gunner's body fell to the ground, watering the dry dust with blood. Pausing for a brief moment to check on the still-living, Bolan continued his escape.

Men appeared from the parking area, aiming AKS-74 Us and AK-47s in the direction of the gunfire. A hail of concentrated slugs tore into the air near Bolan.

The soldier dropped to the ground. A series of side rolls carried him several yards from where lead had torn into the dusty ground.

A long-haired teenager hungry for glory ran toward him, wildly firing his AK-47. Feeling sad about the life the youth would never have, Bolan fired a burst into the young man's chest.

As the dying triad fighter cried loudly for help, the Executioner disappeared into the jungle.

He could hear men yelling and cursing as they crashed through the brush in search of him.

He replaced the nearly empty magazine and fired a 3-round burst at the sudden movement of a bush. A body fell on top of the thorny growth.

The sounds of men rushing toward him from behind some trees alerted Bolan. He pulled a frag grenade from his belt, armed the bomb and tossed it in their direction. The explosion and shrapnel decimated the ranks of his pursuers, and the soldier could hear the moaning of wounded men in the dark.

Tossing another grenade into the woods to slow the enemy, he raced down the makeshift road to where he had parked his vehicle.

In the distance he heard a voice shouting, "In the trucks. After him. Don't let him get away!"

The embassy-owned vehicle was still there. Quickly, he jumped in, started the engine and sped away, not bothering to wait for the explosions that would destroy the heroin.

CHAPTER TWENTY

Chernov finished eating the breakfast he ordered from room service, then looked up and studied Marcel Maracel.

The pair had met in the general's hotel suite.

Wiping away the bits of food on his lips with a linen napkin, Chernov smiled at his visitor.

"I remember you, Borodin. Kabul, wasn't it?"

Maracel carried the farce further.

"Borodin? General Chernov, I think you must be mixing me up with somebody else."

Chernov smiled wearily. "I am not in the mood for these games, Borodin. Five of my best men were killed today. So if you insist on continuing to pretend you are not who we know you are, I will notify the KGB—excuse me, the new, enlightened SVR—who you are and where they can find you. There is still that unwritten rule that nobody quits the KGB. Not even you."

Marcel Maracel considered his reply carefully.

"What would it take to let Borodin stay missing?"

The former general shrugged. "Not much. A little favor."

"What kind of favor? I have only limited connections. Certainly I cannot influence the triads."

"The triads?" Chernov looked surprised. "It takes a real man to confront these people. No. The favor is much simpler." He paused and studied his immaculately manicured fingernails.

"I'll be glad to get back to Moscow. These nails are in desperate need of a good manicurist."

He looked up at the freelance intel op.

"Do you know someone named Michael Belasko?"

"I've heard his name."

"Where?"

"Several places. Someone in the American Embassy happen to mention that a Belasko was coming to Thailand to demonstrate to the triads that the United States was willing to put muscle behind its threats."

"Anyplace else?"

"One of the triad Red Poles—that's their word for chief enforcer—offered me a sum of money to find him."

"Did you?"

"Perhaps. At least I know someone who is in touch with him."

"Who would that be?"

"An American agent for their Drug Enforcement Administration."

Chernov slammed his fist down on the table.

"I want Michael Belasko. I want him dead, and I want it to happen before tomorrow morning."

"Such things take time and money to set up."

The Russian reached inside his jacket pocket and took out a thick wad of bills. Tossing them on the table, he replied, "This should be more than enough to hire men and entice this Belasko to where they can kill him."

Maracel carefully counted the money. After paying off the men he had in mind, there was a handsome profit for him.

"When are you leaving Thailand?"

"When my business here is finished."

"Read the papers," the freelance operative said as he stood. "Michael Belasko's death will be on the front page."

BOLAN MET with Joe Collins at the embassy after destroying the replacement delivery of heroin.

Collins volunteered an update.

"You've got the triads running like crazy trying to buy enough heroin to replace what you destroyed. Each of the three triads has a worldwide network that needs to be fed."

"Anything more specific?"

"A tramp steamer sailed into the Bay of Thailand this morning. Word is out that it's going to be carrying the Yi Kwah Tao's inventory to the United States."

"How does the heroin get to it?"

"Same as usual. A small fleet of trawlers will pick up cartons from one of the triad's warehouses, sail them into the bay, then off-load them to the steamer," Collins explained.

"What kind of cover are they going to be using?"

"Bolts of printed silk. The heroin will be packed under the fabric."

"Does the silk merchant know about it?"

"No. Bill Steman is Mr. Clean. After Jim Thompson, he's the biggest exporter of Thai silk. He's been in Thailand twenty years and never got involved with drugs or teenaged prostitutes. An almost unbelievable feat."

"I need to know where the warehouse is located."

Collins leaned forward in his chair.

"Let's go and ask him," he suggested, then reached for the telephone on his desk.

WILHELM STEMAN TURNED OUT to be a slender, gentle man in his late sixties. He welcomed his guests at the front door of the building that doubled as his home and print shop.

"So you're the embassy official who called me earlier," he said, smiling, when Collins introduced himself.

Steman turned to Bolan.

"I suppose you work for the American government, too."

The soldier remained silent.

Leading the way to the casually furnished living room, Steman pointed to a long couch covered with a bright, flowery fabric. He sat himself in a wicker armchair.

"You wanted to know how I ship the silk fabric I print. Am I right, Mr. Collins?"

"Exactly. Do you handle your own shipments?"

Steman chuckled loudly. "Do I look insane? With all the rules and regulations for exporting from Thailand and the even more complex regulations for importing into the United States, I have a professional shipping broker to handle all that nonsense."

"Who do you use?"

"We used to use Thai Exports. But when a fire put them out of business, we switched to Ameri-Thai Shipping."

Bolan and Collins looked at each other. Organized crime methods didn't change much from country to country. Ameri-Thai was one of the Yi Kwah Tao's legitimate cover companies.

"When was the last time Ameri-Thai picked up a load?"

"This morning. They moved the cartons to the warehouse where they consolidate shipments in freighter loads."

Collins continued his questioning. "Do you have their address?"

Steman gave it to him. Then asked, "Is there some kind of problem with them?"

"Not that we know of," the DEA agent reassured

Steman. "We just like to keep track of who's using who."

He looked at Bolan, who nodded, then stood.

"Thanks for the time."

KHLONGSUNG ROAD WAS a tiny street that dead-ended at the Chao Phraya River. Located on the southern edge of Bangkok, the small road contained several warehouses, including the one whose front door bore the words Ameri-Thai Shipping.

Bolan drove the borrowed car around the corner and parked.

"There's a MAC-10 with several magazines under your seat," he told Collins. "Know how to use it?"

The DEA agent nodded. "I did my training at the Secret Service's shooting range. Their White House detail and the FBI used to have exclusive use of the Ingram weapon until they switched to mini-Uzis. In fact, I've got one under my jacket."

"Now you've got two. You might need both of them and more before we're done."

Collins reached down and retrieved the powerful weapon and the pair of full clips.

"I hope Butch's information was correct," the DEA man commented.

"Butch?"

"The copter pilot who's going to fly us to Chiang Mai. He's Algerian, but he likes the nickname. He just got back from an emergency run for the Yi Kwah Tao from the Thai-China border."

"Heroin?"

Collins nodded. "Lots. Butch guessed the shipment had a street value of thirty million dollars."

Bolan whistled under his breath.

The DEA man pointed to a half-dozen fishing trawlers tied to the dock near the warehouse.

"I'd say they're about to start loading," Collins commented.

Bolan checked his weapons, shouldering the Uzi, and opened the driver's door.

"Let's stop them," he said in a determined voice.

As they worked their way closer to the storage structure, the soldier pointed out strange shadows on the wall and signaled for Collins to take a position against the far side.

The shadows pulled away and became four thickset Asians carrying AK-74 carbines. They were heading for a Mazda parked alongside the warehouse loading dock.

The quartet saw the parked embassy vehicle and stopped. Turning their heads, the guards looked for the driver.

Bolan stepped away from the wall and held his 9 mm Beretta in a two-handed grip.

One of the four sensed the soldier's presence and turned, trying to bring his weapon to bear. But before he could get off a shot, three rounds tore into his mouth and out the back of his head.

Joe Collins had taken the initiative.

There was no time for Bolan to offer his thanks.

The other three fighters required his immediate attention. He dived to his left and out of the direct path of the rifles. Muzzle-flashes winked as all three hardmen fired at his former position.

Bolan returned the fire, washing the space in front of him from left to right in a classic figure eight.

One of the attackers screamed in agony as hot metal shredded his throat and shoved him back against the wall. A second gunner dropped his AK-74 as he fell to the ground, bleeding from a dozen wounds to his chest.

Turning his Kalashnikov submachine gun on Collins, the third street soldier started to unleash the carbine's awesome firepower. Bolan stopped his movement with two lead blasters that chewed into his chest, shoving him backward. Tripping, the gunner fell to the ground, dead.

After checking that the four hardmen were really dead, Bolan quickly scanned the area for additional gunners. Either there were no others in the compound or they were waiting in ambush.

Moving among the shadows, the soldier and the field agent worked their way around to the solid wooden gates that barricaded the compound.

Pushing a hand against one of the doors, Bolan couldn't budge the heavy, teak gates. He pushed a little harder and they gave, the well-oiled hinges preventing the gates from squeaking as they opened.

He led the way inside the walled area, then waited

and listened carefully. The silence was almost overwhelming.

The Executioner decided to move to the rear of the building and try to enter through a back door.

"Wait here and stop anybody who comes out that front door," he whispered.

Collins nodded, and moved into the shadows.

Using the darkness for cover, the Executioner worked his way cautiously against the stone wall of the building. At the corner he exposed his head briefly to check for waiting assassins.

No one.

He stepped into the large, open storage area on the ground floor.

Empty.

But when Bolan emerged out of the shadows, he was surprised to face two terrified triad gunners. Dressed in his blacksuit, his face covered with combat cosmetics, he knew he looked like a creature from hell. Especially when the combat harness around his waist contained devices guaranteed to make a hell out of anyplace he was.

The bulky sound suppressor mounted on the muzzle end of Bolan's pistol reduced the noise of gunfire to soft thuds. The sounds of the bodies falling onto dried leaves were louder.

He had told Collins to check that the triad hardmen were dead. Before he moved closer to the front door of the structure, Bolan had noticed him kneeling and plucking a long-bladed combat knife from one of the bodies.

"One of them is still alive," Collins called out.

"AGAIN," BOLAN STATED, "how many others are there?"

"About twenty," the triad assassin replied.

"Where?"

"All around us." He regained his bravado for a moment. "You can't escape. The ambush was too well planned."

As he lay on the grass, the near-dead triad hit man stared up at the American.

Gasping, he asked, "Who are you?"

But the question remained unanswered as he slipped into Death's embrace.

COLLINS MOVED slowly through the brush, being careful not to make unnecessary noise. In his right hand, he gripped the 9 mm Ingram MAC-10. In his left was the knife he had confiscated from one of the dead men.

Belasko had wanted him to do recon. He planned to do more—much more.

Two shadows separated from the wide tree in front of him. Pausing, he watched the two hardmen start to move in the opposite direction, Skorpion submachine guns held ready in their hands.

He moved swiftly toward the nearer man, then thrust the point of the combat knife into his back, carefully twisting his hand as he pushed the steel blade to sever vital internal organs.

Gulping for air his slit lungs couldn't contain, the street soldier fell against the tree trunk. His partner turned his head and stared at him.

His voice betrayed his concern as he whispered, "Is something wrong?"

The DEA agent pushed his SMG into the second thug's neck and eased back the trigger, stepping sideways to avoid the sudden spring of blood that he knew would jump from the gaping hole.

The echo of the shot reverberated through the trees. Collins knew men would rush to this spot, their guns ready to kill intruders. It was time to move to a different location.

As he turned, two angry-looking gunners jabbed their SMGs at his midsection.

BOLAN SLIPPED into the shadows. As his eyes became accustomed to the dark, he could see the shapes of men and the weapons they were holding.

He checked the extra clips in the pocket of his jacket. Two full magazines.

The sound of a shot broke the silence of the night. Collins had either fired, or somebody had fired at him. There was no time to find out which it was.

THE YI KWAH TAO gunman decided the American wasn't coming. He called out to his superior.

"Li!" he shouted.

No one answered.

The triad enforcer swore loudly. "Where are you, Li?"

The only response he got was a loud "woosh" sound from behind the trees.

The triad hit man recognized the noise immediately—the sound of a silenced weapon being fired.

He grabbed for the Skorpion SMG that sat on the ground next to him and dived to the relative safety of a nearby pile of dirt.

The American had arrived.

The Yi Kwah Tao street fighter swore to himself that the intruder would never leave the compound alive. If one of the other men didn't get him, he would.

Even if it meant sacrificing his own life.

He decided to move to a thick stand of trees on his right. From behind them, he could see anyone approaching.

Checking the area with swiftly darting eyes, he could see no one. In a sudden burst of energy, he threw himself across the dirt road and into the woods.

BOLAN DIDN'T BELIEVE in needless killing, but he could kill an enemy without a second thought when it was necessary to the mission or to his own survival. That was, however, his last choice.

Moving from position to position, the Executioner used the butt of the Uzi to knock out the triad gunners as he encountered them.

More than a dozen dead or unconscious hardmen littered the grass as Bolan moved ahead. One man had spotted the Executioner and attempted to take him out of the play.

Bolan jammed the suppressed Uzi under the gunner's chin and released a single round. Suppressing the muzzle noise of a high-powered weapon didn't have the same effect as silencing it. There was still a clearly audible sound.

The soldier turned and moved behind a wide tree trunk as the report of the Uzi round echoed softly. He could hear the handful of still-living foot soldiers yell in guttural Thai.

"Find him," one of the triad soldiers shouted in rage, "then kill him."

Bolan knelt and steadied the Uzi against his shoulder. He set the extra clip on the ground next to him, and next to it he placed the Beretta 93-R. He started to unclip the grenades from the canvas belt around his waist, then decided they were just as accessible there as they would be on the ground.

The triad horde charged toward him, SMGs firing volleys randomly in front of him. Bolan waited until they drew closer, then freed one of the frag grenades and yanked the pin. Counting quickly to ten, he tossed the metal egg toward the trees ten yards ahead.

The ear-shattering explosion tore branches and leaves from nearby trees, and decimated the ranks of the advancing enemy. Gathering his equipment, Bolan moved cautiously forward.

The gunmen lay dead.

The soldier heard groans from behind one of the trees. Apparently, there was a survivor. Bolan knelt and softly asked a question.

"How did you know I was coming?"

No answer.

"I can stop the pain."

The enforcer tried to stop his screams, but was unsuccessful.

"The Red Pole has many contacts. Someone in your embassy warned us you would come to destroy the white powder."

"Where's the heroin?"

"On a boat," the man replied, his agony plainly visible.

"Who in the American Embassy warned you?"

"I don't know."

Bolan believed him. He placed the 93-R against the other man's temple and gently squeezed the trigger.

CHAPTER TWENTY-ONE

"It was all a setup," Collins commented when they got outside.

"Not totally," Bolan replied, pointing to the departing trawlers. "Your pilot delivered heroin here today. And the cartons of silk fabric were picked up for immediate shipping. The drugs were all on those trawlers."

The DEA agent was furious.

"And no way to get to them."

"Maybe," the warrior said, thinking out loud. "These trawlers will be meeting a freighter in the bay. If we can reach the freighter before it heads to sea, maybe we can cost the Yi Kwah Tao a bundle of money."

"How do you suggest we get there?"

Bolan pondered the question. "Your pilot contact. Butch. Can you reach him?"

"Yeah, I suppose so."

"If he picked us up, the three of us could start looking for a seabound freighter."

"Then what?"

"Then we get to sink it," Bolan replied bluntly.

THE SLIM, Algerian-born helicopter pilot was a practical man. He refused to take off until he was paid.

Bolan reached into an inner pocket and took out a stack of bills.

"This should cover everything," he said.

Butch Gasparque carefully counted the money.

"It is enough," he agreed.

Bolan loaded his bags into the Vietnam War vintage Chinook. Collins followed him aboard.

As the soldier outlined the problem, Butch smiled.

"I think I know where those trawlers were heading. I once had to fly some big men from one of the triads down country to meet with the freighter captain."

Bolan fastened his seat belt and opened the canvas bag that contained his traveling armory. There was enough time for him to clean his weapons.

A BATTERED VAN was waiting for them at the landing strip, a few miles east of the bay. The driver, a neatly dressed Thai, waved to Collins.

The young agent didn't bother introducing the two men. In response to Bolan's questioning glance, the DEA operative explained, "He works part-time for us."

"Here's the rundown," the driver said. "Then I've got to get back to the police station."

Bolan sent a quizzical glance to Collins, who ignored it.

"Just past the village is a string of docks. There's a small motorcraft anchored at the second one. The freighter is called *El Camino*. Panama registry. It is anchored two hundred yards out, far away from the other boats."

"Hang on a moment," the DEA agent said, and walked to the helicopter. He talked to the pilot for a few minutes, then returned.

"He'll wait here for us," he told Bolan, then turned to the van driver. "Can you run us over to the motorboat?"

"Hop in."

This time it was Bolan who called time-out.

Opening his canvas bag, he extracted the items he thought he'd need—extra clips for the two handguns, one of the Uzi SMGs and loaded magazines for it. The combat knife went into the sheath he strapped around his left forearm.

He took out three blocks of C-4, fitted with detonators and timers.

"I'm ready," he announced, then looked at Collins.

The brawny DEA man was wearing a .45 ACP Colt Government Model pistol on his belt, and had an Ingram MAC-10 hanging on his shoulder. His bulging pockets were stuffed with full magazines for the two weapons.

"So am I," Collins announced.

"You carry these," Bolan said, handing him the plastic explosives.

As promised, the small motorboat was tied to the dock. It was a rusty fishing boat, and Bolan checked to make sure it wasn't leaking.

He climbed in and set down his bag, then signaled Collins to join him.

Untying the heavy line, Bolan used one of the oars he found in the boat to move them away from the dock. There was no point alerting anybody to their presence.

Fifty yards later, he started the engine. A loud, droning noise penetrated the area around them.

"It's going to be hard to surprise anyone with this noise," he warned.

"I guess we'd better row," Collins agreed.

Bolan nodded as he shut down the engine and picked up the second oar. Slowly, the boat moved out into the bay.

In the distance the two men could see the outline of the anchored freighter. A dim light from the captain's cabin either meant that some of the crew were still awake, or afraid of sleeping in the dark.

Bolan bet on their being awake.

Moving in the water as quietly as they could, the two men approached the vessel, then dropped the boat's small anchor a few feet from the freighter.

The ship was sitting low in the water, its cargo holds full of goods.

Collins leaned over and whispered in Bolan's ear. "How do we handle this?"

"First we attach the explosives, then we take care of the crew."

The DEA agent opened his duffel bag and took out the explosives the Executioner had given him to carry.

Bolan raised the anchor and moved the boat to within a foot of the rusted ship. He pointed to a place on the hull barely out of the water. "There," he whispered.

The DEA field rep started to reach out with the explosive, but Bolan stopped him.

"Set the timer first," he whispered. "Twenty minutes."

The pair repeated the procedure two more times as Bolan steered the small boat around the freighter's hull.

The soldier was so engrossed in watching the DEA man handle the C-4 that he didn't notice that their boat was drifting until it banged into the freighter.

"Damn," the Executioner cursed under his breath. "Get your hardware out. We'll be getting company."

Bolan grabbed the 9 mm Uzi, while Collins primed his MAC-10.

Three hard-faced men rushed from the cabin, each armed with an AK-47.

"Bring that searchlight over here," one of them

yelled from where he stood, just above where the small motor craft was floating.

A large searchlight began to sweep the waters below.

Bolan snapped the lever to continuous fire and hosed the railing above him with a hail of 9 mm Parabellum slugs.

The light went dark, and from the deck there was a thud as a body tumbled to the deck.

Bolan reached for one of the oars and shoved the boat toward the bow. Just behind him, the water jumped in two dozen places as someone above emptied a magazine at them.

A rope ladder from the deck hung down into the water.

"Wait here," Bolan ordered in a harsh whisper, then climbed onto the deck.

Two men with swarthy features were staring into the water, looking for the intruders. Without a sound, Bolan swept his blazing Uzi from left to right in a blistering figure eight. Both men fell to the deck and didn't move.

Bolan forward-rolled on the deck, just as a heavy-set man wearing a sweat-stained captain's cap rushed out of the cabin. The AK-47 in the man's hands ripped a series of holes into the deck.

Bolan knew he couldn't turn fast enough to avoid the next wave of lead from the assault rifle.

A triple burst coughed discreetly behind him. The

fat man dropped the weapon and stared past the soldier with glazed eyes, then crumpled to the deck.

Bolan turned his head. Joe Collins was holding the Ingram MAC-10 in his hands.

"I'm getting better at this," he commented.

The Executioner scrambled to his feet. "We can talk about that later. Let's get out of here! Get this thing up to top speed right away."

The DEA field agent cranked the motor and raced the motorboat back to the dock.

As they climbed onto the wooden platform, the force of the explosion out in the bay shoved the two men forward. A shower of exploding diesel fuel hurtled into the sky as the freighter erupted.

The two men lapsed into silence as they docked the boat and then hiked back to where the helicopter was waiting. There wasn't much more to say or do until they got to their destination.

Struggling to maintain his balance, Collins asked, "What else were they carrying on that ship?"

"It doesn't matter," Bolan replied. "They won't be using it."

CHAPTER TWENTY-TWO

"One more stop," Bolan told the DEA agent, as they got into the embassy vehicle. "But I'll drop you at your apartment first."

Collins rejected the offer. Then asked, "The 14K?"

"If the other triads had to buy new supplies, so did the 14K."

"I thought you hit them."

"Not hard enough," Bolan replied.

"But which warehouse?"

"We'll know it when we get there," Bolan replied, rechecking his artillery.

"This could be a long search," Collins warned. "The 14K own a lot of buildings in Bangkok."

"I've got an idea where it is. On Mahai Sawan Road, right next to the river."

"Not the best neighborhood," Collins commented.

Bolan was too busy checking and reloading his arsenal to reply.

He had replenished the supplies in the combat vest

he wore. They now contained an ample supply of
clips for the Uzi, the Beretta and the Desert Eagle.
In addition, four delay fragmentation grenades hung
from clips, ready to be launched in fractions of a
second. And several blocks of C-4 were primed and
ready.

BOLAN PARKED HIS VEHICLE a short distance from
the small building. The only hint that it wasn't just
another run-down warehouse were the bars mounted
on all the windows.

The two men could smell the stagnant odor of the
Chao Phraya River nearby.

"I forgot to tell you I got a call from Maracel
today."

The soldier remembered the name. One of the
DEA agent's best sources.

"What about?"

"The Russian who tried to buy you is setting up
some kind of a buy later tonight. Maracel has the
details. If you're interested, you can meet with him
later."

Collins handed Bolan a sheet of paper.

Without reading it, the soldier folded the paper and
shoved it into a pocket.

"Right now we've got something else to do."

The locks on the front door looked formidable.
Bolan decided it would take too long to force them
open. He moved quietly around the building, looking
for another way into the warehouse.

There was none.

Momentarily stymied, he remembered several other weapons in his carryall. Returning to the car, he reached inside the canvas bag and found them—a glass cutter and an incendiary grenade.

"This is risky, but I can't think of another way to get inside," he told the DEA agent.

Collins fingered the MAC-10 and nodded.

Using the cutter, Bolan carved a circle in one of the side windows, then gently pushed at the severed piece. It fell inside with a soft noise.

Pulling the pin on the grenade, he pitched it through the opening and moved down along the wall of the warehouse. Seconds later, he could see smoke and flames churning up from the floor. Hopefully, whoever was inside would also see them.

ONE OF THE TRIAD GUNNERS sniffed the air. "You smell that?"

"Yes," the other foot soldiers replied. "What is it?"

"Smells like something is on fire."

One of them opened the office door. Hot smoke swirled in, choking the men. The door was slammed shut.

"We got to get out of here," the first said, panicking.

The six men grabbed their jackets and opened the door again.

Flames shot at them through the smoke.

Terrified, they held their breaths and ran through the black fog to the front door. The first hardman rifled through his pockets, searching for the key. Finally, he found it and felt his way to the lock. The key jammed momentarily, then finally slid into the slot. Tearing open the heavy metal door, the two rushed into the fresh night air, coughing and gagging.

Bolan had been waiting for them. He aimed his Uzi at the chest of the wide hardman, and drove a pair of shots into the man's chest, shattering breastbone before fracturing the heart muscle.

The foot soldier slid to the ground, dead.

The second raised his hands above his head.

"Who are you?"

"You don't want to know," the warrior replied coldly.

One of the other triad members grabbed for the SIG-Sauer P-226 in his waistband holster. A short burst from Collins's SMG tore the thug's face apart.

The three surviving hardmen kept their hands above their heads.

"Is the new heroin shipment inside?"

The triads looked at one another. Each seemed too frightened to be the one who answered.

Bolan punctured the pavement in front of them with a short stream of lead.

"I asked you a question."

"No," one of the captives replied nervously. "We were sent here to stop you before you found the white powder."

"Where is it?"

"Gone by now."

"Which warehouse?"

Shaking with fear, the small wiry man gave him the address. As Bolan leaned forward to haul the man up, the hardman tucked his chin to his neck and bit on the cyanide capsule that hung around his neck on a chain.

"Why?" Bolan asked.

"Easier than the Red Pole..." The dead man's lips were twisted into a smile.

Washington, D.C.

THE MAN BEHIND the large desk signaled Hal Brognola to take a seat in one of the pair of easy chairs facing him.

"I got a call from Senator Firestone," the President said.

"How are things going on his end?"

"Not good, Hal. He met with all the parties involved and was accused of setting them up for a series of explosions that destroyed their warehouses."

"I guess my man is holding up his end of the mission," Brognola commented.

"Perhaps too well. Next time you talk to him, suggest he ease off on the amount of damage he does."

"It doesn't work that way, Mr. President. With Striker, it's all or nothing." He reached into his briefcase and brought out a folder. Opening it, he shared information with the Man.

"According to the DEA, the street price of heroin has almost doubled in the past twenty-four hours, which means supplies to the United States have been drastically reduced or eliminated."

The President did some thinking.

"Should we bring the CIA in Bangkok into the picture to help him?"

"No."

"They *are* our foreign intelligence arm," the man behind the desk reminded Brognola.

"At least one of them isn't anymore. He was caught trying to sell information on Striker and the operation to the triads."

The Man shook his head in disgust.

"Let the operation continue as it has been. Only, I will order the senator back home if he can't get the others to agree to our offer."

Brognola looked skeptical.

"Even if they do, you can be sure they'll find a way to break the agreement and blame it on us."

The President sighed in frustration.

"What's the solution?"

"Getting addicts off the street and into treatment centers. That will put the drug kings out of business faster than any other action."

"And what do we do while we're trying to make that happen?"

"Let Striker carry on. He's got them looking desperately for enough poison to keep their pipelines supplied.''

"Like I said, tell your man to continue,'' the man behind the desk agreed.

"I've got something else to tell him. It's about the Russians.''

Brognola could tell he suddenly got the President's full attention.

"What have the Russians go to do with the mission?''

"The godfather of their biggest drug operation offered to help our man eliminate the drug barons.''

"Why?''

"I guess he hates competition like any other cold-blooded businessman.''

Thailand

IT WAS AFTER MIDNIGHT when the two men approached the hidden warehouse. The front door, when Bolan checked it, was locked.

"Wait here,'' he whispered. "If I hear gunfire, I'll know they're coming out the front door.''

Collins replaced the half-empty magazine in the MAC-10 and nodded.

"Good luck,'' he whispered back.

"I'll see you when I see you,'' Bolan commented, and vanished around the corner of the building.

With his carryall slung over a shoulder, he worked his way to the rear of the building.

A pair of metal cutters from his bag severed the hasp that secured the padlock. Swinging open the doors, the soldier shone the beam of his flashlight in front of him and moved down the metal steps.

The underground storage area was larger than it had appeared when he was there earlier. Almost two football fields in length.

Silently he moved through the aisles of the concrete-block enclosure. No one was hidden in the basement. Only stacks of one-kilo bags of heroin were there to greet him.

He wasted no time as he started placing explosive packets around the huge room. Setting the timers for thirty minutes, he finished his task in short order and headed back to the steps.

From above he heard male voices and saw the metal doors close. He was trapped.

Shining the flashlight in every corner, he looked for a solution. The weapons in his bag were useless, even the fragmentation grenades. Thrown against the metal doors, they would cause more damage in the basement than outside. He searched for another exit.

The sound of gunfire got his attention.

COLLINS HAD SEEN the pack of triad wolves work its way to the rear of the warehouse. His MAC-10 primed and ready, the DEA agent followed them.

One of the foot soldiers pointed to the open hatch that led to an underground storage area, then gestured for one of the men to set down his AK-47 carbine and help him close it.

Unless Belasko had the ability to walk through metal, Collins suspected he was trapped in the underground room. There was only one way to help him get out.

Switching to burst mode, Collins studied the nearest pair of gunners in the open sights, then pumped a short burst at them.

The closest man looked stunned as the first of two rounds punched open his stomach and exposed the twisting intestines to the night air. The foot soldier turned to his companion with a helpless expression on his face and fell forward, dead.

A pair of Collins's rounds had dug in the second thug's forearm, causing him to drop the AK-47 he was carrying. The DEA man's next dose of lead was better placed.

Two of the three churners cored their way into the chest of the triad mobster. From the soundless expression of agony on the hardman's face, Collins knew he was already as good as dead.

The DEA agent hosed the area in front of him with a steady rain of death.

Two more triad hardmen ate lead and died. The remaining eight raced from the closed hatch and vanished around the far corner of the warehouse.

BOLAN KNEW Collins was nearby. Climbing the metal steps, the soldier pushed open the hatch doors and checked outside.

Only Collins and four dead bodies were visible.

The DEA field agent pointed to the far corner.

"They went that way," he snapped.

Bolan nodded. "Keep them busy if they return. There's something I want to take care of down here."

A small cache of weapons and ammo were stacked in a corner of the underground room. Bolan scrounged through the boxes and found loaded magazines for both his Uzi and Collins's MAC-10. Pocketing them, he scrambled up the metal steps and joined the DEA man outside.

"Any sign of them?"

Collins shook his head.

"Maybe they took off."

"Not their style. They're more afraid of being treated like cowards by their superiors than they are of facing us.

"Stay alert. These boys have learned some nasty tricks."

Sitting back-to-back, the two men scanned the area for any sign of movement.

Nothing.

Bolan decided to bring the triad members into the open where they could be fought.

Checking the height of the small building, he pulled the pin on one of the delay fragmentation grenades that hung from his combat vest, then tossed a spiraling pass to the roof.

"Let's make tracks for the woods," he shouted, pointing to the overgrown area behind the warehouse.

The two men dived into the underbrush.

The muffled thunder of the detonated grenade shook the one-story structure, and brought the triad gunners into view.

Bolan sent the front four to an early grave by lobbing a fragmentation grenade into their midst. Body parts mingled with fluid spraying from shattered blood vessels to stain the rear of the building, and the ground around it.

The remaining four started to flee, then changed their minds and turned back, ready to fight.

A spray of tumblers from Collins's weapon tattered one of the assailants and wounded a second.

Bolan joined in, emptying the Uzi's magazine at the still-living duo.

Then, as the triad hardmen scattered back around the corner, Bolan checked his wristwatch.

"Let's get out of here," he shouted, then took off at a fast trot, hoping Collins was right behind him.

There was no time to place the canvas carryall in the back seat. Even as Collins opened the passenger door, the soldier, with the arms bag still on his shoulder, had the engine cranked, and took off at top speed.

Collins turned his head to check if anyone was

following them. He heard the awesome blast as a shower of building materials and white powder shot into the air, then fell to the ground.

He turned to Bolan. "Got anything else in mind for tonight?"

"Just meeting with Maracel. Besides, it's not tonight anymore, it's tomorrow. All I really want is a shower and a few winks."

"I think you'd better use my place. By now, your hotel room must have a lot of men in it wanting to welcome you home."

Bolan nodded. Collins's apartment sounded like the safest choice. And he could call Brognola and see if he'd gotten a line on the Russian yet.

"I've got to make a quick stop at the embassy and get my notes together for tomorrow's hearing. But I shouldn't be long," the DEA man said.

"I'll drop you off and pick you up in an hour. I just want to cruise for a while."

The soldier needed to do some thinking. The triads were running out of places to hide their heroin. He couldn't help feeling uneasy about how they were going to respond to that reality.

With a lot of killing, if their history was any guide.

CHAPTER TWENTY-THREE

The Thai hit man didn't know why Marcel Maracel wanted to kill the man named Michael Belasko, nor did he care. It wasn't his business.

He had worked for the man before, when he used another name—Borodin.

Sriyanonda had never questioned him about changing his name and identity. All he ever asked of his sometimes employer was how much he was willing to pay, and when the money was going to change hands.

He had hired a dozen professionals. Gripping the cheap, plastic gym bags that contained the Skorpion SMGs he'd provided, they were trying their best to blend into the crowds that jammed the streets.

It was supposed to look like an indiscriminate massacre ordered by one of the Chinese triads. The assault would kill more people than just the American, but the resulting panic and confusion would make it easier for all of them to escape.

Finding the American hadn't been difficult. Several of his men had canvassed the hotels and learned that a big American had been registered at a place, on Silom Road.

One of his men had spotted a vehicle with American Embassy markings. Using a shortwave radio, he had broadcast the information to Sriyanonda. It was moving down Silom Road, slowed by the typically heavy volume of traffic. The Thai hit man walked quickly to the corner to see who was behind the wheel.

A large, expressionless man was driving. No one else was in the car.

Excitement ran through the Thai assassin. It had to be him. The man called Belasko.

Belasko looked even more powerful in person than in the grainy photograph that been circulated to all the street hustlers in the Patpong District.

The gray-haired man signaled for the Lexus at the curb to start moving.

Then he took up a position against the outside wall of a small tourist shop and knelt to open his bag.

STARING INTENTLY at the faces on the streets, Bolan didn't notice the car that had pulled out behind him. He was too busy looking for Collins's informant, Marcel Maracel.

He had dropped Collins at his apartment, and was now on the prowl.

According to the DEA man, the freelancer had information on some secret heroin storage depots the triads maintained.

The meet was to happen near his hotel, just off Silom Road. The two would meet on the street, exchange money for information outside a popular local restaurant, then part company.

Collins had given him a detailed description of Maracel. Bolan searched through the crowded side street for a man who fit the description.

He decided to continue his search on foot.

Bolan started to get out of the car when he spotted an ancient British sedan parked at the curb, with its engine running. He looked at the trio of men standing next to it and knew them for what they were the minute he saw them—professional hit men.

This was a setup, and he was the target.

One of them stared at him, then gestured to the others. Reaching under his jacket, the soldier took out the .44 Desert Eagle from its holster and slipped it inside his waistband.

He left his car at the curb and started to stroll toward the trio, then stopped.

A Lexus was parked behind his vehicle, and a pair of hard-faced locals got out and started walking toward him.

He made a choice of who would be his first target.

The three men standing beside the Ford were stunned at the sight of Bolan suddenly running toward them.

From underneath his opened jacket, one of the trio pulled out an AKS-74 U submachine gun. The compact weapon could pump a full 30-round clip of 5.45 mm rounds in seconds.

The assailant knew he had plenty of replacement magazines. He didn't have to wait until the American got closer.

He started to squeeze the trigger, spraying hot lead at the fast-moving target.

Yanking the Israeli-created mammoth from his waistband, Bolan juked to the right and wasted no time with precise aim. He slid into a two-handed gun stance and squeezed off two shots.

The first of the lead wallops cored into the shoulder of the SMG-toting thug, forcing him to spin. The second ricocheted off the metal trim of the rear windshield and slammed into his head, tearing a hole in the back of his skull.

The AKS-74 U fell to the ground as the man tumbled out of sight.

Stunned, the other two dropped behind the gray sedan and poked the muzzles of their submachine guns into view. Inside the Ford, the terrified leather-jacketed teenaged driver slid down in his seat. This was his first job, and no one had mentioned anything about dying.

The soldier moved to his left and fired at the second man near the ancient Ford. The first hollowpoint round chopped into the gunner's side. Roaring with pain, the would-be killer turned and swept the area around Bolan with a continuous burst of lead death.

In the hands of a wounded shootist, the AKS-74 U

proved unreliable. Lead ricocheted off cars, the brick walls and asphalt paving, slamming indiscriminately into terrified restaurant patrons and passengers in passing cars.

One of the wildly fired slugs skinned the fleshy part of Bolan's upper right arm, near where he'd been grazed before. Ignoring the pain, he fired another round at the hit man's chest, which ruptured the would-be killer's collarbone. The next two rounds carved a path through his cheekbone and exited through a newly created crater in the side of his skull.

Trying to get a clearer shot, the last gunman popped up and sprayed an endless burst at the American.

Ducking away from the path of the lead projectiles saved the soldier's life.

Bolan focused on his attacker with unswerving concentration. The Eagle barked once and delivered a death blow to the center of the gunner's forehead. Suddenly he collapsed like an empty hot-air balloon.

Keeping his body close to the ground, Bolan carefully worked his way around the bullet-fractured vehicle.

Inside the Lexus, the driver realized he had to escape. He panicked and threw the car in reverse, then stomped his foot on the gas pedal instead of the brakes. The imported car rammed into the handful of hypnotized patrons who had huddled just outside the restaurant entrance to watch the gun battle.

Terrified, the driver threw the car into forward gear and raced toward the intersection.

Bracing himself against the anticipated crash, the driver saw Bolan's face first. It was cold and unforgiving. The face had a body, a muscular body that stood between him and escape.

The driver didn't feel the three slugs that tore open his body. Without a guiding hand on the wheel, the sedan crashed into a parked Mercedes 500. The driver of the Ford wasn't upset. Nothing in life would ever bother him again.

BOLAN RELOADED HIS PISTOL and turned his attention to the two men hovering near the Lexus.

In unison, the pair pointed their AKS-74 U submachine guns at the soldier, venting their rage with continuous bursts of heated metal.

The soldier dropped into a roll and came up near the Japanese vehicle, firing, while the slugs from the automatic rifles carved into the concrete.

The nearer of the pair screamed in fury as he felt the burning sensation of the .44 slug cutting a deep groove across his forehead. Angrily turning his weapon on the American, he squeezed the trigger and sprayed the area in front of him with metal-jacketed rounds.

Bolan did a side jump and landed almost two feet away from where he had been standing. Pushing his Desert Eagle forward, he let two more slugs race at the livid gunmen.

The first plowed its way through the neck of the nearest hit man. The second gouged out his left eye and penetrated the thick skull, rupturing vessels in the front lobe.

The soldier took advantage of the momentary shock and ducked behind a nearby Isuzu, narrowly missing the hail of hot lead unleashed by the final attacker.

There was no way to reach him without exposing himself. It was a risk he would have to take.

Unleathering the Beretta 93-R, he jacked a round into the chamber and stood, firing rapidly at the enraged gunner.

The first two slugs penetrated the man's chest, while the third drilled into his abdomen, rapidly tearing its way into his pancreas. Bits of bloody tissue and splintered bone exploded onto the asphalt ground.

Screaming, the thug tried to rush at the big American, but was only able to manage a half-dozen steps before he collapsed dead.

Bolan heard a noise to his right. Pivoting, he spotted a tall, armed young man who was vomiting. The pedestrians nearby rushed at the young hit man and tore into him, like dogs tearing apart a rag doll.

Turning back, the Executioner saw a skinny, gray-haired man ram the muzzle of his mini-Uzi into the back of a terrified, sloe-eyed girl. He demanded, in clipped Thai curses, that she walk in front of him.

Confusion and terror ran through the street. Panicked men and women grabbed the hands of their loved ones and pushed through open doors to restaurants and shops, trampling anyone who came between them and escape.

Bolan ignored them and focused his attention on the gunman and his now-hysterical hostage. With constant prodding from the lethal weapon in the small of her back, the weeping young woman kept moving toward him.

He stood still until the hostage was almost next to him. The angry gunman shoved her aside and braced his body as he pulled back on the trigger of the weapon in his hands.

With the ease of years of practice, the Executioner lunged for the ground in a forward roll. Above him, he heard the burst of gunfire and the screams of the woman. Then he felt her blood spray his face as he leaped to his feet behind the hit man.

Bolan glanced at the fallen body of the hostage.

"I surrender," the street fighter screamed, but instead of dropping his weapon he attempted to target Bolan.

The Executioner pumped three loads of lead into Phenom Sriyanonda.

Bolan quickly searched through the corpse's pockets. In his wallet was a Thai driver's license and a slip of paper. He scanned the note.

"See Borodin for balance of money." The name, Borodin, had been crossed out. In its place was another name—Marcel Maracel. Obviously, Collins's source sold his information and assistance to anyone willing to pay for it.

The soldier got into his vehicle and sped from the scene of the shoot-out. Sooner or later someone would think to call the police. It was time to leave.

CHAPTER TWENTY-FOUR

The Executioner briefed Collins on the attempted assassination.

The DEA agent groaned.

"Was Maracel there?"

"Not that I could see."

"He just signed his own death warrant," Collins commented grimly. "If not from me, from the intelligence community. In Bangkok, you don't sell your information to both sides at the same time."

"Later. There's a location on your list I want to check out right now."

He handed over the page Collins had prepared.

"Third from the bottom."

The DEA man studied the address, then remembered.

"The Chui Chao used to use the place as a temporary storage depot. But none of my local police contacts have seen the triads go near the place in months."

"All the more reason to check it out now."

Bolan drove along the Petkasem Expressway until

Bangkok was only a shimmer of bright lights glowing behind them. Exiting the main highway, he followed a narrow paved road until it dead-ended, then turned into a packed-dirt road and parked.

Tightening his grip on the silenced Uzi SMG in his right hand, the big American scoured the nearby area, searching for signs of life. Collins, MAC-10 in hand, was right behind him.

He saw nothing. Perhaps his combat senses were dulled because he was tired. His fatigue could be finally catching up with him.

Bolan studied the ground for signs of truck tire tracks. There were tracks, but not those made by trucks with cargo. Glancing at the DEA agent, he realized Collins was showing signs of exhaustion, too.

Through the trees he could see the small structure. There were no signs of life in or around it. Not a single electric light was showing. No muffled voices. Only the sounds of birds and night animals.

He sensed the enemy just before two shadows separated from the shadowy stands of teak trees.

A pair of small figures tried to use the jungle brush as a blind while they crouched and worked their way past the banyan tree the Executioner was using for cover.

The first of the slender shadows sprinted for the bushes on Bolan's left. The soldier suspected the assailant wasn't sure where the enemy was hiding.

The Executioner could make out the shape of the

7.62 mm AK-47 tightly gripped in the man's hands. Bolan slipped the Applegate-Fairbairn combat knife from the thin leather sheath strapped to his forearm, waited patiently until the man came close, then moved behind a thick stand of foliage. As the attacker moved past him, the soldier clamped a hand over his mouth.

The knife made no sound as it carved a bloody path across the slender man's throat. Easing the now-still form to the ground, Bolan heard a faint noise behind him. Whipping the Beretta from its harness, he spun and unleashed a pair of 9 mm rounds that drilled through the second assailant's sternum.

Only a short grunt of pain and a small geyser of blood from severed blood vessels announced the end of his life.

He examined the dead pair. Both were wearing the uniforms of the People's Revolutionary Army.

Bolan was puzzled. What were they doing this far south? The Communists had a hands-off policy when it came to Thailand. More important, how did they know where to find him?

Answers to both questions would have to wait for another time. Right now, he was in no mood to play cat and mouse with the enemy force hidden in the jungle around him. He didn't know how many there were or where they were hiding.

It was time to flush them.

Signaling Collins to join him, he moved behind a boulder.

"Keep your head down," he whispered, then pulled a frag grenade from his combat vest, armed the bomb and lobbed it like a small football into the bushes in front of him. Flattening himself against the leaf-padded ground, he could hear the explosion and the shrieks of the dying and wounded as burning shards of metal tore into hidden assailants.

"My turn," the DEA agent stated and tossed a second grenade to his left. The pair waited for the ensuing explosion, then rose and in a crouching position ran twenty yards to their left.

A third grenade pitched by Bolan exploded and scattered another group of hidden PRA soldiers.

There were cries of pain from the woods, but no hint of movement.

Bolan and Collins waited patiently, making sure none of the attackers were watching for them to expose themselves.

Ten minutes later, the jungle around them exploded with fury. From all sides, the two Americans heard the crackling of gunfire. Bullets pounded the trees and bushes but miraculously missed them.

Movement on their left got their attention. Two uniformed men raced into the open space in front of them. Both, the Executioner noted, were dripping blood as they charged. Their faces were fixed in terror.

From experience Bolan knew that fear could pump the adrenaline and move fighters to irrational actions.

It would take more than a well-placed pair of slugs to stop the two men tearing toward him.

The soldier stood and waited for the duo to get closer, then hosed them with the rest of the Uzi's clip. The slugs ripped into the throat of the closer man, nearly severing his head from his body, while the second, the taller of the two, clutched his midsection, trying to stop his exposed intestines from oozing to the ground.

As Bolan watched, the first attacker tried to keep moving, but stumbled and fell. The Executioner snapped a fresh clip into the Uzi and waited.

The second attacker pulled his hands away from his ruptured body and pointed his AK-47 to where Bolan had been standing. In one last desperate effort, he squeezed the trigger and emptied the clip. The force of the recoil shoved him backward. He fell to the ground and lay there, his blood soaking into the vegetation beneath him.

Battlewise, the soldier had signaled the DEA agent to move. The 9 mm slugs from the AK-47 tore holes into the huge Elephant Ear plants that covered the jungle, rather than into Collins or him.

Bolan wasn't sure who had sent the hit team. These weren't guerrillas; they were regular army.

He knew this wasn't the time to worry about it. Right now, they had to find out if there were any Communist soldiers still alive.

His question was answered when three shadows raced into the dense underbrush. Weighing his options, the soldier reached into the canvas carryall and dug out an incendiary grenade. Pulling the pin, Bolan lobbed the bomb after the soldiers.

Within seconds, a flaming torch darted out into the open area. Collins fired a mercy round into the burning man's chest and watched as the scorched body fell to the ground.

Cries of agony from the underbrush pierced the quiet night. The Executioner waited until a second assailant, fatigues scorched and clinging to his flesh, staggered out of the deep brush.

Clenching his Kalashnikov carbine, the crazed attacker fired wildly, then turned the gun on himself and chiseled a 7.62 mm hole in his skull, spilling gray matter and blood down his slumping body.

Now the Executioner knew what kind of adversaries he was facing. They weren't the best combat soldiers, but were either so dedicated to their cause or so afraid of their superiors that they would kill themselves rather than be captured.

Collins signaled that he would scout the brush surrounding them for any signs of the fourth shadow. He could see none.

Some sixth sense warned the DEA agent they weren't alone. He moved forward and triggered his MAC-10, aiming at the low brush. But there were no cries of pain, no hint of life.

Suddenly an explosion behind Collins made him turn.

A body lay on the ground, a soldier in fatigues.

What was left of his face was covered by a mask of blood. In his limp hands was an AK-47.

The DEA man was crawling to him on his hands and knees, when he heard a whining sound race over his head. Collins started to get up, but Bolan pushed him down again.

"What the hell are you—"

"Stay down!"

The forest behind resounded with an explosion that sounded like a bolt of thunder. Large chunks of timber and branches were propelled in every direction by the force of the eruption. Flames began to consume the trees and the brush.

The soldier watched as Collins stood, then asked, "Any injuries?"

He felt his arms and face. "No, I don't think so."

Staring in horror at the flaming inferno, Collins turned and looked at Bolan.

"How did you know?"

"I've heard the sound before. A fragmentation grenade launched from a Kalashnikov combo assault rifle."

"So not all of them were dead," the DEA field op said in disbelief.

"Wait here," Bolan ordered in a low voice, as he hauled the .44 Magnum Desert Eagle from its leather holster. "They soon will be."

CHAPTER TWENTY-FIVE

As they drove away from the scene of the attack, Bolan started to wonder again how the troops had known where to find them.

"Somebody must have followed us," Bolan stated.

"One of us would have seen him."

What the DEA man said bothered the soldier. He *would* have spotted anyone following them.

"Pull over," he ordered.

Surprised at the harshness in his voice, Collins pulled off the road and stopped the vehicle, then turned to Bolan.

"Is something wrong?"

The soldier tried to listen past the usual night sounds. Nothing. Was it fatigue? he wondered. The last time he thought it was a lack of sleep, he had ignored that convenient explanation and, as a result, was still alive.

Reaching for the canvas bags, he took out the M-16 A-2 he had packed and a handful of clips, which he shoved into the pockets of the combat vest.

Checking the clip of the carbine, he snapped in a fresh magazine and jacked the first round into the chamber. Then he loaded an incendiary grenade into the M-203 launcher mounted beneath the powerful assault rifle.

The Executioner was intimate with the combo weapon. He had used it on countless missions.

Not only was the M-16 A-2 capable of pouring 800 rounds of high velocity 5.56 mm ammo per minute at a muzzle velocity of 1000 feet per second with virtually no jamming, but the launcher made it possible to hurtle a 40 mm grenade accurately as far as four hundred yards.

Seemingly satisfied, Bolan started to rise, then changed his mind and reached into the bag again. As he brought out a long tube, the DEA operative recognized the weapon.

"Why on earth would you need a LAW 80?"

"I might not," Bolan replied, slinging the antitank rocket over a shoulder. "But then again, I might."

There was something else in the bag—a shiny black button. Bolan took it out and studied it, then dropped it on the ground and crushed it with the heel of his combat boots.

"I found the snitch," he told Collins. "Someone planted a tracking device in my bag."

"Who?"

"It could have been almost any interested party." Feeling more secure, he added, "Let's get out of here."

As Collins resumed driving, the soldier could feel the heat of tension radiating from him again.

"It may be nothing," he said, trying to reassure him.

Collins smiled weakly. "I trust your instincts," he replied, checking the magazine in his .45-caliber Colt Government Model pistol.

"If there is an attack, follow my orders pronto. Every minute you delay may cost us our—"

The rest of his sentence was punctuated by automatic fire pouring like a sudden rainstorm from both sides of the road.

"Get this car into the woods," he shouted, grabbing the M-16 A-2 combo.

Without hesitation, Collins spun the steering wheel hard and plunged into an open space in the bushes. The vehicle bucked as it bounced on the uneven forest ground. But the DEA field man managed to hold on to the steering wheel.

"Stop," Bolan shouted.

Stomping down on the brake, Collins stopped the car suddenly, causing it to stall.

"Get out and find someplace to stay under cover," Bolan told him sharply.

Gripping the Colt in his right hand and the MAC-10 in his left, the DEA operative threw himself out of the car and behind a wide banyan tree.

Out of the car, the Executioner glanced at where the DEA man had taken refuge and decided he was safe for the moment.

With determination, he pushed his way into the thick brush and moved toward the source of the gunfire. Two Chinese soldiers had their backs to him.

The sound of a snapping twig made them spin. At the sight of the large American, the pair squeezed the triggers of their subguns.

Bolan had anticipated their actions. Twisting to the left, he fired a burst of 5.56 mm rounds at the closer of the pair. The bullets carved a path through the gunner's neck and up into his brain.

The second army recruit recovered quickly from the shock of seeing the other torn apart, and quickly emptied the magazine of 7.62 mm ammo at Bolan's former position. The Executioner had spun out of the path of the lead killers as the rounds from the trooper's SMG chopped chunks of wood from a tree behind him.

While the young soldier tried to force a fresh magazine into his weapon, Bolan turned his weapon on the man and swept his carbine in a left-to-right path across the gunner's midsection. Screaming curses in Cantonese, the army fighter dropped his SMG and tried desperately to stop his intestines from spilling to the ground.

Looking down at the huge cavity where his stomach and digestive organs had been seconds earlier, the dying fighter saw the blood from his body wash over his hands. Then he sat on the ground and calmly waited for death to come for him.

Scanning the nearby woods for hidden enemies,

Bolan sensed the presence of a large force on both sides of the highway, more than Collins and he could handle.

It was time to retreat.

As they approached the parked car, Bolan stopped.

"Get the car started. I'll be there in a minute," he ordered.

Collins was about to argue, but changed his mind. His instincts told him he could trust the man's combat judgment.

Bolan listened for a moment, then focused carefully through the sight mounted on the left, adjusted the setting. Mounting a frag grenade, he squeezed the trigger on the M-203 and watched the metal missile travel above the treetops. Then he turned and ran for the car.

Collins started to get out and let him take over the wheel.

"You drive," Bolan told him. "I might be busy keeping us alive."

Getting behind the wheel of the vehicle, the DEA agent waited until the soldier got in, then started the engine and floored the gas pedal.

As the car raced in the direction of Bangkok, Bolan and Collins could hear the loud explosions of ammo set off by the grenade he'd delivered.

"That takes care of that group," the DEA man commented in a calmer voice.

"We're not there yet," Bolan warned.

As if his words had been prophecy, an armored

personnel carrier lumbered out of the woods in front of them.

Bolan recognized it as a Chinese copy of the Soviet GAZ-69 four by four. Sitting behind the driver with his back to him was a fatigue-clad soldier staring down the sight of the Chinese-manufactured 7.62 mm RP-46 machine gun.

The light armored vehicle started to make a U-turn so the gunner could have a clear target.

"Weave!" Bolan shouted.

Responding instantly, Collins swerved the embassy-issued car into a series of loops.

A steady stream of lead wasps stuttered from the mounted machine gun, missing the vehicle and its occupants by scant inches.

"The gunner's getting too accurate. Into the woods!"

"Can't we outrun him?"

"Not with the range of that machine gun. And we don't know what other weapons they're carrying."

Collins drove the car over the low curb and headed for a clearing in the underbrush.

Bolan jumped out before the DEA man had stopped.

"Hide. I'll be back," he promised.

MAJOR SUNG TURNED to the young gunner behind him.

"Why did you stop firing?"

"They ran into the forest, Comrade Major," the gunner explained.

"We will follow them," the Chinese officer replied, already sensing a promotion in rank as a result of the battle.

He didn't know how the general had arranged it, but several military vehicles were parked and waiting for his troops when their helicopter had landed. Probably the work of one of the corrupt Thai Military Police officials, in exchange for money. It didn't matter. All Sung cared about was killing the American mercenary and winning a promotion.

He could see the faint outline of the enemy vehicle hiding behind some banyan trees twenty yards in front of them.

"Stop here," he ordered, and got out when the carrier came to a halt.

"Maintain a stream of fire at the car," Sung ordered. "General Lu will be pleased with our success.

BOLAN HAD SLIPPED behind the trees until he had a clear view of the GAZ-69. Slipping the LAW 80 from his shoulder, he pulled the safety pin. The end caps fell away and the weapon telescoped another six inches, while it armed itself.

The nearly three-foot-long, shoulder-held missile launcher carried a 66 mm round with a hollowpoint nose, shaped like a small teacup. The whole unit weighed about five pounds.

Sighting through the eyepiece that moved into position on top of the launcher, Bolan knew he had to move fast and accurately or he and Collins would be memories.

Focusing on the vintage military vehicle, he pulled the trigger and mentally crossed his fingers. The missile raced out of the tube at a speed of almost 500 feet per second and easily cut a hole through the GAZ-69 as if it were made of paper.

He could hear the missile exploding with the deafening sound of thunder, tearing the armored vehicle in two. Molten bits of metal from the warhead and flames shot back at him, scorching trees in their path.

Over the exploding ammo, Bolan could hear muffled screams as superheated chunks of metal and flame consumed the men in and around the vehicle. The smell of burning flesh fouled the air.

He waited for the intensive heat to dissipate, then worked his way back to where Collins had parked. He hoped the DEA agent hadn't been injured in the intense battle.

Collins was waiting for him near the vehicle. He started to point his pistol at him, then lowered it when he realized it was Bolan.

"Next time, I go with you," he snapped. "I felt like a helpless bystander watching a war being fought."

Getting into the car, Bolan pointed to the wheel. "Drive. It's been a very long day."

"At least we're coming out alive," the DEA operative commented.

CHAPTER TWENTY-SIX

The sun was threatening to break through the night clouds. Bolan could feel fatigue draining him. He needed a shower and at least three hours of sleep. Collins had warned him that his hotel room would probably be under surveillance, and he had been right.

But the DEA agent had a shower and a couch. Bolan decided to make use of both.

A Mitsubishi van was parked across the street from the apartment building where Joe Collins lived. Its windows were heavily tinted, making it almost impossible to see if anyone was in the large vehicle.

Bolan noticed the van as he approached the four-story building, and kept moving.

Collins looked at him. "Something wrong?"

"Maybe not. Just being careful. Is there a back entrance to the building?"

The DEA agent nodded. "There's an alley just around the corner that leads to the rear."

Bolan entered the narrow alleyway, watching carefully for possible assailants.

Nobody was waiting in hiding.

He parked the car, then locked the bag containing the money in the trunk of the vehicle, and carried the arms bag on the same shoulder as the Uzi SMG.

"Lead the way," he said.

Collins slung the MAC-10, then, using a key, he opened a door that led to a flight of stairs. Bolan followed him upstairs to the second landing.

The field agent stopped at a wooden door, then thumbed through a large number of keys on a ring until he found the right one. As he started to insert it into the lock, the Executioner grabbed his hand and pulled it away.

"Something feels wrong."

Bolan inspected the lock, which looked like any of the other ones on the second floor. But some sixth sense warned him someone had tampered with it.

He studied it, searching for something that would give credence to his sense of danger.

Then he found it—tiny scratches on the brass colored lock. Someone had picked it open.

Turning to the DEA operative, he asked, "Is there another way to get into your apartment?"

"There's a fire escape that goes from the roof to the ground level. But it's pretty old and shaky."

The soldier pointed to the MAC-10 slung on Collins's shoulder.

"Stand guard here in case somebody comes hunting. I'll be back in a few minutes."

Slipping back out through the rear door, Bolan

searched for the fire escape. As Collins had warned, it was old and rusty.

Carefully, Uzi gripped in his right hand, weapons bag on his shoulder, Bolan worked his way up the metal steps to the second level.

He tried to open the window, but it was securely locked. Closed curtains made it impossible to check if anyone was waiting inside.

He looked down and saw two Asian men enter the alley. They walked to the parked embassy car and stared inside.

Bolan eased the Uzi from his shoulder and raised it to eye level. Just in case.

The pair below him searched the area, checking doorways and windows. One of them looked up and spotted Bolan.

There was no time to explain what he was doing on the fire escape, and no reason.

The Executioner chugged three rounds at the street soldier. Two carved paths into the man's stomach, while the third found a way into his chest.

As the hit man fell to the ground, the second thug aimed a Skorpion SMG in Bolan's direction.

The soldier zoned in on the gunner and washed the area with the rest of the rounds in the magazine.

Several ripped into the gunman's face and punched him to the ground, never to rise again.

The wolves were getting hungry, Bolan decided. There was no time to waste trying to create some clever battle strategy. He had to get inside Collins's apartment, check it out, then come up with a battle strategy.

He used the butt of the Uzi to break the window, then reached inside and released the locking mechanism.

Bolan paused and listened for any sounds of life. There was none. Whoever had picked his way into the apartment was gone. Lifting the shattered window, Bolan climbed inside and looked around.

Nothing looked disturbed.

He moved to the front door and reached to open it, then spied the clay pressed into the doorjamb, all the way to the carpet. A thin, almost invisible wire ran under the door.

Bolan recognized the setup—plastic explosive with a trip trigger, set to detonate when the door opened.

The explosive trigger was a simple device. Opening the door to the room set off a small electrical charge that triggered a detonator, which in turn set off the explosive.

Dismantling the device was easy. Bolan carefully freed the wire from the electric connection, then removed the detonator. Opening the door, he pulled the claylike explosive from the doorframe and dropped the components into a wastebasket.

Collins stared at him from the hallway.

"Booby trap?"

"Something like that."

"First time anyone has brought the drug war to

my apartment,'' the DEA agent commented angrily. ''I'd like to reciprocate.''

Bolan reached into the wastebasket and retrieved the bomb components. Carefully, he molded the plastic explosive into a small brick, then reinserted the detonator.

Searching in his canvas bag, the soldier found a tiny timer. He connected it to the detonator, then left his bag on the carpeted floor and walked to the front door of the apartment.

''I'll be back,'' he stated, then added, ''If I'm not, have your people in Washington, D.C., find a man named Harold Brognola and tell him what we accomplished so far.''

''Need help?''

''Right now more than one would be a crowd,'' Bolan said, disappearing down the corridor.

BOLAN KEPT to the shadows of the buildings on the street. The Mitsubishi van was still there. This time he was sure that a squad of hit men were inside, waiting for Collins and him to return and self-destruct at the apartment door.

Despite the rapidly rising morning sun, the soldier managed to move toward the van without being spotted.

Slipping behind the large vehicle, Bolan crawled underneath and attached the plastic block to the fuel tank, started the timer and slipped back across the street.

As far as he knew, nobody had detected his presence. He'd know if he was right in ten minutes, when the timer set off the plastic explosive.

Until then, there was nothing he could do but wait. But not on the street.

WHEN HE RETURNED to the apartment, he smelled a familiar aroma. Collins had brewed a pot of coffee.

"Marcel Maracel called."

"What did he want?"

"Just to say goodbye. He was leaving Thailand."

"Did you ask him about somebody named Borodin?"

"Yes. He said it was someone he knew a long time ago. Someone who's dead."

"Anything else?"

Collins nodded. "Something strange. He said there are those who pay for killing and those who kill. He didn't like being the one between them."

"Sounds like an apology," Bolan commented.

"That's what I thought. He also said General Chernov was on his way to Chiang Mai. But this time he'd have to do his own killing."

"Not if we beat him to it," Bolan replied.

The DEA man held up an empty cup.

"Want some?"

The soldier nodded. "Black."

"Mission accomplished?"

Bolan checked his watch.

"We'll know in eight minutes."

"Good. I need a shower and a nap," Collins said.

"Sounds like a plan. We should be safe here for a while."

"Your Mr. Brognola called," Collins reported. "Bad news. Chernov turns out to be the godfather of the Russian drug syndicate. I wonder why he came to Thailand?"

It made good sense to Bolan.

"To wipe out as much of the competition as he can."

He focused his attention on his watch.

Six minutes.

Five, four, three, two, one.

"Thirty seconds to go," he warned.

Collins was confused by Bolan's words.

"To go where?"

As if it were answering the DEA agent's question, the room shivered as a huge explosion rocked the street outside.

Bolan sipped the coffee. Then said, "Now about that shower."

TWENTY-SEVEN

Chiang Mai

A freak late-afternoon thunderstorm had delayed their takeoff by ninety minutes. Bolan had come close to commanding the helicopter pilot to ignore the wild streaks of lightning and lift the surplus military warship into the air.

Bolan was frustrated with the weather. The reason he was there kept flashing in his mind: make sure the President's message was delivered and the senator was alive.

Nothing else mattered.

For the first time he was going to have to face different enemies at the same time: the triad street fighters, the Communist troops and, finally, if his guess was right, the former Russian commandos Chernov had brought with him.

Bolan picked up the topographical map as the freelance pilot finally lifted the helicopter off the concrete pad.

As the pair of T58-GE turboshaft engines pulled

the chopper up at the rate of 1300 feet per minute, Bolan studied the map he held.

Leveling at ten thousand feet, the Sikorsky moved through the afternoon sky at 141 knots. As the converted assault ship worked its way along the Thailand coast toward the city of Chiang Mai, Collins pointed to a red dot printed at the top of the map of Thailand.

"That's where we're heading."

"I know," Bolan replied. "I've been there before."

Collins looked surprised. There was so much about Mike Belasko he wanted to know. But he suspected it would take a lifetime to learn it all.

Bolan stared at the map.

Chiang Mai had worked hard to earn its nickname of The City of Opium. The large metropolis would be in sight in forty-five minutes, then it was just a simple matter to follow the map toward the remote area where the villa was located.

Bolan had been here a number of times in the past, during various missions to destroy the power of the Chinese triads who controlled the distribution of heroin from The Golden Triangle.

The corner where Thailand, Myanmar, Laos and southern China met in the mountains produced seventy percent of the world's supply of heroin. Even with Bolan's previous efforts, resuming the growing, processing and shipping of the morphine derivative had taken less than two years.

The soldier hoped the current effort would have a

more permanent effect on the availability of the white powder that killed thousands of addicts monthly.

The muffled engines of the twin-bladed Sikorsky still emitted a harsh whining sound that pierced the night skies. Fortunately, a thick cloud cover made the gunship less visible from vessels sailing on the Andaman Sea.

Bolan checked the canvas carryall he had brought with him. In addition to the Uzi SMG and M-16 A-2/M-203 combo, he had packed a rocket launcher he had confiscated and several HEAT rockets, along with a supply of fragmentation and incendiary grenades.

The soldier's favorite handguns sat on top of the bag, the silenced 9 mm Beretta 93-R and the Israeli .44 Magnum Desert Eagle. The Applegate-Fairbairn combat knife Bolan carried on missions was in its stiff sheath, ready to be strapped to his arm or leg.

Bolan took out the plastic-wrapped package stored at the bottom of the bag. Carefully opening it, he checked the six bricks of C-4 plastic explosives and the miniaturized timers and detonators he had wrapped with them. Satisfied that his equipment was in operational condition, the soldier repacked his bag, leaving out the handguns, one of the UZI SMGs, an M-16 combo, a quartet of antipersonnel grenades and a supply of magazines for the weapons.

He had planned to leave the combat knife in the bag, but changed his mind and took it out.

The pilot's voice rasped over the speaker system.

"Coming up on Chiang Mai."

Bolan moved to the front of the combat helicopter and leaned over the pilot.

"Where are we landing?"

"In a clearing about three miles from General Lu's compound," Butch said. "I had a friend leave a Land Rover parked nearby. Its tank is full and the keys are under the driver's seat."

"What about patrols?"

"There won't be any," the pilot replied.

"Why not?"

"The People's Revolutionary Army soldiers will be too busy keeping an eye on the triad squads to worry about intruders."

The soldier wasn't satisfied. Something was wrong with the pilot's explanation.

Turning to the DEA agent, he asked, "Are you certain this is where the American senator is holding his meetings?"

"That's what my contacts told me."

Stripping his outer clothes, the warrior pulled on the blacksuit, which he had removed from the carryall, then covered his face with combat cosmetics.

He loaded his combat vest pockets with small bricks of C-4, and detonators and timers to set them off. An assortment of fragmentation grenades were clipped to the web belt he'd cinched around his waist.

As the Executioner slipped into the stiff harness

that held the silenced 9 mm Beretta pistol, the pain of the bandaged shoulder wounds made him wince. Loading the pockets of the vest with filled magazines for the Beretta, the M-16 and the .44-caliber Desert Eagle he had slipped into a rear belt holster, he remembered the telephone instructions Hal Brognola delivered before takeoff.

"This comes directly from the Man," the big Fed had told him. "You've made it clear to the Chinese godfathers that we mean business. Now make sure Bob Firestone is alive to deliver the message. If he isn't, you deliver it for him."

"FROM WHAT I'VE been told," the DEA man warned, "there'll be a lot of hostiles waiting for you."

Bolan nodded. "What else is new?"

"I don't know who you've had to face in the past, but the triads are bringing their own street fighters, General Lu never travels without his soldiers, and, if the Russians show up, they're all former Spetsnaz— the best of their commandos. How do we handle them?"

"One at a time, if possible," the Executioner replied, as he watched Collins reload his pair of MAC-10s and his .45 ACP Colt.

THE TEAK-AND-STUCCO compound on the outskirts of Chiang Mai was heavily guarded. Only twelve miles from the center of the northern Thai city, the structure was the current host to the leading drug barons in Southeast Asia, and the warlord who supplied them with the white powder they sold.

A tall, stone wall surrounded the property. Machine guns were set in concrete emplacements on all four sides, and the several dozen People's Revolutionary Army soldiers General Lu had brought with him manned them twenty-four hours a day.

The guards the three triad godfathers had brought were bivouacked in dormitory buildings outside the compound walls.

Except for the CIA agents who guarded the visiting American senator, no weapons were allowed in the main house or the courtyard.

General Lu's troops were housed in a small structure that connected to the main building by a long, covered passageway.

A small landing pad, which could handle up to four helicopters, was carved out of the jungle, northwest of the compound. And near it was a leveled field that could accommodate an additional six parked choppers.

Transportation to and from the compound was provided by a fleet of military and civilian vehicles.

The dozen PRA soldiers on duty carried identical weapons—Chinese copies of the M-16 A-1, which handled 5.56 mm cartridges. The chilly evening had descended on them, and their thin cotton uniforms did little to help them stay warm. The men rubbed their arms and shoulders to stave off the cold of night.

Inside the main building, a series of rooms surrounded a large living room. A two-room suite had been set aside for the exclusive use of General Lu's mother, Mai Ling.

The general himself slept in a large room with windows that faced the helicopter landing pad to the north.

There were other bedrooms for guests who didn't want to risk being seen at one of the luxury hotels in the nearby city.

General Lu's guests, the Elder Brothers and Incense Masters of the three major triads with whom he did business, had made their own living arrangements. Especially since there wasn't enough room in the compound to house the squads of foot soldiers they had brought with them.

Their initial reaction to the letter the senator had brought from the American President wasn't unexpected by the general. Each group had a worldwide network to supply and protect. While his responsibility ended when he delivered and got paid for the heroin grown on the vast poppy fields of Yunnan Province, theirs only began then.

The senator had left them and returned to his hotel. He had promised to be available to anyone who wanted to meet with him and discuss the proposal.

Lu had studied the problems of distribution for more than a year. The lion's share of the profits were kept by the triads, even under the competitive arrangement he had introduced.

Now it was time for him to make a decision. Should he continue the distribution arrangements or make new ones? If he decided to stick with the triads, the senator's presence was purposeless. If he didn't, Senator Firestone would be a valuable asset.

This was the dilemma he brought to Mai Ling's suite.

"One possibility would be to increase the prices charged to the triads," she suggested, leaning back in the brocaded easy chair.

"I've already thought of that," Lu replied, sitting on the edge of the long couch. "At some point, it would be cheaper for the triads to increase their efforts to assassinate me than pay higher prices. Whatever I decide to do must be done quickly before the Elder Brothers have time to come up with a counterplan."

"Have you discussed this with the senator?"

"Not yet. Is this the right time?"

"He will have to be brought into the picture sometime," she reminded her son.

"Do you really think blackmail will work?"

"Senator Firestone has spent his adult life building an image of firm but kind leadership. It is rumored that he will probably be his party's next candidate for President. Given that, do you believe he would want the world to know that the son he brought into the world was the most important grower of opium in the world?"

Mai Ling smiled.

"One possibility would be for you to suggest that you will reduce the amount of heroin shipped to the United States in exchange for a secret distribution arrangement." She paused and did some rapid calculations in her head. "Even if you only shipped fifty percent of the heroin now being smuggled into America, you would have increased profits considerably."

Lu looked concerned. "Would you talk to him first, Mother?"

The handsome woman smiled and patted her son's shoulder.

"Of course. If that is what you want."

The young warlord got to his feet.

"Thank you, Mother."

"I hope I can be of help, my son."

Lu leaned over and kissed her cheek.

"As always, you have come up with the logical solution to the problem."

He walked to the door that led to the corridor. The triads could wait. He had to make arrangements to have his mother driven to the hotel for a talk with the American senator.

With his father.

CHAPTER TWENTY-EIGHT

It was almost evening when they landed in Chiang Mai.

The vehicle was waiting for them at the makeshift helicopter pad as Butch had promised—a battered Land Rover.

Butch walked with them to the helicopter door. Turning to Collins, he said, "Call me when you want me to pick you up."

The DEA man nodded.

Looking at Bolan, the Algerian pilot held out his hand. Bolan dug into an inside pocket, took out a thick wad of bills and handed one third of it to the pilot.

Then he jumped to the ground.

Something was wrong. The Executioner could feel it in the air. As Collins joined him, Bolan shouted, "Into the woods. Fast!"

With an expression of confusion, the DEA agent started to hesitate, then changed his mind and threw himself into the underbrush.

Bolan slipped the M-16 combo from his shoulder and slammed a round into the chamber.

There was a five-gallon can filled with fuel on the back rim of the vintage vehicle. The soldier grabbed it and tossed the can at the nearest wooded area, then fired at it until the gasoline exploded.

A storm of lead raced from behind the trees and tore into the surplus military vehicle. The soldier looked at the helicopter pilot standing in the open doorway of the Sikorsky.

There was no look of surprise on his face, only disappointment.

Bolan decided to change that.

Unleashing a pair of hollowpoints at the Algerian pilot, he watched the man's expression turn to shock, then blank as the rounds shattered his neck and death took possession of his body.

Focusing the M-16 on the sector pummeling the Land Rover with a continuous stream of rounds, Bolan launched a frag grenade from the M-203 slung under the carbine.

Screams cracked the jungle air as shards of superheated metal pierced the bodies of hidden assailants.

The Executioner jerked another fragger from his vest, armed the bomb and tossed it into another area. Cries of pain erupted as the grenade scattered its metal death needles.

The rustling sounds of the fleeing ambushers followed the second grenade explosion.

Then it was quiet.

Bolan turned to Collins.

"Any scratches?"

The DEA man shook his head.

"How did you know?"

"Your buddy kept searching the woods for something. I figured he had to be looking for men waiting for us."

Collins shook his head in disgust.

"He was always so reliable."

"The other side must have thought so, too."

Collins got to his feet. "What do we do now?"

"See if the Land Rover is operational, then go after the ones who didn't die."

The DEA agent nodded, and followed Bolan to the military vehicle.

Dozens of bullet holes scarred the transport. The soldier lifted the hood and peered inside. None of the rounds had punctured the radiator or engine block. He slammed the hood and climbed into the driver's seat.

The ignition key was under a worn floor mat. Two five-gallon gasoline tanks sat on the floor behind the driver's seat. Bolan checked them, and they were full.

There was also a map under the driver's seat.

The Executioner studied it and saw that a small dirt road ran through the forest. He put the vehicle in gear and kept his fingers crossed that it would still run.

As he engaged the engine, Bolan turned to Collins.

"Shoot at anything that moves."

Collins nodded and gripped one of his two MAC-10s.

SENATOR FIRESTONE WAS waiting for someone to pick him up and take him back to the villa. He kept staring at the telephone in his hotel room, tempted to place a call to the White House and tell the President the truth about his past. He had wrestled with his conscience ever since Lu had him driven back to the hotel.

There was a knock at his door. The American politician assumed it was one of his CIA bodyguards, so he opened it.

The woman who smiled at him from the corridor was breathtaking.

"It has been a very long time," she said.

The senator was momentarily puzzled, then realized who she was.

"Come in Mai Ling," he said, opening the door wide.

THEY SAT AND TALKED about the brief time they had spent together in the hills of northern Thailand.

"More than thirty years ago," he commented, shaking his head. "And if anything, you are more beautiful today than you were then."

Mai Ling smiled. "And you have become a very important man in your country," she replied. "As has our son here."

"I have a problem with that," Senator Firestone said. "What he is selling kills many thousands of men and women each year."

The woman's voice became cold. "They are not obligated to buy the heroin."

"At some point," Firestone said, trying to control the sudden rage he felt, "they have to have the drug, no matter what they have to do to pay for it."

She stood and held out a hand.

"I'm sure our son and you can find a mutually acceptable basis for negotiating," she said, and left.

Firestone stared at the door. Emotions ranging from anger to guilt raced through him. This was going to be more difficult than he had imagined.

It was ironic, Firestone reminded himself, that he and the man he had helped create were in the same business.

Only on opposite sides.

There was only one possible answer to give his son.

No.

THE ELDER BROTHERS MET privately in one of the smaller rooms in the villa. After checking for eavesdropping devices, they discussed the American's proposal and what they should do about it.

"Kill the senator," the Chui Chao head suggested.

"The President of the United States will just send some other politician to replace him," the godfather of the Yi Kwah Tao replied.

"Ignore the letter from the American President," the 14K Triad chief said.

"Then what?"

"We release the information about the senator's son to the scandal newspapers around the world," Tan Suan Chi, of the Yi Kwah Tao, replied.

The Chui Chao chief looked puzzled.

"What information?"

"Your Intelligence people have let you down again, Sun Jee," Tan Suan Chi commented sarcastically. "General Lu is the son of the American senator. Illegitimate, of course."

Sun Jee looked concerned. "Then it is obvious that General Lu and the senator are working together to eliminate us as distributors."

Luk Sang interrupted the three godfathers.

"I beg your forgiveness in speaking, but the senator has left the compound to return to the hotel."

Sun Jee nodded and addressed the other triad godfathers.

"May I suggest that we get out of here and continue our conversation in my suite. I smell death all around us."

The heads of the Yi Kwah Tao and the 14K got to their feet and quickly left the room. Sun Jee waited until they had left, then studied his Incense Master's expression.

Luk Sang was the Chui Chao Incense Master for Bangkok. He had worked up through the ranks of the triad, starting as a foot soldier.

With a long string of successful kills against traitors and undercover police, Luk was elevated to territorial commander—Incense Master—when his predecessor was killed in a street fight with the Thai military police. As had been the tradition for the century-and-a-half history of the Chui Chao, Luk had been accepted after going through the lengthy ceremony that all leaders of the triad had submitted to when so honored.

Under Luk's command, drug traffic from the Golden Triangle to foreign ports had tripled in five years. Sharing in the profits, members of the Chui Chao had acquired villas in Bangkok, Hong Kong and London.

Chui Chao profits went down when the new warlord, General Lu, decided to share heroin distribution rights among the three triads.

Attempts to assassinate the young upstart had proved fruitless, and Lu threatened to cut the triads from the refined opium supply if they continued their attempts.

The change in the Golden Triangle distribution policy had done something even worse. It had delayed Luk's official appointment as heir to Chui Chao leadership.

SUN JEE WAITED for the other godfathers to leave, then asked, "Is there something you wished to say to me in private Luk Sang?"

Luk hesitated a moment, then, looking around as

if he expected there to be somebody else in the room, made a suggestion.

"The problem of shared distribution could be solved easily, Master, if our partners were without leaders."

"An excellent thought, but not easily achieved. We have the same number of men with us as each of them."

"But we have something they do not, Master. The element of surprise."

"General Lu may step in with his soldiers to stop the battle," Sun Jee warned. "He has the backing of the province governor."

"Not if it was over before they knew it was happening," Luk commented.

Sun Jee weighed the suggestion.

"Make it be so," he said softly.

THE ELDER BROTHERS and their entourages had left the compound in separate cars. When they hadn't returned to the compound, Lu suspected they were meeting in private to come up with some unified response.

He summoned Major Hon, the representative the People's Revolutionary Army sent to replace the now-dead Major Sung, and General Tuan Weh, his Myanmar partner.

"We are at an important point tonight," he told the pair. "There might be some trouble with the triads."

Turning to Hon, he warned, "Make sure your troops keep a careful eye on the foot soldiers the triads brought with them. At the first sign of trouble, kill them."

The young general remembered something.

"There is also an American mercenary who had been destroying the triad warehouses in Bangkok. While this has temporarily increased our profits, I don't know who sent him. We would be better off with him dead."

He glared at the major.

"And be more skillful than your predecessor was when he encountered him."

The major nodded and left the living room to alert the soldiers they had brought with them.

Lu smiled at his Myanmar counterpart. "I believe that the source of the attacks on your laboratories are competitors."

General Tuan was furious. "Who?"

"A group of Russians arrived in Rangoon yesterday. The man leading them, my contact in the Russian embassy tells me, is a former general who has taken control of the poppy fields in the once-Soviet republics. Evidently, the triads created an enemy when they started distributing the white powder in his country, and the countries near Russia."

He remembered what the Russian "attaché" had told him by phone in exchange for a bonus in Swiss francs.

"What pushed him over the edge was the death

of his own son due to an overdose of Golden Triangle heroin.''

"What do we do?"

"We separate ourselves from the triads.''

Tuan looked puzzled. "Then how do we get the product from my laboratories to distributors?''

"I have a plan. It involves killing the triad foot soldiers—feeding them to the Russian's men. If it works, we will make new arrangements for distribution. If it doesn't, we will resume our business arrangements with the triads.''

Lu started walking to the door leading into the corridor.

"I have somebody I need to see about the new arrangement. I should be back before the triad leaders return.''

CHAPTER TWENTY-NINE

As the modified Mi-24 gunship moved north through
the night skies to Chiang Mai, Chernov turned to his
Karin army guide.

"Ask the pilot how long before we land in Chiang
Mai."

Colonel Ne Win asked the question in one of the
Myanmar dialects, waited for the response and turned
back to the Russian.

"Twenty minutes at most," Ne Win reported.

"Does he know a place where we can land? It
wouldn't be smart to land at the commercial airport
without visas."

Ne Win repeated the question to the pilot, who
grinned and shouted something back in the unfamil-
iar dialect.

"He has landed many times in Chiang Mai, and
he has cousins who live in the highlands north of the
city. He's already radioed them to meet him at the
landing site and bring several military transport vehicles."

"Tell him there will be a bonus for him when we're finished," Chernov said.

Before the colonel could translate the message, the pilot nodded happily. Chernov smiled. Some things didn't need translating. Like making some extra money.

He leaned forward and gazed out of the Plexiglas bubble at the colorful rural scenery below.

Leaning his head against the inner skin of the Russian warship, Chernov reviewed what he knew of the situation.

The heads and their seconds in command of the three triads that distributed the Golden Triangle heroin were inside the house. They were meeting with the general who controlled the poppy fields in Yunnan Province and the American senator.

There weren't as many troops as the Russian had expected to find, but the several dozen men from the triads who were here were trained killers.

Then there was the American mercenary, cold-blooded and ruthless. A dangerous enemy. Chernov suspected that he was here, too, or would be soon.

The two dozen former Spetsnaz commandos he had brought were the best-trained fighters the Soviet army had had. They outmatched anything the other side could offer. He'd stake his life on it. And had, many times before this.

Then Chernov remembered the American mercenary had killed six of his men. Probably a lucky break, he decided. No American could kill a Spetsnaz commando without resorting to trickery.

THE LAND ROVER traveled along the dirt road that led to an estate. Parking on the edge of the forest, the soldier surveyed the area with his binoculars.

A dozen People's Revolutionary Army troops stood guard outside a high stucco wall, concentrated around the two heavy wooden doors that led into the front courtyard.

Getting out of the British vehicle, he told the DEA man, "Wait here."

"I'm going with you."

"No. You represent the United States government."

"I could write a letter of resignation," Collins suggested.

"You're more valuable doing what you've been doing."

"But what if you don't come back?"

"Get out of Thailand as fast as you can," he replied, "and contact Hal Brognola. Tell him what happened."

The soldier couldn't be burdened with the responsibility of another life. Not when he wasn't certain his would be there in a few hours.

"Belasko," Collins called out, "whether or not you want me, I'm going to be there at your side, getting rid of the drug bastards."

Bolan knew there was no point arguing.

"Just keep out of my way," he growled and watched Collins get out of the transport, while trying to balance a pair of MAC-10s on his shoulders.

Bolan had to check if the senator was being detained in the general's villa. Working his way along the edge of the thick underbrush, he led the way to the villa.

Moving behind him, Collins complained, "They never told us about this in training."

"It gets worse," Bolan warned without stopping. "If you want to drop out, now is the time."

"No way," the DEA man gasped, breathless from trying to keep up with Bolan's relentless pace. "I'm in for the duration."

Five minutes later they ran into a patrol.

Six men in People's Revolutionary Army uniforms moved silently through the forest, searching for intruders. The Executioner saw them first.

Grabbing the DEA agent's arm, he pulled him behind a tree and waited for the patrol to pass.

"WHOEVER YOU THOUGHT you saw has left," the Communist noncom snapped at one of the patrol.

The soldier, a teenager, argued, "I saw two men riding in a British-made vehicle along this road. They looked like Americans."

"Perhaps, Yang. Or perhaps you have a good imagination," the sergeant replied sarcastically.

"Let's proceed on the basis that Yang did see two

men and that they are someplace in the forest,'' a second soldier suggested. "What do we do now?"

"Wait," the sergeant replied.

"For what?"

"For further instructions."

"Not me," Yang said arrogantly. "We are six. They were only two. I say we find them and finish them off. If need be, I will go by myself."

Reluctantly the sergeant gave in. He didn't want one of his men filing a formal complaint about his leadership.

The six soldiers gathered their weapons.

"We will search for them in two teams," the sergeant said.

The others nodded, then paired off and moved cautiously into the forest.

BOLAN WORKED his way through the brush, keeping the sounds of his movements to a minimum. Behind him, Collins imitated his companion's steps.

For a big man, Bolan was amazingly light-footed. Years of moving through the world's battlefields had trained him to move with the silence of a cat.

His eyes had become adjusted to the relative darkness of the thick forest. He could make out obstacles on the ground and avoid them. Jungle warfare experience had sharpened his hearing. Focusing his ears to go beyond the birdcalls, the animal coughs and cackling, he listened for sounds of human enemies.

Hushed whispers beyond the stand of teak trees

made him stop for a moment. He couldn't make out the words, but somebody was speaking in one of the Chinese dialects. And someone else was replying in the same dialect.

The soldier wasn't sure how many were hidden behind the tall hardwood trees. Two or three, he assumed, armed with the automatic weapons issued to People's Revolutionary Army troops.

Collins joined him.

"What do we do now?"

In response, Bolan shouldered his M-16 A-2 and eased the suppressed 9 mm Beretta 93-R into his right hand.

"You keep a lookout for any more troops. I'll be back."

NERVOUSLY, the trio of soldiers checked carefully behind every tree before moving forward.

"We'll follow this trail," the sergeant stated, pointing to a dirt path. "It leads to—"

His words were interrupted by a large charging form.

Before they could shoulder their weapons, Bolan let loose a pair of 9 mm deathseekers. The slugs shattered the face of the youth who wanted to find and kill Bolan and Collins. Deflected by his thick jawbone, the lead ricocheted and drove bone splinters into the PRA soldier's brain.

There was no time for crying out. Death was instant.

The Executioner wasted no time pitying the new corpse. He made a half turn and fired three slugs through the sergeant's breastbone and into his heart muscle.

Blood spurted from severed vessels and poured out of the newly created chest cavity.

In a rage, the remaining PRA soldier threw himself at Bolan.

Stepping aside, the big American let the attacker hit the ground, then pointed his 93-R Beretta at the fallen soldier's face and fired. Bits of skull pushed their way up and into the soft tissue that had been his brain. He'd never face another enemy.

THE SECOND TEAM of soldiers heard the soft sounds and charged toward the muffled noise. The first team had to have found and killed the Americans.

"It will not hurt our careers if we are there to share in the success," one of them suggested.

Smiling, the other two soldiers gripped their Kalashnikov carbines and crashed through the bushes.

One of them shouted a question. "Are the Americans still alive?"

Mack Bolan was very much alive, and ready for the glory-seekers.

The three new arrivals, pushing their way through the thick undergrowth, stared in horror at the still-standing American. Ramming their AK-47 carbines against their shoulders, they fired wildly, unleashing a torrent of 7.62 mm death in front of them.

Unfortunately for them, Bolan had anticipated their movement and darted to the right. Lead shredded large leaves and sped into the darkness of the undergrowth.

Bolan turned and faced them. He wanted to keep one of them alive for questioning. The other two were expendable.

Perforating the bodies of the first two attackers with an accurate burst of 9 mm slugs, the Executioner turned to the survivor of the trio.

The hard-faced jungle fighter gestured for the terrified soldier to drop his weapon. Slowly, the man bent and started to place the carbine on the ground. His right-hand index finger was still planted against the trigger.

Bolan was about to give the order to move the finger when he heard the ear-splitting sound of a weapon unloading its clip. As the soldier fell to the ground, Bolan turned quickly, Desert Eagle in hand, and saw Collins. The Colt Government Model pistol was gripped tightly in the DEA operative's hand.

"I hope he's alive. He can tell us what's going on," Bolan snarled, relaxing his trigger finger.

"He would die before he betrayed the Communist Party," the DEA man replied coldly, and knelt to remove a chain from around the wounded youth's neck. "But yeah, he's alive."

Collins handed the Executioner a necklace. A cyanide capsule was attached.

Bolan now knew he was facing enemies who were not only willing to fight for the Party, but die for it, too.

If he was successful, many of them would.

CHAPTER THIRTY

Bobby Firestone wasn't expecting any more company, so he was startled when he heard the knocking on his hotel-room door.

He had just finished talking to the President's aide and reporting on the reaction to the President's letter. There was no reason for him to stay in Thailand, given how the triad leaders—and Lu—had reacted.

There was a flight to Bangkok in ninety minutes, and he had reserved a seat on the flight.

The senator opened the door.

General Lu was standing in the corridor, looking embarrassed.

"If you are busy, I can come back later."

Firestone felt as awkward as his illegitimate son looked.

"No, no. Come in. Perhaps we can get a little better acquainted without the presence of other people."

Firestone opened the door wide and let the general enter, then closed the door and pointed to a pair of upholstered chairs placed around a small circular table.

Lu sat, and the senator joined him.

There was silence for several minutes. Finally, Firestone spoke.

"You know, I had no idea I had a son until your mother contacted me. The woman I married was unable to have children."

"Your identity was kept from me until recently," Lu replied. "But I came to discuss your President's letter."

"Your mother left a little while ago. She came to discuss the same subject," Firestone replied. "And, by the way, he's your President, too," Firestone reminded the younger man, "if you choose to claim American citizenship."

"No. I am perfectly happy with what and who I am," the young warlord replied. "The proposals in the letter are totally unacceptable. Not only will the triads not agree to the terms, but I too reject them."

"What do you suggest?"

"How many know I am your son?"

"Nobody yet."

"There is no need for anyone else to know," Lu said. "It will make doing business with your country easier."

Firestone exploded.

"I won't let myself be blackmailed. I'd rather resign my seat in the Senate and tell the world who you are, than turn against my country!"

"Think of the benefits my suggestions bring to your country. The triads are immediately put out of business. The volume of drugs is reduced substantially. And you are viewed as a great hero." He smiled. "There are rumors that you would like to be the next President."

"I'll give your proposition to the President," the senator said coldly.

Lu became the warlord again, hard and without any display of emotion.

"It is only that someone he trusts needs to tell the President what I offer that you are allowed to live," Lu replied icily. "But leave Thailand before I change my mind."

Then he stood and walked out of the hotel room without looking back.

BEFORE LEAVING for the hotel where Sun Jee was staying, Luk Sang had reviewed his plan with the Chui Chao enforcer. Hiding any misgivings he might have, Chen Chi-Li had put his backup man, Chan Tse Chao, in charge of the attack.

Gathering together the half-dozen Chui Chao foot soldiers, Chan handed out assignments.

"You two," he ordered, pointing to a pair of older fighters, "will plant explosives around the buildings the Yi Kwah Tao and the 14K occupy. The rest will divide into two teams and station themselves at the entrances to the buildings. Kill anyone entering or leaving."

The Chui Chao hardmen checked their weapons and stuffed their pockets with extra magazines. The explosive handlers gathered their explosives, detonators and timers and started out the door.

"By this time tomorrow, we should be the only distribution source available to the general," Chan told the triad soldiers. "Which means more money for all."

WITH DUSK COVERING the sky above Chiang Mai, Chan Tse Chao signaled the men to start the attack.

The two handling the explosives set their timers to zero, then planted the plastique in the dormitories of the Yi Kwah Tao and 14K. They waited until street soldiers of the rival triads opened the doors, then flattened themselves against the ground.

A series of violent blasts fractured the otherwise quiet evening. Shattered fighters inside the buildings screamed in pain as explosives tore them to pieces. Through the ruptured doorways, bloody bodies raced into the night, desperate to escape the hell that had just visited them.

Chui Chao submachine gunners patiently waited for the signal to start firing, then began to pummel the survivors with sustained bursts.

Bodies fell, clogging the doorways.

Those able to move shoved aside the dead and ran into the darkness, only to be greeted with waves of lead tearing into their bodies.

Finally, the screams ceased. So did the firing.

Chan signaled his men to retreat. It was time for their next targets: the Incense Masters and the godfathers themselves, the Elder Brothers of the 14K and the Yi Kwah Tao.

But that honor would be left to the Elder Brother, the Incense Master and the Red Pole of the clan.

THE SOUNDS OF BATTLE carried to the two Americans.

"What's that?" Collins asked.

"I'd say somebody just went to war," he suggested.

Exploding gunpowder filled the night with flashes of light from the area of the dormitory buildings.

"Shouldn't we check it out?"

Bolan rejected the suggestion.

"I've got enough on my hands without getting involved. Besides, it isn't our fight."

When they reached the compound, the Executioner left Collins to watch the front entrance, while he searched for other opposition.

The first man Bolan encountered was a sour-faced Asian whose thick features identified him as a native of Sinkiang Province. The uniformed guard was leaning against a small road marker, scanning the area for possible intruders.

The soldier was watching the flashes of gunfire, looking unsure about what he should do.

Moving quietly behind him, the Executioner dispatched him with an expert thrust of the Applegate-

Fairbairn blade between his ribs, then a twist and push upward into the heart muscle.

Easing the body to the ground, Bolan surveyed the area.

Collins moved to Bolan's side, a MAC-10 clasped in his right hand.

"There was another hit man hiding behind the wall."

"Where is he?"

"Dead," the DEA man whispered, "but he talked first."

Bolan suddenly remembered that Collins spoke several Chinese dialects. "What'd he say?"

"There were twenty-one triad troops here, including their Red Poles. Or at least there were the last time he checked.

"He was with the Chui Chao. Those gunshots we heard was his clan attacking troops of the other triad fighters," Collins replied.

"Did he say anything about the PRA soldiers from Yunnan Province?"

"Thirty of them flew in with General Lu. They're guarding the compound and the house. The general went out a while ago. But before he left he ordered squads of his men to constantly check the area for intruders and kill any they encountered. Especially some American who thinks he's bulletproof."

Bolan now knew that he wasn't just the target for triad hit men. The general had just moved him up in stature to "personal enemy number one."

"Did he say anything about the senator?"

Collins nodded. "Firestone is back at his hotel. Some of the Chui Chao were supposed to go there after the battle and make sure he doesn't leave Thailand alive."

"Is the CIA still guarding him?"

"As far as I know," the DEA man replied.

"We've got to find a telephone and alert them."

"The Chui Chao must have lost a lot of their manpower in the war we saw coming here," Collins reminded him.

"Not their leaders. It's up to us." He remembered something. "By the way, what did you do with the man you captured?"

Collins's face twisted into a smile.

"He won't bother us."

Bolan glanced at the expression on the DEA man's face. He looked like an avenging angel.

The Executioner didn't bother asking the government agent what he meant. He already knew.

Bolan did some estimating. There were more than forty armed men ready to blast him out of existence. Too many to kill in direct battle, and he had a senator to keep alive.

CLUSTERING INTO SQUADS, the PRA soldiers gripped their automatic rifles and searched the immediate area for intruders. A side door opened, and another half-dozen armed men poured into the night, led by a uniformed lieutenant, and pumped for combat.

The Executioner didn't make them wait. A high-explosive grenade fell into their midst. Before they could escape, the bomb exploded, killing four of the soldiers.

"The Thai military police are attacking," the lieutenant shouted in terror. "Take cover."

Wave after wave of lead rained on the troops from two directions. Each round unleashed by the Executioner and DEA agent tore into a body.

The battle was becoming a rout. The remaining soldiers tried to escape over the compound walls. Their bodies crackled with electricity as they made contact with the high-voltage wires reinforcing the tall wall.

One of the men ran back into the building and shut off the line that fed electricity to the wall. Bodies that had been glued to the metal of the barrier were now freed to fall back to the ground.

After Bolan and the DEA man left the compound, almost a dozen did.

CHAPTER THIRTY-ONE

"It is getting late. It is time we returned to the general's house," Cheng Ah Kuo said to his Incense Master and started to rise from his chair. The head of the 14K felt uneasy, as if he sensed something was wrong. The sooner he left the Chui Chao Elder Brother's hotel suite, the safer he would feel.

The godfather of the Yi Kwah Tao agreed with him. Tan Suan Chi started to stand. But looking as portly as statues of the Lord Buddha he was said to resemble, he had to force his wide frame free of the armrests.

He gestured to his Incense Master to get ready.

"An interesting proposal, Sun Jee, but one that must be weighed very carefully,"

The 14K Elder Brother started to walk toward the front door of the hotel suite, then stopped to make an observation.

"If the general were dead, who would take his place? And how cooperative would he be?"

Sun Jee stood, signaling Luk Sang to do the same.

"Good questions, brothers. Unfortunately, none of you will be here to hear the answers."

The Chui Chao Incense Master yanked a 9 mm micro-Uzi machine pistol from under his jacket.

Facing the leaders of the other triads, he pulled back gently on the trigger before the rival leaders could retrieve their weapons.

The portly godfather of the Yi Kwah Tao looked stunned as high-powered rounds penetrated his breastbone and robbed him of life. His Incense Master had gotten his hand on the 9 mm Smith & Wesson 459 when lead zingers tore a large hole in his intestines.

The Yi Kwah Tao head ignored his age and raced for the front door. He managed to get a hand on the knob before Sun Jee stopped him with three rounds to the spine.

Chan Tse Chao revealed the Skorpion SMG he had worn beneath his casual cotton jacket. Teeth in a tight smile of hatred, the Incense Master shoved the auto at Sun Jee and started to pull the trigger.

Luk Sang stopped the rival Incense Master's movement with a rising corkscrew burst that shredded the 14K official's torso.

Glancing at the four bodies saturating the rugs with blood, the Red Pole, Chan Tse Chao, was pleased that he hadn't forgotten his combat skills.

The Incense Master opened the door of the suite.

"Time we leave, Master," he said, suddenly sounding humble.

The aged godfather held a .45 ACP Colt Commander in his left hand, while he knelt and checked the four bodies for signs of life. Satisfied they were really dead, he stared at the silk jacket he wore, then turned to Luk Sang.

"Next time," he admonished the younger man, "be more careful. Cleaning a fine jacket like the one I am wearing is very expensive."

THE SHOTS BROUGHT two of the four CIA agents guarding the senator on the run. Mini-Uzis in hand, they turned the corner and saw two Asians, one a stooped and gray-haired man and the other younger, well-dressed.

"The gunshots," one of them yelled. "Did you hear where they came from?"

The younger man turned to face the Americans. The micro-Uzi submachine gun in his hand moved smoothly across the midsections of the CIA men, spitting flame. Both fell in pools of their own blood.

A third American turned the corner, mini-Uzi in hand, and ground his heels into the carpet. Swinging his SMG into position, Rockne Horne yelled, "Hands up!"

Luk Sang ignored the order and emptied the clip in his micro-Uzi into the face of the attacker.

Still in motion, the CIA official looked stunned, as if he couldn't believe what had just happened. Then he collapsed in a heap.

JOE COLLINS POINTED to the Mercedes-Benz parked outside the hotel.

"Are you sure the car belongs to Sun Jee?"

"I know the driver. His name is Cheng Chi-Li, the chief enforcer for the Bangkok branch of the Chui Chao."

The DEA man pointed to two other men loitering at opposite sides of the parking lot.

"Those two work for the 14K and Yi Kwah Tao."

The Executioner waited until the Chui Chao driver went inside the hotel, then watched as the other men followed.

Reaching into his bag, he took out three small rectangles of C-4, detonators and triggering devices.

"Keep me covered," he said, as he got out of the British-made vehicle and moved quickly to the Mercedes.

Sliding under the front of the luxury car, he tinkered with wires and cables, then affixed the plastic explosive under the driver's seat. He repeated the operation on each of the other cars Collins had identified as belonging to the triads.

As he pulled himself out from under the third vehicle, he heard a gunshot from inside the hotel. Jumping to his feet, he grabbed the Beretta 93-R and signaled Collins to follow him, then rushed inside.

Racing to the second floor, he shoved the fire door open and ran into the corridor. Three bodies lay on the bloodstained carpet. The stench of cordite poured out of an open door. He started to run to it, when he heard an angry voice shout.

"Drop that gun," a hard voice called.

Collins stepped between Bolan and the other man. "It's okay, Carl," he shouted. "He's with us."

Begrudgingly, the man lowered his weapon and held out his hand. Bolan shook it.

"Carl Madison," the CIA man said, introducing himself.

Bolan didn't respond. Instead he asked, "What's going on?"

"Somebody took out Horne and two men we imported from Rangoon. At first I thought they were after the senator. Then I looked in there," he added, pointing to the open door.

Bolan led the way into the room.

Walls, furniture and carpets were saturated with blood and bloody body parts.

Collins forced himself to control his stomach as he studied the four dead.

"I know them," he said in a hushed tone, as he continued to stare at the bodies. "The heads of two of the biggest triads in Bangkok and their backup men. They both do...did business with General Lu."

Bolan hurried to the windows that faced the parking lot. As he, Collins and the CIA agent watched, a well-dressed Asian greeted two men who ran from the hotel.

"There they are," the DEA man shouted, pointing to the men.

The three got into the Mercedes and waited for the driver to start the engine.

Car and human body parts flew in every direction as the German-built car exploded with a clap of ear-piercing thunder. Shredded metal parts struck the hotel wall and nearby cars.

At almost the same instant, the other two drivers rushed out of the hotel and jumped into their vehicles. A pair of two explosions shattered the air. Nearby buildings shivered when shock waves from the planted plastic explosives raced past them.

The paved lot shattered, leaving only a crater, which swallowed several parked vehicles.

"Good Lord," the CIA man gasped at the sight of the instant holocaust.

When Collins finally calmed down, he turned to Bolan and asked, "What now?"

"Get the senator out of here and on a plane home before the drug bosses regroup and go after him."

The DEA agent whispered something to the CIA field man. Almost instantly, the agent got on the telephone and started to make calls.

Collins turned to Bolan. "What's our next move?"

"I get back to the general's compound and take care of business there. You stick with Firestone and make sure he gets out of Thailand in one piece."

"The CIA can handle that," the DEA field man insisted. Then added, "Like it or not, we're a team until this is over."

Bolan looked at the determined expression on Collins's face.

He didn't like it, but he was stuck with the DEA agent until the last round was fired.

FORMER CAPTAIN Tremenko gathered the ex-Spetsnaz commandos in a circle behind the recently landed Mi-24 to review the mission.

"In that house," he said, pointing to the villa in the distance, "is an American politician who is representing his government in making a deal with the warlord who controls the poppy fields of the Golden Triangle. Your job is to eliminate the politician and the general—and any of the general's trained troops who try to get in your way..."

One of the ex-Spetsnaz—a native of Chechnya—started to laugh.

Annoyed at the interruption, Tremenko glared at him and asked, "What is so funny, Kamil?"

"Sorry, Captain. But the idea you could train these Asian bastards how to fight struck my funny bone."

"Perhaps we should take their soldiers back with us and put them on exhibit in the Moscow zoo," one of the other commandos cracked, grinning.

"Do not treat them as anything less than expert killers," General Chernov warned, as he joined the conference. "Remember what the Asian bastards did to us in Afghanistan. We will treat this as we do any mission. We move in, we destroy, we kill and we move out. Understood?"

Suddenly quieted by his somber tone, the commandos nodded.

CHERNOV WATCHED his men get ready for the mission. Donning dark fatigues, they covered their faces with camouflage cosmetics, then started to check their weapons and ammo supplies.

"With the fighting between the triads that we saw from the air, we should have no interference in killing the general, the American politician and that mercenary."

Tremenko could sense that the general had something else on his mind. He waited until Chernov spoke again.

"I am very disappointed in Borodin's failing to fulfill his contract," Chernov commented. "For all we know, the American mercenary may even be here right now.

"Borodin won't mess up any more assignments," Tremenko promised. "Not when I'm done with him."

The former general understood. Borodin—or whatever he now called himself—hadn't killed the American mercenary as promised. But had kept the money Chernov had given him.

It was an obvious violation of ethics, even in the killing trade.

"Maybe we should let it go…for now. After all, there is a business waiting to be run back in Russia."

The Karin army colonel leaned out of the open

door of the Hind. "Somebody is trying to reach you," he shouted to Chernov.

The Russian drug syndicate boss climbed the steps and picked up the microphone. He knew who was calling. The Russian "attaché" in Rangoon, looking to squeeze money out of him for some more useless information.

"This is Maracel," the voice said.

Chernov was surprised. He would have thought the former Soviet Intelligence operative would have found a place to hide until he felt it was safe to surface again.

"Yes?"

"The triad chiefs you are hunting are dead," the freelancer reported.

The Russian wondered what kind of game Borodin was playing. "How do you know this?"

"Contacts. They were killed in and around the Dusit Inn less than an hour ago."

"You are confident the information is correct?"

"Yes, General. My sources are impeccable," the freelancer replied.

"Their troops are still here."

"Without their leaders, they'll be running back to Bangkok as fast as they can."

"What about the American politician and this General Lu?"

"Sorry. No information on them."

"Anything on the American mercenary?"

"Only that he seems to thrive on battle. In ancient times they would have called Belasko a berserker."

"Never mind that," Chernov snapped. "Keep me informed if you learn anything more."

HE REPEATED the freelance intelligence operative's information to Tremenko.

"Maybe Borodin is trying to earn the money you gave him. My question is, do we abandon the mission and go home, General?"

Chernov shook his head.

"There is a good chance the general and the American politician are still in the house. We get rid of both of them."

The Russian had worked out a combat strategy, and he shared it with his aide.

"There will be no unnecessary contact with the street gangsters who work for these Chinese drug bosses."

Tremenko nodded. "Anything else, General?"

"I will stay here with six of the men to guard the pilots and the Karin army colonel so they don't decide to take off and leave us here.

"The rest of the men go with you. And I want them ready for combat if the triad assassins try to attack."

"How soon, General?"

"Now, Oskar, now," Chernov snapped, impatient.

USING THE COVER of night, the Russians moved past the triad dormitory structures.

The air around the small buildings was drenched with the stench of the freshly dead. More than a dozen bodies were scattered in heaps, like broken mannequins from a store window. Shattered heads, some still attached to bodies, were everywhere. So were puddles of thick red fluid and shreds of skin and tissue.

One of the ex-commandos turned his head away and vomited. Others stopped and stared at the broken corpses.

One of the ex-sergeants moved to Tremenko's side.

"Who would have wanted them dead?"

The former captain shook his head. Like everything he had encountered on the mission, it made no sense.

A commando ran up and tapped Tremenko on the shoulder.

"We found one of them alive," he reported.

The former captain followed the ex-Spetsnaz to a dying youth.

"Who did this to you?"

The triad soldier didn't seem to understand.

"Get Colonel Ne Win over here," Tremenko ordered.

NE WIN KNELT, trying to avoid soaking his knees in blood, and repeated the question.

The young triad shook his head, but Ne Win persisted.

"I can make your dying easier," he offered.

A long moment of silence.

"Chui Chao," the youngster gasped in a Chinese dialect. "Broke the pledge. Triads do not attack one another."

Colonel Ne Win translated the triad fighter's words for the Russians.

"Ask him why," Tremenko ordered.

The Karin army officer turned back to the young foot soldier to translate the question, but it was too late.

Death had come before the next question.

Chernov's aide sent the Karin officer back to the helicopter to tell the general what they had learned, then resumed the mission.

A half-dozen of the elite Russian commandos cradling Skorpion SMGs in their arms followed.

Combat blade in hand, Tremenko was as silent as a cat as he slipped up behind the nearest of the guards at the main gate.

In one swift motion, the ex-captain slit the throat of one of the pair of PRA soldiers guarding the doors that led into the villa. Then moving quickly, Tremenko wrapped his thick arm around the neck of the second soldier and twisted the man's neck until he heard the bone snap. He then let the limp body slide to the ground.

He signaled to the front pair of commandos.

"Get rid of these so nobody sees their bodies."

NE WIN'S REPORT only confused the former general. He had never heard of triads warring with one another. He wondered if the Golden Triangle warlord was behind the killings.

Or was it the American?

Chernov paced back and forth thinking about the American mercenary. The man reminded him of someone other Mafia leaders had encountered.

From what they had told him, Chernov thought Borodin's description of the mercenary was probably accurate. He was a berserker. The former Spetsnaz general could imagine the mercenary in combat, destroying anyone and everyone who got in his way.

Had Belasko left Thailand? That was what worried the Russian leader. What had the man been hired to do? Chernov wondered who Belasko's employer was. The American Mafia? The Turks? The Afghans?

In the end, it didn't matter. The American would have to die.

His concerns were interrupted by the sudden cacophony of gunshots coming from the area around the compound, which was where the general and the American senator were supposed to be meeting.

He pointed to a nervous Spetsnaz sergeant.

"Have two of your men check out the gunfire," he ordered.

Chernov wondered who the troops of the Golden Triangle general were trying to kill. It didn't make sense, but nothing these people did was intelligent.

They owned a perpetual gold mine in the vast poppy crops they grew. More than enough for everyone to profit. America and Europe offered vast markets for their heroin.

But they had to arouse his anger by trying to take over markets that were exclusively his.

A stupid waste of time and lives.

CHAPTER THIRTY-TWO

Bolan led the way around the corner of the wall that surrounded the compound.

"I'll be back. You wait here."

"I'll go with you."

"Collins, stay here and keep an eye out for anyone trying to break in."

"And...?"

The soldier looked at the MAC-10 the DEA operative was gripping. Collins glanced at the weapon and nodded. Bolan didn't have to explain. The DEA man knew what he was expected to do.

As he moved closer to the villa, Bolan saw eight black-clad figures moving toward the main building. Gesturing for Collins to stay back, he moved closer and studied the squad. The hardmen weren't Chinese or Thai. If anything, they looked European. Or Russian. Their movements reminded him of the American Special Forces.

Suddenly he identified them—Spetsnaz, well-trained Russian commandos.

He remembered the Russian general who had offered to hire him. Chernov. Hal Brognola had sent a message that the Russian had headed a battalion of Spetsnaz in Afghanistan.

"Time's up," Bolan growled.

The eight men turned, surprised at the presence of the ominous figure in black. They reached for their side arms, then saw the M-16 A-2 combo in his hands.

Slowly they raised their hands.

"Who are you working for?" Bolan asked in Russian.

The commandos looked at one another, then stared at the intruder, but didn't reply.

"We can do this easy, or we can do this hard," Bolan warned. "Who sent you?"

"This has nothing to do with you," one of the hardmen snapped.

Bolan thought of the American senator.

"Yes, it does," Bolan replied coldly. "So start talking."

The hardman remembered the official line the general had used.

"We are on a mercy mission. To protect our young people from the poison these animals are selling them."

The Executioner thought of the message Brognola had left for him.

"The same garbage you sell them. I think this is about not wanting competition," he growled.

One of the Spetsnaz let his hand drift to the holster

mounted on his web belt. With a sudden movement, the Russian yanked the pistol from its leather case and turned it on Bolan.

Without wasting a motion, the Executioner fed the would-be assailant three high-powered deathseekers.

Blood rushed from the ruptured body, intestines spilling on the ground. With a stunned expression on his face, the commando slid to the ground. The Spetsnaz managed to get off a round before he fell. The projectile skidded fractions of an inch from Bolan's shoulder.

The remaining seven men went for their weapons. There was no time to change the selector switch on the M-16 to bursts. Bolan washed the trio on the left with a wall of lead. Death took them instantly.

The two black-clad commandos on the far right jumped at Bolan, but a pair of shots from behind tore past him and punctured the chests of the two attackers.

One of the Spetsnaz took advantage of the distraction and palmed his 5.45 mm PSM, his forefinger easing back on the sensitive trigger.

As Bolan knew, the small, self-loading pistol had a remarkable penetration capability, easily defeating standard bulletproof vests, and was capable of penetrating more than forty layers of Kevlar at fifteen yards or less.

Bolan dived to the left and out of the path of the rounds the commando unleashed. Then, firing from the ground, the Executioner drilled two hollowpoint bullets into the Russian's face.

With a permanent expression of surprise, the commando spun, propelled by the force of the shots, and slid down the wall to the ground.

Bolan turned. Collins was right behind him, his Colt .45 pistol locked in his right hand.

"I thought I told you to wait," he said.

"I've always been lousy at taking orders," the DEA agent replied.

Bolan looked at the bodies. "Wait here. I'll be right back."

He moved cautiously to a small side door, using the shadows to mask his presence, opened it, then stopped and listened. There was no sound from inside the house. Only the whistling of nocturnal birds disturbed the silence outside.

Still, the soldier wondered how many gunmen were hiding inside. It made no difference to him whether they were PRA soldiers, triad thugs or Russian commandos. They all had the same thing in mind.

Death.

His, among others.

Easing a pair of HE grenades from his combat harness, he pulled their pins and counted to five, then tossed the bombs in a high pass inside the door and flattened himself against the stone wall.

The exploding fragments shredded four Russians hiding inside and shot heated darts of shrapnel into three more. Their screams shattered the still night, and confusion and panic permeated the area.

Soldiers on guard duty loitering outside the compound rushed toward the explosions, firing their weapons at every moving shadow. Four uniformed troopers fell to the waves of lead sprayed by their own men.

Bolan could see Collins cutting loose in long bursts. From the expression on the DEA agent's face, the Executioner knew that each killing round was a memorial candle to the man's dead family.

The big American crouched and moved swiftly to the nearest machine-gun site. Pulling the pin on a delay fragmentation grenade, he lobbed the deadly egg like a softball. Exploding as it made contact, the missile dismembered the body of the soldier who had sat behind the 7.62 mm RPK light machine gun.

Bolan started to move toward the other manned emplacement, then saw Collins walk up behind the machine gunner and slit the man's throat. Even in the darkness, Bolan could see the expression of revenge on the DEA operative's face.

The Executioner turned away from the image of Collins and his need to get even for the death of his family. He had to pay attention to the action around him, if they were going to come out of this alive.

Something was wrong, and what it was became apparent. Two Russians had moved out from behind the main house, and one of them had a long tube propped against his shoulder—an RPG-16, the Russians' portable rocket launcher.

The Spetsnaz fired the weapon and unleashed a PG-7M HEAT rocket. With a muzzle velocity of 120 meters per second, the 2.25 kilogram missile was capable of penetrating the walls of Lu's villa.

As the launcher released the rocket, Bolan yelled, "Down!"

The hastily fired HEAT rocket missed the building and dug through a banyan tree, setting the forest around it on fire.

Bolan knew the two of them were dead if he didn't take the initiative. Dropping the canvas bag, he transferred the M-16 combo from his shoulder to his hands.

Turning to face the Russian team, he stunned them momentarily by racing right at their weapons. Before they could respond, the Executioner sprayed the area in front of him with a sustained burst.

A pair of body shredders had chewed up the face of the rocket launcher. The man with him dropped his Skorpion SMG and tried, unsuccessfully, to stop his intestines from escaping through the cavity Bolan's rounds had carved.

By the time the Executioner reached the pair, both had fallen to the ground. Cautiously, he knelt and checked both bodies, his M-16 combo poised ready to respond if either was faking. They weren't. Both were dead.

He got to his feet and walked back to the bushes where Collins was waiting.

The DEA man pointed to the M-16 combo slung on Bolan's shoulder. "How come you threw the grenades instead of using the launcher?"

"No time to load them," Bolan explained, then warned, "Keep your eyes open. We're far from finished."

As if to reinforce his comment, a submachine gun started to chatter from the area of the small structures outside the compound. Other submachine guns returned fire.

Bolan climbed the narrow steps to the machine-gun tower. A large-scale battle had begun. Triad fought triad with whatever weapons they'd had handy, and took on the PRA troops when the soldiers got in their way.

He remembered the vow men joining a triad took—not to attack members of another triad, no matter what their personal feelings. The honor of their clan was at stake. Like most Mafia types, however, the triad thugs obviously followed the rules only when they suited their cause.

Soon the area shook with the staccato sounds of weapons being fired. Screams of pain and loud cursing boomed across the open fields. Uniformed soldiers forced into the battle were being torn apart by ricocheting lead from triad weapons.

Collins crawled to Bolan's side and looked up.

"Did we start all that?"

"No. The triad hit men seem to be trying to eliminate each other," the Executioner replied quietly. "They've been waiting a long time for some excuse to kill the competition."

The DEA man nodded. "Ever since General Lu made them share distribution rights."

"With any luck," the Executioner replied, nodding, "there won't be anybody to distribute the poison—at least not for a while."

"Are we going to help the odds?"

"That's not the main reason I'm here," Bolan replied.

Signaling the DEA operative to wait, the soldier began his surveillance of the area. He could see nothing that resembled a living human being. Finally, he was satisfied that nobody was waiting in hiding—at least outside. He waved for Collins to join him.

"Stay behind me," he said quietly when the man joined him.

Switching to the M-16 combo, Bolan eased his way to the building. He wore the web belt around his waist, festooned with an array of grenades. The canvas carryall was slung over a shoulder, and under his jacket was the Beretta, fully loaded and ready for war.

He could hear Collins's heavy breathing as the agent stayed close to him.

"Wait here."

The Executioner went ahead alone. When he reached the building, he ducked beneath the nearest window and lifted his head briefly so he could peer inside.

The living room was empty. He moved from window to window, risking a quick look.

As far as he could determine, none of the protection forces were in the building.

He turned to gesture for the DEA agent to join him, but Collins wasn't behind him. Instead, there was a human form lying prone on the ground. Even in the dark, he could see Collins's light-colored hair. Kneeling, he felt the pulse in the DEA agent's neck. He wasn't dead, but a large red patch covered the right side of his shirt. Collins had taken a lot of lead.

The soldier gently touched the other man's shoulder. Suddenly, a muzzle stared at him.

"Die—" the DEA man started to yell as he tried to sit up. Bolan clamped his hand over Collins's mouth.

"It's me."

Collins let his head fall back.

"I screwed up," he moaned. "One of them got behind me. But I took care of him."

"You'd better wait here," Bolan warned.

"No." The word came out as a statement of fact.

Collins moved to his side, his finger resting against the trigger of the MAC-10 SMG in his hands.

"Do we go inside?"

Bolan shook his head. "Not we. Me."

The Executioner looked at the shirt covering the

DEA man's wound. The bleeding had slowed, but hadn't stopped.

"You stay here and try to stop the bleeding."

Something was wrong. He wasn't sure what yet, but all his survival instincts warned him to be careful.

As Bolan headed out, the DEA agent followed behind him.

The blond man looked around. "Nothing in here. No men, no equipment."

"Something is definitely wrong," Bolan agreed. "They must have known we were coming."

As Collins grabbed for the doorknob, the Executioner pulled his arm away.

"Remember your apartment?"

Shivering in the night air, the DEA man nodded.

"First, we make sure it's safe."

The soldier led the way outside, stopped at a large tree forty yards from the front door and pulled one of the frag grenades from his belt. Then he yanked the pin and spiraled the bomb like a football at the front door.

He pulled Collins to the ground with him as the grenade exploded. The violent explosion blew the thick wooden front door off its hinges and onto the ground. Shock waves slapped at the two men.

"Semtex, probably," Bolan commented. "Not very original, but it can be effective."

"Then they are all gone from here," Collins said with frustration.

"Check around outside. See if you can find fresh tracks of vehicles driving away from here."

Collins was about to protest, but Bolan's hard stare stopped him. He nodded instead and moved toward the forest.

The Executioner stopped at the doorway, listened for a moment, then sprayed the inside with a burst of rounds. A huge Asian wearing the stripes of a sergeant tumbled to the ground, clutching an AK-47 assault rifle in his left hand. Blood from his ruptured neck splattered his shirtfront and drenched his weapon.

Two more men leaped out of hiding, wildly waving AK-47s, as they rushed to the front door.

There was no time to develop a battle strategy. Bolan spun and emptied the M-16's clip at the pair.

At the rear entrance to the front room, a face appeared belonging to a thin man with a permanent smirk and an AK-47.

He saw the bodies on the floor, looked at the face of the man they'd been sent to kill and aimed the Russian assault rifle at the Executioner.

Someone fired a pair of rounds from behind Bolan, which tore the thug's chest open. As the Russian commando fell backward, the Executioner turned and saw Collins, clutching the MAC-10.

"There were car tracks. But they were all coming in, not going out."

As he rammed a fresh clip into the M-16, Bolan nodded.

"I'm not sure we've got them all. There's still the rest of the house."

"I'll check around in the back," the DEA man announced, and vanished.

The soldier moved into the foyer. A short barrage of flaming ammo greeted his entrance. Plunging into a diving shoulder roll, the Executioner came up firing, sweeping his M-16 in an arc, left to right and back again. Two of the attackers stumbled as if over invisible wires, sprawling into awkward poses in death. The others scattered, fanning out, falling to the ground. Within a heartbeat, they returned fire again.

Bolan repeated his evasive maneuver—rolling, rising and firing, again and again, matching the hostile fire with calculated bursts. Each time he fired, fewer weapons answered. Finally, there was no one left alive to reply.

Beyond the outer wall of the compound, Bolan could see a few of the Russian commandos running toward the forested area. There was no point chasing them and running into what might be a trap.

Instead he cautiously crossed to where the prostrate bodies were huddled. Having faced hostiles who pretended to be dead before, the Executioner transferred the M-16 to his left hand and pulled the silenced 9 mm Beretta from its holster. He gripped the weapon, a finger inside the trigger guard, holding it in front of him, ready to dispense instant death to any pretenders.

CHAPTER THIRTY-THREE

A vintage military-style jeep, still covered with the markings of the Vietnam War, was parked against the wall surrounding the compound. One of the soldiers Lu had brought with him from his base in Yunnan Province stood guard near it.

Bolan signaled the DEA agent to wait, then froze until the PRA soldier turned his back on him and moved swiftly. Instantly, the combat blade left its sleeve sheath and was in the Executioner's hand.

Wrapping his left forearm around the neck of the surprised guard, Bolan severed the man's carotid artery, then let the suddenly limp form slide to the ground.

Bolan grabbed his canvas carryall, then turned and signaled Collins to get into the jeep.

The keys were still in the ignition. Bolan started the engine.

"Where next?"

Collins was pale, which worried Bolan. But there was also a mission to complete.

Bolan looked at the DEA man. His workshirt was

drenched in blood. There was a large hole in it, in the area where flesh met intestines.

"I can run you over to one of the hospitals in Chiang Mai," the soldier offered.

Collins waved away the offer. "I don't think the lead hit anything vital."

"Bleeding to death is serious."

"Hey, I'm the trained medical professional. I'm not going to bleed to death."

Reluctantly, the Executioner decided the mission came first. There was a lot left to do, and not much time remained.

The leaders of the triad drug distributors were dead. Bolan knew replacements would come into power, but at least they had been slowed for a year or two.

The head of the viper was still alive, General Lu, and he was probably going after Senator Firestone.

It was time to take the war to him.

"You okay to drive?"

Collins nodded. The two men switched places, and the DEA agent pushed down on the gas pedal.

As they drove on the dirt road, Bolan listened for any sounds that would signal the presence of an enemy.

Except for the sounds of birds and animals calling to their species, he heard nothing.

He knew—not guessed or feared—that somebody was waiting for the right moment to strike.

A soft sound came from behind the trees. Bolan

turned to see where the sound came from and saw a half-dozen armed men running toward him, screaming guttural curses in Chinese. He could see the blood lust in their expressions as they charged recklessly, ignoring the large puddles of water as they crossed the field from the jungle several hundred yards away. The AK-47s they carried sprayed a wall of lead in his direction.

These weren't well-trained fighters, or they would have held their fire until they were closer so that their rounds wouldn't fall short of their target.

"Out!" he shouted.

Ignoring his wounds, the DEA man dived from the jeep, not wasting time to put the gears in neutral. The surplus military vehicle ran into a wide banyan tree with resounding force.

Quickly, Bolan led the way into the forest. It was a poor shield. Trees were no protection against high-powered ammunition. But at least they would provide them temporary cover until he could calculate the next move.

Collins pointed to one of the attackers.

"Chan Tse Chao," he whispered. "Second in command of the Chui Chao thugs. Looks like he's planning to wipe out the other triad hoods."

Bolan nodded. "Wait here."

Like a wraith, the Executioner streaked toward the startled triad thugs, pitching an M-40 grenade, then switched to a two-handed grip on the M-16 combo.

As the bomb ripped the center flank of the enemy,

shrill cries of agony shattered the stillness of the night. The handful of shadows started to vanish behind trees.

Someone hollered an order in Cantonese. The other men stopped and turned back.

Bolan could count four still living. Obedience rather than combat skill seemed to spark their willingness to risk their lives. The soldier thought they were local teenagers, still in training and pressed into service at the last minute.

The first of the group charged at Bolan in a burst of bravado, accompanied by loud incoherent shouting.

Bolan set his M-16 on burst mode, tracked the movement of the lead attacker and fired. As he had intended, the shots chewed the gunner to shreds. His head burst open like a ripe fruit. The Executioner turned to face another charging hardman.

Firing as he raced at the American, another killer-in-training emptied the clip of his Chinese-manufactured assault rifle. Bolan dived to the ground and rolled out of the path of the rounds, firing as he did.

The burst drilled into the attacker's neck, almost severing his head from his shoulders.

Dropping his rifle, the youth pressed his hand against the wound and tried to keep his head attached. Blood poured down the dying youth's shirt and painted the torn fabric red. He fell to the ground and let what was left of his life run down his side and leg onto the leaf-cushioned ground.

The two surviving gunners fled back into the forest.

As he got to his feet and moved behind a thicket to check the burning sensation in his right shoulder, Bolan realized he hadn't seen Collins in the past few minutes.

Had the DEA man been hit again? There was no way to find out until he took out the rest of the defense forces.

His shoulder began to ache, and the soldier glanced at it. The collar of his blacksuit had been tattered by a bullet, and a red patch began to stain the fabric.

The soft sounds of movement from behind the thick underbrush caught his attention. He'd have to think about Collins later.

The bushes exploded as the triad squad attempted an ambush, spraying 7.62 mm death toward Bolan as they rushed forward.

The Executioner had moved to the right in anticipation of the attack, then hunched to wait until the four came closer. Jumping to his feet, M-16 combo gripped in both hands, Bolan didn't waste time sighting the carbine. At the twenty yards that separated the four triad chargers from him, he knew he didn't have time to carefully sight the assault weapon. He set the rifle on automatic and, firing the powerhouse rounds from the hip, turned the four into lifeless bags of bleeding skin and shattered bones in less than five seconds.

Bolan hurried forward, kicked the weapons away from the bodies, knelt and felt the neck artery of each before being satisfied that they were truly dead.

Behind the brush, Bolan heard the sounds of a coughing engine coming closer. Sprinting through the undergrowth, he saw a jeep and two People's Revolutionary Army soldiers studying the bodies of the four men he'd killed.

The tall man in the passenger seat reached for a shortwave radio mike mounted on the dashboard. Bolan suspected he was going to call for backup.

In an easy motion, the Executioner raised the M-16 combo to his shoulder and carefully lined up through the sight of the M-203 launcher. Fifty yards separated Bolan from the vehicle. In a matter of minutes, help would be on the way.

Releasing the delay frag grenade, Bolan dropped to the ground, let the combo fall from his hands and covered his head with his arms.

He could hear the ear-shattering explosion as the grenade met the jeep, and the ammo and grenades in it, and consumed them in a hurricane-force hail of shredded metal. Waiting to let the shrapnel settle to the ground, Bolan got to his feet and looked at where the vehicle had been standing.

Only the car's frame was intact. The other parts had scattered in different directions. Bolan doubted the PRA soldier had had time to contact his command center before he was chewed up by the hurtling metal shards.

Cautiously searching the area, the Executioner found the jeep driver's body still intact. Soft moans struggled from the shattered voice box. The scorched face turned slowly in Bolan's direction.

"Please help me."

Bolan eased the Beretta 93-R from the shoulder rig and knelt beside the dying man.

"Please help me," the tortured voice repeated.

"I will," Bolan promised, then placed the handgun against the temple of the man and pulled the trigger.

He stood and went to search for Collins.

The sandy-haired man was sitting on the ground, his back against a tree, staring at the body of a freshly dead soldier. He looked up as Bolan approached and smiled weakly. "I figured I might as well make myself useful," he said, as he changed magazines in his Ingram.

Forcing himself to his feet, Collins tried not to wince.

"What's our next stop?"

CHAPTER THIRTY-FOUR

The former Russian general kept looking over his shoulder as if he expected someone he didn't want to see to be there. Tremenko noticed Chernov's nervousness.

"Is something wrong, General?"

"No," the Russian Mafia boss replied hastily, as they boarded the lead helicopter.

"What about the men, General? Should we wait and see how many more make it back to the helicopters?"

"They knew the risk. We can always recruit more men, Captain. That is the reality of life."

Tremenko made no comment.

"I'll tell you this," Chernov stated once they boarded the Mi-24. "If you want something done properly, you have to do it yourself."

CHERNOV STUDIED the men in the military vehicle traveling along the dirt road. Borrowing a pair of binoculars, he made a closer examination of the two men. One of them was the American mercenary he had met with in Bangkok.

The former general would have liked to find out for whom Belasko worked, but he'd have to forego that information.

He moved to a position directly behind the pilot. Then pointing to the vehicle moving on the ground, ordered him to follow.

"Oskar," he said, turning to his aide, "it is time to get rid of them."

The captain nodded and went back to where the remainder of the Spetsnaz commandos were sitting.

"Which of you is the most expert at firing a HEAT missile?"

All six of the men raised their hands.

"To miss is to forfeit your life," Tremenko warned.

Five hands moved back to laps. Only one of the ex-soldiers kept his hand raised.

"Your name?"

"Katchenkov, sir. Mischa Katchenkov."

"You have fired the HEAT missile before?"

"Many times in Afghanistan."

"With successful results?"

"Always, sir. I am considered an expert on missiles."

"Good. Then move to the front of the helicopter and show me," Tremenko ordered.

When they got behind the general, Tremenko

pointed through the windshield to the moving vehicle on the ground.

"You can hit that?"

"Like shooting wolves from the air," the commando bragged.

Tremenko grinned, then turned to Chernov for approval.

The general nodded.

BOLAN HEARD the faint rotor throbs coming from above. A chopper.

From the vague outline, the helicopter was a Russian Hind—an Mi-24 warship. There was a second one in the sky, not far behind it.

"We've got company," he told the DEA man.

Collins glanced up and saw the approaching chopper.

"Who's in that?"

"Chernov is my bet," Bolan replied. "Let's not make it easy for them."

The DEA agent nodded. He twisted the wheel and pulled the transport off the roadway. The military vehicle bumped across the open field, heading for the forest in the distance.

When they reached a dirt intersection, Collins turned the wheel sharply and accelerated.

The noisy chopper closed the distance to overfly the moving car, banking to hover about sixty yards overhead.

The hovering warship continued to track the military transport for several more minutes.

Bolan knew that the men in the Hind would take some sort of action soon unless he seized the initiative. Loading a high explosive grenade into the M-203 launcher slung under the M-16, he twisted into a low crouch as he swung the weapon skyward, tracking the chopper.

The helicopter was practically on top of them, the throbbing of its rotors causing him to blink rapidly.

He saw one of the crew aboard the chopper leaning well out from the aircraft as the pilot maintained his holding position above and just off to the vehicle's left. There was a rocket launcher in the man's hand—an RPG-16, he guessed. The rocket man was trying to lock on to the erratic path of the military vehicle.

Bolan registered one split-second impression of eyes and mouths widening inside the chopper, reacting when they saw his quick turning of the M-16 combo. The pilot worked his stick into an evasive maneuver. The big bird wobbled slightly and started to bank up and away.

But it was too late.

Bolan released the HE grenade. The studded oblong bomb skidded along the skin of the chopper and detonated when it made contact with the Mi-24's fuel tanks.

The eruption started inside the tanks and spread

quickly over the entire exterior of the Russian warship.

"Keep weaving," Bolan shouted, as the rotor tore away from the frame of the Hind.

Collins began a series of figure-eight half turns.

Adjusting to the weaving motion of the military vehicle, Bolan emptied the rounds of his assault rifle at the hole in the melted Plexiglas window. The soldier holding the rocket launcher screamed as several shots tore into his face.

The shock waves from the exploding Mi-24 almost shoved the racing vehicle off the dirt road. Bolan grabbed on to the door frame as Collins dodged flaming debris from the exploding chopper.

A ball of flame scorched the trees. The charred remains of the helicopter dropped into a nearby wooded area, vanishing into the thick brush as the flames spurted like a volcano for a moment, then died.

Looking at the remaining Hind in the distant sky, Bolan knew there was always the possibility that it would also attack. He tore open his canvas bag and retrieved the second rocket launcher. Inserting a HEAT rocket, the Executioner sighted on the distant Mi-24 and waited for it to come into range.

Suddenly, the second Mi-24 changed direction and flew toward the Myanmar border.

CHAPTER THIRTY-FIVE

Bolan had Collins turn the jeep and return to the villa. From the distance they could hear the remnants of battle.

They drew closer, and tightening his grip on the micro-Uzi he had confiscated, Bolan could see the dead and wounded strewed on the ground outside the compound wall.

What was left of the triad attackers was rushing the front entrance of the villa. The sound of the vehicle he was driving attracted their attention. They turned the carbines they were holding in his direction.

One of them held up a sheet of paper and shouted something to the others. Bolan suspected it was the photo with the reward offer the Dragon Lady had distributed in Bangkok.

As the triad thugs charged the military transport, Bolan slowed the vehicle and ordered the DEA operative out. Gripping the MAC-10, Collins stumbled, then got up and plunged into the underbrush.

Before the lead they started to unleash could reach

him, Bolan plunged into a diving shoulder roll from the moving vehicle.

As he turned, he swung the Uzi into target acquisition, firing at the charging men.

Bodies fell, shoved to one side by the impact of the Uzi burst. Those behind them trampled the prostrate corpses in their attempts to capture Bolan, and the prize money attached to his killing.

Seven men charged. The Executioner fired seven times, and seven men died.

FROM THE EDGE of the forest, Chan Tse Chao had watched the slaughter silently, only his dark eyes revealing the fury he felt at the incompetence of the men the Red Pole had put under his command. He feared Chen Chi Li's reaction when he learned how badly the Chui Chao fighters had performed.

"Let's take the American alive. We can turn him over to the Red Pole for questioning," the street soldier at his side said, showing him the AK-47 he was holding. "This should convince him."

Checking the clip of the Czech-made 9 mm Skorpion SMG, Chan nodded his approval of the attack and started to ease his way across the field back to the large villa.

The tall grass made it difficult to see clearly. The triad enforcer depended on his memory of how the area was laid out to guide him.

Bolan came up behind him. He had worked his way around the wooded area.

"Drop the gun," he snapped, gripping the stubby Uzi in his right hand.

The small man in fatigues reacted to the command with an ill-aimed burst of rounds. None hit the warrior, but they drilled into several teak trees.

Bolan cut down the triad hit man with a short burst from the Uzi. Each round chewed its way into the man's chest, carving a path to his heart valve. Then he focused his attention on the man with him.

Without a sound, the small man slid down to the leafy ground and tried to hide in the tall grass.

"Drop the gun," Bolan ordered, looking at the second assailant.

He waited for him to ease his grip, but saw only a cold smile of hate, and watched the man's finger as it began to tighten.

The negotiations were over.

The Executioner punched out a pair of rounds. The first tore into the man's side. Before he could fire back, the second destroyed his stomach.

Blood colored the gunner's fatigues. Despite the pain in his face, he tried to shoot back.

"Don't," Bolan yelled.

Stubbornly, he kept trying.

There wasn't time for pity. The warrior let loose another short burst. The man's head exploded like an overripe melon.

Bolan turned and moved away quickly, but some instinct made him pivot back. There was someone behind him. Another triad soldier. Younger than the other two, but just as deadly.

The fatigue-clad man stood in the clearing pointing an AK-47 at him.

His eyes were filled with hate.

"Drop gun," he spit in English.

Bolan lowered the suppressed Uzi SMG, trying to figure out how to stay alive.

Shots rang out from behind the triad thug. He fell forward, dead.

Bolan didn't have to wait to find out who had fired the shot. Collins was standing there, his side still covered with his own blood, the smell of freshly detonated cordite swirling around him.

The soldier led the way to where they had parked the jeep. His two bags were still on the floor in the back of the military vehicle. Neither Collins nor he said anything as they got into the transport.

Collins saw the grim determination in the soldier's face and slid behind the driver's seat. Bolan looked down at the DEA man's lap. The .45-caliber Colt pistol was resting in it.

"Do you always drive with a loaded weapon in your lap?"

"Only when I'm in a war zone," Collins said bluntly.

Bolan knew he was right. This was a war zone, and he had invited himself to join in the battle.

CLUSTERING INTO SQUADS, the remaining Communist troops gripped their automatic rifles and followed their officers to the compound gates to search for the missing American.

The Executioner didn't make them wait. He had slipped into the courtyard through a side gate. Gripping his M-16/M-203, he fired an HE grenade.

The missile fell into their midst, and before they could escape, the bomb exploded, the shrapnel killing another four soldiers.

"Take cover," one of Lu's junior officers shouted in terror. "Take cover."

Three more HE grenades were launched as quickly as Bolan could load them into the M-203. Waves of superheated metal bits chewed into the already confused soldiers.

Out of missiles, Bolan unleashed rapidly fired high-powered rounds at the PRA soldiers. Following the Executioner's lead, Collins emptied the magazine in his MAC-10 at the enemy.

The battle had become a rout. What remained of Lu's troops and the PRA soldiers shoved the compound doors open and rushed into the night. The Executioner accelerated their race from the area with a spray of well-placed zingers from his M-16. Four more guards fell. No one stopped to help them to their feet or check if they were dead.

RETURNING FROM his meeting with the American senator, the young warlord had told the sergeant who was his driver to drive through the countryside north of Chiang Mai so that he could think through his next moves.

General Lu was depressed. The great plans he had put together were fast fading into daydreams.

The car radio, filled with news of the slayings and car bombings at the Dusit Inn, didn't improve his mood.

His sources of distribution were gone. The triads would find replacements for their leaders, but that would take time—perhaps three or four years before the distribution networks were again fully operational.

The Russians were becoming a threat to his control of the heroin trade. Their production had grown rapidly since the Soviet Union ceased to exist. Now they were second in volume, and hungrily seeking new markets.

The American mercenary had been seen at the Dusit Inn. But whether the person spotted was the supposedly omnipotent mercenary or merely an American vacationer visiting Chiang Mai was not clear.

Lu's biggest concern was the Beijing government. The corrupt ones in the central government wouldn't be satisfied with any explanation he or his connection—the governor of Yunnan Province—could give them.

They wanted money. That was the only acceptable explanation.

Driving up to the compound gates, he viewed the

piles of freshly dead scattered around the fields inside and outside the walls.

He realized he had to come to a decision. And quickly.

Perhaps this was the right time for his mother and him to vanish from Southeast Asia and relocate. There was enough money hidden in bank accounts abroad for them to live like royalty anyplace in the world.

He would discuss it with her as soon as possible.

"Take me to the back entrance," he ordered his driver.

Lu wasn't concerned about the safety of his troops. It was Mai Ling for whom he felt concern.

Grabbing the 7.62 mm Type 54 pistol he wore at his side, he entered the villa. The Chinese copy of the TT-33 Tokarev held an 8-round magazine and was as accurate as the Soviet original.

Signs of a pitched battle fought within the villa were evident everywhere—shattered windows, walls smashed by bullets and explosives, bloodstains on the once-priceless Oriental carpets. Paintings had been torn from the walls and, in some cases, slashed by knife blades.

None of that mattered to Lu, as long as Mai Ling was unharmed.

A number of bodies, some still bleeding, were strewed on the floor. Asian and European corpses lay near each other.

The general glanced at the Caucasian bodies and

knew instinctively that they were some of the Russians he had been warned were coming to Chiang Mai.

Cautiously, he moved up the stairs to Mai Ling's quarters.

FROM THE DARKNESS, Bolan could hear the sounds of firearms and the screams of dying men, as soldier fought soldier in a fear-driven struggle to survive.

"Looks like we really got the bastards," the DEA agent gloated as he joined Bolan.

"We're not there yet," the soldier warned.

As if his words had been prophecy, an armored personnel carrier lumbered out of the woods in front of them.

Bolan recognized it as a Chinese copy of the American jeep. Sitting behind the driver in a small swivel seat, a fatigue-clad PRA soldier squinted carefully through the sight of the 7.62 mm RP-46 machine gun mounted in the rear.

A steady stream of rounds were fired from the mounted machine gun, missing the two attackers by scant inches.

There was too much distance between the armored car and the Executioner for his shots to be effective. He had to get closer.

"Get behind some trees," Bolan ordered.

Then he jumped into the jeep and raced at the armored vehicle, absorbing round after round of lead from the mounted submachine gun.

A second gunman popped up in the rear of the small military vehicle. Bolan recognized the weapon jammed against the second man's shoulder—a 40 mm BG-15 grenade launcher mounted beneath an AK-74 carbine. Loaded and ready to fire was the Russian 7 P-17, an impact HE fragmentation grenade.

Grabbing his bags, he opened his door and threw himself as far from the surplus military vehicle as he could.

The grenade smashed through the front windshield of Bolan's vehicle and tore the interior into shredded remnants. Burning chunks of metal flew in every direction, narrowly missing him.

He lifted his head and saw the gunner refocusing his mounted weapon. Rounds from the machine gun shredded the foliage.

The gunner was getting too accurate, Bolan decided as he slipped behind the trees. He stopped when he had a clear view of the Chinese armored car. Raising the LAW 80 he had selected from his canvas carryall to eye level, he pulled the safety pin. The end caps fell away, and the weapon telescoped another six inches while it armed itself.

Bolan knew he had to move fast and accurately, or he would become bits of memory. He pulled back on the trigger and watched the missile fly from the tube.

The missile exploded with a deafening, thunderous sound, tearing the armored vehicle in two. Molten bits of metal from the warhead and flames shot back at him, scorching trees in their path.

Over the exploding ammo stored in the armored vehicle, Bolan could hear muffled screams as chunks of metal and flame consumed the men in the military transport.

He waited for the intensive heat to dissipate, then worked his way to the wreckage. The charred carcass of what had once been a military officer still held the remains of the Chinese submachine gun he'd been carrying. It was difficult to recognize that the other remains had once been living humans.

Grimly, the Executioner had begun what he suspected was the final battle. The hordes who worked for the Communists and the drug barons had been taught a lesson about killing.

There was one more thing he had to do to complete his mission. Find the Golden Triangle warlord and kill him.

He had searched the grounds for him, then spotted the armored Mercedes-Benz parked at the rear of the main house.

General Lu Shu-Shui was home.

He found Collins leaning against the outer wall of the villa.

"I'll be right back," he promised, then headed inside and climbed the stairs to the second floor. Checking carefully, he looked into each room for the missing drug emperor. The suppressed Beretta 93-R was gripped firmly in his right hand.

All he could find were bodies—triad hardmen intermingled with PRA soldiers and a handful of Russians.

There was one door left to open.

A young uniformed soldier sat on the floor, the head of a dead woman resting on his lap.

Bolan recognized her—Mai Ling.

He looked at the young Asian.

"General Lu Shu-Shui?"

The officer held a Chinese copy of the Tokarev in his right hand.

"You must be Belasko. I was starting to believe you were only a legend," Lu said coldly.

"No, I'm real."

"And dead," the warlord replied, pulling back on the trigger of his pistol.

Bolan had anticipated the action and threw himself into a roll at a right angle, out of the path of the two rounds the general had fired.

Coming up on one knee, Bolan released a pair of rounds from his Beretta at the drug lord.

The first ripped a canyon in Lu's chest, shattering his breastbone. The second channeled its way into his lungs.

The weapon in Lu's hand fell to the floor as he stared at the Executioner.

"Now it is really finished," he gasped. "My mother is dead, and my father has rejected me."

A sad smile covered his face as his eyes became glazed by death.

Bolan looked around the room at the rich trappings. Meaningless. At least to the two who were dead.

Something Lu said puzzled him. Something about his father. It didn't make sense. Who was Lu's father? Suddenly the pieces of the puzzle came together.

He'd have to confirm it, if it was important. He didn't think it was, not anymore.

Senator Firestone had fathered a son.

General Lu Shu-Shui.

The game was over. At least this inning was.

The Executioner knew there would be many more innings that had to be played before the game was won. And the games never ended, it seemed.

He'd have to think about that later. For now there was a DEA agent to get to the hospital, and a plane leaving Thailand he had to catch.

There would be respite from the heroin dealers for a certain time. At least until the Asian and the Russian drug cartels got new masters.

That was enough to be thankful for.

At least for now.

James Axler

OUTLANDERS™

OUTER DARKNESS

Kane and his companions are transported to an alternate reality where the global conflagration didn't happen—and humanity had expelled the Archons from the planet. Things are not as rosy as they may seem, as the Archons return for a final confrontation....

Book #3 in the new Lost Earth Saga, a trilogy that chronicles our heroes' paths through three very different alternative realities...where the struggle against the evil Archons goes on....

An old enemy poses a new threat....

JAMES AXLER

DEATH LANDS®

Gaia's Demise

Ryan Cawdor's old nemesis, Dr. Silas Jamaisvous, is behind a deadly new weapon that uses electromagnetic pulses to control the weather and the gateways, and even disrupts human thinking processes.

As these waves doom psi-sensitive Krysty, Ryan challenges Jamaisvous to a daring showdown for America's survival....

Book 2 in the Baronies Trilogy, three books that chronicle the strange attempts to unify the East Coast baronies—a bid for power in the midst of anarchy....

Shadow THE EXECUTIONER®
as he battles evil for 352 pages of heart-stopping action!

SuperBolan®

#61452	DAY OF THE VULTURE	$5.50 U.S. ☐	$6.50 CAN. ☐
#61453	FLAMES OF WRATH	$5.50 U.S. ☐	$6.50 CAN. ☐
#61454	HIGH AGGRESSION	$5.50 U.S. ☐	$6.50 CAN. ☐
#61455	CODE OF BUSHIDO	$5.50 U.S. ☐	$6.50 CAN. ☐
#61456	TERROR SPIN	$5.50 U.S. ☐	$6.50 CAN. ☐

(limited quantities available on certain titles)

TOTAL AMOUNT	$
POSTAGE & HANDLING	$
($1.00 for one book, 50¢ for each additional)	
APPLICABLE TAXES*	$ _____
TOTAL PAYABLE	$ _____
(check or money order—please do not send cash)	

To order, complete this form and send it, along with a check or money order for the total above, payable to Gold Eagle Books, to: **In the U.S.:** 3010 Walden Avenue, P.O. Box 9077, Buffalo, NY 14269-9077; **In Canada:** P.O. Box 636, Fort Erie, Ontario, L2A 5X3.

Name: _____

Address: _____ City: _____

State/Prov.: _____ Zip/Postal Code: _____

*New York residents remit applicable sales taxes.
 Canadian residents remit applicable GST and provincial taxes.

GSBBACK1